THE LONE STAR
COLLECTION II

Featuring….

Dena Blake

Kris Bryant

Julie Cannon

Renee MacKenzie

Annette Mori

Yvette Murray

Del Robertson

Lacey Schmidt

Barbara Ann Wright

MJ Williamz

Affinity
Rainbow Publications

2021

The Lone Star Collection 11
© 2021 by Various Authors

Affinity E-Book Press NZ LTD.
Canterbury, New Zealand

1st Edition

ISBN: 978-1-99-004931-6 (PAPERBACK)
ISBN: 978-1-99-004928-6 (EPUB)
ISBN: 978-1-99-004929-3 (PDF)
ISBN: 978-1-99-004930-9 (KINDLE)

Editor: Angela Koenig
Proof Editor: Alexis Smith
Cover Design: Irish Dragon Designs
Production Design: Affinity Publication Services

ACKNOWLEDGMENTS

Thanks to the generosity of authors and fans of lesbian fiction, our first anthology, *The Lone Star Collection*, was extremely successful. Proceeds from sales ensured that the Lone Star Literary Society could continue to sponsor lesfic events.

Unfortunately, last year, concerns about the health risks of COVID-19 forced cancellation of the Spring LesFic Literary Fest. In the interim, since it has not been safe to hold group activities, we decided to continue raising funds for future events. Eight of the authors from the original anthology: Julie Cannon, Renee MacKenzie, Annette Mori, Yvette Murray, Del Robertson, Lacey L. Schmidt, MJ Williamz, and Barbara Ann Wright enthusiastically supported the idea of a second collection. They were joined by Dena Blake and Kris Bryant. A Texas-sized thank you to these wonderful storytellers for donating their time, creative talents, and royalties to support this fund-raising effort.

Once again, JM Dragon and her marvelous crew at Affinity eBook Press have been instrumental in publishing an anthology for us. We are tremendously grateful for their limitless patience and expertise.

Lastly, in recognition of her many years of support, we dedicate *The Lone Star Collection II to* our dear friend and Sapphic Reading Group member, Erin O'Reilly.

Yvette Murray

DEDICATION

Erin O'Reilly

*Author, Co-Publisher of Affinity eBook Press, and
founding member of the Sapphic Reading Group of Austin,
TX*

TABLE OF CONTENTS

THE LONE STAR
COLLECTION II

Affinity
Rainbow Publications

2021

Various Authors

INTRODUCTION

THE LONE STAR LITERARY SOCIETY AND SAPPHIC READING GROUP

PRESENT:

THE LONE STAR COLLECTION II

FEATURING...

Various Authors

Heat by Kris Bryant

A chance encounter with a good Samaritan on a deserted highway leads Sidney Weston to an outcome she never expected.

Lured to the Rocks by Barbara Ann Wright

Sophia faces an ominous dilemma, remain trapped as the dangerous Sirens' pawn, or risk their wrath by attempting to escape.

Horse Play by Dena Blake

Her daughter's fascination with Beckett's horses' spurs Jen to reconsider her feelings toward the obstinate rancher.

50 By 50 by Renee MacKenzie

Newly single at age 45, Megan pursues an adventurous list of 50 things to do in 50 states.

Rainstorm by Annette Mori

Sarah asks the love of her life to break the rules and give her the pleasure of a parting wish.

The Lone Star Collection II

Pins and Needles by Julie Cannon

What secret does seamstress Mary Alice discover about the new banker in town?

The Devil's Backbone by Lacey L. Schmidt

Can love emerge from the ashes of tragedy caused by the evil beast on the Devil's Backbone?

Take Me All the Way by MJ Williamz

What is Tanya willing to do to find everlasting love?

Return to Me by Del Robertson

Pirate captain Jeanne de Bouchard captures a reluctant lady and finds unexpected booty.

Ghostly Galleons by Yvette Murray

During a sabbatical in Galveston, Kerry explores a mysterious connection to Dr. Danika Lester, her attractive Amazonian landlady.

HEAT

KRIS BRYANT

I watched the temperature gauge on my rental car climb the farther south I drove. When I took the traveling sales job, my territory was only the upper Midwest. Since Jim Beaumont, the regional manager for the southern region of Paxton Company retired, they split up his territory instead of hiring another representative, and I got Texas. Some people were jealous, but most of them laughed.

"Oh, you're going to love Texas. It's a heat you've never experienced before. Especially in August," Jim said. He shook my hand while balancing his box of personal belongings that threatened to spill over if I shook his hand too hard. I was tempted.

"I can handle a little heat." That wasn't true. I was born and bred in upper Minnesota and learned to ice skate when I was three. I really wanted to play ice hockey, but my parents put me into figure skating, thinking it was the gentler sport. After two knee surgeries and the obvious realization that the Olympics weren't in my future, I quit. The cold never bothered me.

I steered with my knee while I twisted my hair up in a bun. Fuck. This heat was unbearable for a girl who wore a coat only when the thermometer hit twenty or below. I looked at the digital readout of the outside temperature. One hundred and four. I'd left Kansas City this morning after spending the first part of the week with clients. After a solid seven hours of sleep and a decent continental breakfast, I slipped into the car, excited to take a nice leisurely drive and enjoy the scenery. News flash. Nothing was between Kansas City and Dallas except open fields dotted with cows, oil pumps, and suddenly, out of nowhere, Oklahoma City. I spotted a large casino and was itching to gamble, but I kept going, anxious to get to know the Dallas area and find my customers before the meetings. I hated not having a plan, and even though my meetings didn't start until late tomorrow morning, I wanted to know the lay of the land first so I would arrive on time.

"What the fuck?"

I looked down at the gauges of the rental, a 2021 Ford Escape, and grasped the steering wheel as the SUV jerked hard several times for unknown reasons. Warning lights lit up the dashboard like a Christmas tree. My begging was futile, and I had no choice other than to pull over and let the car coast to its death on the side of I35. Thirty seconds in the hot Texas sun and I was starting to melt. I scrolled through my emails until I found the rental agreement and called the emergency roadside-assistant number highlighted.

"Hello? My name is Sidney Weston. I rented a car from you earlier this week, and now it's dead on the side of the road in the middle of Nowhere, Texas."

"Do you have gas?" The dullness of the agent's voice told me he didn't share my concern.

For a split second, I doubted everything. Did I have gas? Did I put diesel in by mistake at the last stop? I took a deep breath. I'd gassed up less than a hundred miles ago. And the nozzle for diesel wouldn't fit in an unleaded car.

"Of course I have gas. This car has less than ten thousand miles on it. Perhaps your mechanics failed to add oil."

"Where are you right now?"

I threw my hands in the air as if he could see me and my frustration. "Somewhere in Texas along I35 in the middle of the afternoon on the hottest day of the year."

"You rented the car in Minneapolis, correct?"

"Yes. Unlimited miles are a wonderful thing. Is that a problem?"

"No. Do you know the closest mile marker? We can send a tow truck to you if you know where you are."

I saw a green sign about fifty feet from the car and read off the number. "I just crossed into Texas. A giant casino is about fifteen miles back. Don't you have a tracker on the car?" I heard clicking as the agent typed on his keyboard. Sweat gathered on the small of my back, and I shielded my hand over my eyes and squinted as I looked around at nothing but asphalt and brown grass.

"We should have somebody to you in an hour. Is this the best number to reach you?"

"Are you serious right now? I'm in a dead car on the side of the road. Of course, this is the best number to reach me."

"I'm sorry you're frustrated. I'm doing my best."

I took a deep breath. "Please hurry. It's over a hundred degrees and there's nothing around." I disconnected the call and tried to figure out a way to stay cool. Black metal with black leather interior. Awesome choice. I popped the hatchback to provide shade and stood staring at the road, waving a pamphlet for any kind of air flow. The driver of the first car that pulled over was a young man driving a beat-up truck that I doubted could get us to the next town. With all the windows open, he for sure didn't have air conditioning either.

"Do you need some help, ma'am?"

He seemed nice enough, but I wanted to wait with my things. "Oh, thank you for the offer, but the car-rental company will be here in a few minutes." I wasn't scared because cars were steadily passing us on the interstate, and any attempt of kidnaping would be heavily witnessed. He nodded, tipped his cowboy hat, and merged back into traffic.

By the time the fourth car stopped, my anxiety was at an all-time high. I had drunk the last of my water ten minutes ago and hadn't heard from the car-rental company in twenty minutes. I almost rolled my eyes at the black sports car that pulled up behind me, even though I really did need help. I didn't expect the well-dressed soft butch who exited the car. I stood a little taller.

"Do you need some help?"

She was gorgeous and confident, and approached me carefully. I looked her up and down and tried not to openly gape at her sexiness. Her pressed white shirt with the cuffs rolled up revealed ink on her forearms, and the slim-fitting pants showed off her lithe and fit form. She slipped her hands into her front pockets and slowly made her way over to me.

"I love your shoes." That's what I say? This beautiful woman shows up to save me, and the first words out of my mouth are *I love your shoes*? I raised my voice as a semi rolled past us. "I mean, help is on the way." Her shoes, coffee-color wingtips, really were amazing. I was a shoe snob, and I knew quality and fashion.

"Thanks. They're my favorite pair. You have good taste. Hi. I'm Jamie Wagner. I can take you wherever you want go, or you can cool off in my car while we wait for your help."

"Sitting in your car would be wonderful. I think I melted a bit. Or a lot."

She laughed and pointed to the passenger-side door. I slid into the cold car and almost wept with relief. "Thank you so much for stopping. I can't believe how hot it is."

Jamie angled herself so that she could face me. "I'm guessing you aren't from around here."

I laughed and my voice hitched. "I'm from Littlefork, Minnesota, but I live in Minneapolis."

"Damn. What brings you down here?"

She was entirely too close to me in the small confinement of the cabin. I was acutely aware of how badly I was sweating, and inwardly prayed I didn't look as awful as I felt. "Work. I figured I'd drive down instead of flying for a change of scenery."

"From Minnesota?" Jamie gave a low whistle. "That's a lot of driving."

I smiled and tried to make it sound like it was my choice, but truthfully, I was scared of flying. Not "just have a drink and hang on" scared of flying, but genuinely "oh, my God, we're going to die." I gave up flying a long time ago. "I'm getting to learn our country pretty well."

Jamie laughed and sobered up quickly. "I'm not laughing at you, but the decision to drive to Dallas is ambitious and not very exciting."

"I'm listening to audio books. That helps pass the time." Even though the air conditioning was doing a nice job of cooling me off, the sweat on my upper lip and by my temples wouldn't subside.

As if reading my mind, Jamie handed me a tissue she pulled from the center console. "Here. Let me get you a cold drink from my cooler. I was at a conference in Oklahoma City, and even I know this drive is awful. Hang on. I'll be right back."

She slipped out of the car and walked to the trunk. The minute the trunk opened and I was partially hidden, I quickly flipped down the sun visor to check myself out in the tiny mirror. Other than my entire face and neck being flushed, I didn't look as bad as I felt. My makeup hadn't smeared or melted, which was amazing. I hated that my hair wasn't styled anymore, but at least it still had body, even though it was up in a messy bun. I dabbed the perspiration from my face and tucked the tissue into my pants pocket. The last thing she needed was my discarded tissue balled up in her car. I flipped up the visor just as she opened the door and handed me a bottle of cold water with condensation dripping down the sides. I almost moaned with appreciation and wrapped my hot, swollen fingers around it.

"You really are a lifesaver."

She cocked her head a bit and studied me. "I'm doing what I think is right. A woman stranded on the side of the road. If I hadn't stopped, I would have never forgiven myself."

"I owe you dinner or a drink for stopping and offering me your car. I feel so bad. I'm sure you have places to be and people to see." I couldn't believe I was trying to bait information out of her. What was I thinking?

"Where are you staying?" She held her hands up. "Not that I'm going to stalk you, but just in case you feel obligated to buy me a drink after all this, I'll know where to go. I live in downtown Dallas and know the area well."

Something was happening inside the car. I'd classify it as very subtle flirting, but it was there in the way she tilted her head and smiled at me. I felt like we were in a bar somewhere, not in her two-seater car that was getting smaller by the minute, but I trusted Jamie for some inexplicable reason.

"Hyatt Regency."

"Oh, that's a nice hotel. It's near my work," she said.

"What do you do for a living? I'm in sales. It's not glamorous, but I don't have a family or pets, so it's nice to get in a car and see the country at my leisure." Did I just purposely confess I was single?

"I'm in finance. Boring, but it pays the bills."

"I doubt it's boring at all." I looked at the Mercedes emblem on the steering wheel. "And it affords you nice things."

Her genuine laughed warmed me. "Most of the time when I talk shop, people get that faraway look in their eyes, so I never mention it."

"Same with sales. Apparently, it's not exciting."

"Somebody has to do our jobs, right? It might as well be us." Jamie rested her wrist on the top of the steering wheel as if we were on the road driving somewhere. "So, when the tow truck shows up, rather than drive with them, I can take you to the hotel, and they can drop off another rental there. But only if you want. No pressure."

My stomach tightened at her intense stare. "I would love that, but only if you have the time. I don't want to put you out." Her smile released the butterflies. I prayed she wasn't a murderer and that my story would end up on *20/20* where. ten years from now, they find me in a fifty-five-gallon drum on a remote ranch or, worse, eaten by coyotes. My mother would never forgive me. She hated having her picture taken, so I couldn't even imagine an entire news crew shining bright lights and asking her personal details about my sad life.

"This might be for you." Jamie pointed to a tow truck that raced past us but quickly swerved onto the shoulder and backed up to the front of my rental.

I popped out of the car and leaned inside before closing the door. "I'd like to accept your offer. I just need to tell him my plans. Is your offer still good?"

Jamie nodded and turned off her car. "I'll load your luggage."

I greeted the stocky thirty-something with paperwork from the rental company, wondering how he could wear coveralls in this brutal heat.

"I'm Tucker, from A-Plus Cowboy Tow. The rental company asked that I tow your car to my shop, and they'll drop off a rental there." He wiped his sweaty face several times before nodding at me and lowering the lift. He looked like the photo the agency had texted me after they told me a tow truck was en route. I called the rental agency and told them to deliver the car to the Hyatt because I had a ride. I sure as fuck wasn't going to ride in a greasy tow truck littered with candy wrappers and fast-food bags. He shimmied under the car with a large chain and connected it to the SUV. Jamie loaded my two suitcases and messenger bag while I waited to sign paperwork.

"I've got a ride, thank you, and I've already called the rental place. They're going to deliver the new rental to my hotel. Thanks for your help."

He shrugged. "Whatever works. Have a good day."

I was anxious to slip back into the air conditioning. Texas was going to be a state I visited only in the spring and fall. Lesson learned.

"Ready?" Jamie waited for me to buckle up and get situated before merging into traffic. The Mercedes was so smooth that I barely felt the acceleration or the gears shifting. I ran my hand along the soft cream-colored leather armrest.

"You rarely see a light-colored interior in a black-exterior car," I said.

She quirked her eyebrow. "Now you know why I ordered it this way. It's too hot to have a black car with black leather."

"Agreed." I shook my head, thinking about the headache my rental had caused me. Then I changed the subject. "Have you lived in Texas your entire life?"

She nodded. "Born and raised. But I've traveled and have spent many winters in Colorado because I love skiing."

"I do, too." I told Jamie about our family cabin that we shared near the Lutsen Mountains. They weren't massive or steep, but close, and we always had a great time.

"I guess I never really thought of Minnesota as the go-to place for skiing. Everyone always heads to Colorado or Utah," she said. She slowed down as the traffic thickened when we got closer to Dallas.

"Traffic is pretty heavy."

"Dallas is tricky. The only time it's not super busy is five in the morning."

"It's a lot bigger than Kansas City or Oklahoma City, that's for sure." I looked around in amazement at all the lanes of traffic. "I'm sorry this is completely out of your way."

Jamie waved me off. "My condo's in downtown Dallas. Your hotel isn't far from where I live. Ten minutes, even in traffic. Everyone's headed out of the city, and we're driving into it."

I hadn't noticed the soft Southern twang of her voice until right then. She was relaxing around me. I could tell if a meeting was going to be a success just by reading the expressions and mannerisms of the people in the room. The body language in this car yelled trust, and it made me smile. I was completely attracted to Jamie and felt both at ease and excited.

"Have you been to Dallas before? It's such a fun city. If you want suggestions of places to hit, let me know."

"This is a quick trip for me. I'm meeting a few customers to introduce myself and will be headed home Friday."

"That's too bad. We have great restaurants and several festivals going on this month."

I looked at her in disbelief. "You mean in this heat? Outside? That just seems torturous."

She laughed. "It's not that bad."

I focused on my surroundings. The city was beautiful even in the sweltering heat. Jamie took the exit, darted across several lanes of traffic, and slipped into the Hyatt parking lot with ease. I breathed a sigh of relief. Dallas traffic was heavier than I'd imagined.

"I can't thank you enough for rescuing me."

I opened the car door and stretched. Jamie popped the trunk and pulled out my two bags. "Do you need help with anything?"

"No, thank you. I just need to check in. Would you like take me up on my drink offer?"

She checked her watch. "I have a better idea. Why don't I come back in an hour, and we can have dinner here and hit the rooftop bar after that. I promise the heat will be bearable then."

A long shower to wipe away my sweat and put on fresh clothes sounded wonderful. "That sounds like a better idea." We exchanged phones and input our contact information. "I'll see you in an hour. Thanks again."

Jamie slipped back into her smooth sports car and smiled. "It was completely my pleasure. See you soon."

I dragged my bags inside to the front desk and checked in. I didn't even fight the bellhop when he reached for my luggage. I was tired of trying to save myself today. I opened the door, slipped him some money, and fell facedown on the bed after he left. I was tired but excited to see Jamie again. Who knew what the night would bring?

†

She was at the bar sipping on what looked like a gin and tonic when I made my way to the restaurant. "Hi. It's good to see you again." She was wearing a black, short-sleeve, button-down shirt with skinny jeans, both accentuating her muscles. She wore the same wingtips, and her hair was coiffed taller than it'd been earlier.

"You look great." I was a hugger and automatically leaned in for a quick hug and smelled a familiar Jo Malone peppery scent that I loved. "Is that Grapefruit?"

"You know the Jo Malone line?" She leaned back in seeming surprise. "I'm impressed."

"It's one of my favorites." I was slightly embarrassed that I was close enough to recognize the smell and quickly changed the subject. "What are you drinking?"

"A mojito with a little mint. What would you like?"

The bartender slid over to us and looked at me expectantly while wiping clean the spot in front of me. "I'll take a lemon-drop martini."

Jamie smiled at me. "I almost ordered that for you. I like to try to guess what people like to drink. It's kind of a game I invented to pass the time."

I slid onto the stool next to her. "After today, I'm going to need at least two."

"Did the rental place drop off another car?"

I dangled a fob. "A white SUV, with light interior. It was a requirement after what just happened."

"I completely understand. Let's hope this one doesn't die on your way home. But if it does and you're still in Texas or Oklahoma, give me a call."

Jamie had a great smile that curved up more on one side than the other. The effect was charming. She was charming.

"So, tell me about you. What are your hobbies? Are you married? Do you have kids?" It was a bold line of questioning, but I was curious, and I was only in town for a few days. I was expected to visit quarterly, and the trip would be a lot easier if I knew I had somebody I could hang out with, romantically or not. There was that smile again.

"Just got out of a relationship of three years. Tracy. She has a seven-year-old boy, Brock. We stayed together too long. We broke up this past spring."

"I'm sorry." I didn't know what else to say. It was always awkward to hear about a breakup, even though I had asked.

She waved me off. "It was an amicable split. I still attend his soccer games. The little dude is fairly good. Tracy and I didn't live together or anything like that, but I was involved in their lives. What about you?"

"I haven't had a girlfriend in a while. I've been too busy trying to get ahead in my company. And honestly, my freedom works for me. I travel Monday through Friday and have a feeling that will be an issue in any relationship." Just like that, I made it known that I was available. I made an appreciative noise after the bartender delivered the lemon drop. I held my glass next to hers and said again, "Thank you for rescuing me today."

"It truly was my pleasure. So many people don't like to ask for help, so it's nice that you accepted it."

"One hundred and four degrees will make anybody forget their pride." I had drunk three ice-cold bottles of water when I got to the room. A cooler was always going to be in my backseat from now on, full of ice and water, when I traveled down to Texas. Lesson learned. Another one.

When they called us for our table, we moved our conversation to the dining room. Jamie mentioned a rooftop bar with live music that we could hit after the sun went down if I was still interested in hanging out. I wasn't into country music, but I was into Jamie, and that meant I was in. Following her advice, I ordered a steak because, according to her, it was the best in the country. The fish tacos had caught my interest, but she was right. I eyed the loaded baked potato, but even I knew that was going to be too much food, so I stuck with a salad as my side. Jamie ordered a medium rib eye with asparagus and garlic mashed potatoes.

"So, down in Texas we have beef. What is Minnesota known for?"

"Definitely fish. A lot of mushrooms. And any and all the casseroles you can think of," I said. "Just last week my mother sent me a tater-tot recipe, my favorite childhood thing to eat."

"Fish is good. Do you fish?"

"I used to go fishing with my dad all the time, but then I moved to the city and haven't fished since."

"So, you're not the person to lean on in case of a zombie apocalypse?" Jamie asked.

I laughed. "Obviously. I mean you found me in heels by the side of the road. I'm not ready for any setback. I'd last a day, maybe two in an apocalypse."

"Do you watch the show *Alone*?" Jamie asked. At my nod, she continued. "I feel like I would last maybe a full week. I could build a shelter, but I'm going to need somebody to fish and collect nonpoisonous mushrooms."

"My dad watches it and likes to tell me what the contestants are doing wrong. He would love to do it, but he's in his late sixties, and my mother would kill him if he signed up for that." Evidently, my rustic upbringing in the middle of nowhere wasn't so awful after all.

"Plus, your family is used to the cold, and I'm not," Jamie said.

"As is evident by your great tan." Her skin was at least five shades darker than my creamy natural tone. It gave me an excuse to stare at her tattoos. "And fantastic art." I wanted to run my fingers over each brightly colored image. "Tell me the stories of your ink."

Jamie explained how her college roommate was an artist and they'd started dabbling in the different types and styles of tattoos. It had been hard to stop. Her tats were of things in her life that made her stop and think. Several books, movies, events, a death, a birth. They were all representations of such things, so unless she explained each one, they just looked like cool collages. I'd never seen watercolor tattoos up close.

"They're beautiful, Jamie."

She blushed. "Thanks. It's nice to show them off. At work I wear long sleeves because I work for such a conservative business."

"Finance," I said.

"Finance."

Two hours flew by, and when Jamie suggested hitting the rooftop bar since the sun had set, I was surprised to see it was dark outside.

"Okay, one drink. I have a big day ahead of me tomorrow." I paid, insisting it was my treat for her saving me by the side of the road.

"Okay, but the drinks are on me upstairs," Jamie said.

I nodded, grabbed the receipt, and followed her out of the restaurant. "It's so cold in the hotel, but it feels wonderful after today."

"This bar has an outdoor misting system that really cools down the place. I promise. You won't be miserable." She pointed to a set of elevators to our left with a sign on an easel marked *Rooftop Bar*. When the doors opened, I felt her hand at the small of my back. The contact sent a jolt of tingles throughout my body. I knew I was attracted to Jamie; I just didn't expect the rush of blood to every sensitive part of my body.

"I don't know a lot of country songs. I'm at your mercy," I said.

"It'll be fun. I promise." She said.

Her eyes dropped down to my lips and then met my gaze. Her lips were only inches from mine, and I think she would have kissed me if four young cowboys hadn't yelled at us to hold the elevator. Jamie pressed the button until they jumped in. They all tipped their Stetsons at me, politely said "ma'am" to me, and nodded at Jamie. A wave of spicy cologne washed over us in the tiny space, and I had to hold my breath for fear of coughing. At least it was a somewhat pleasant smell, albeit overpowering. When the elevator doors opened, the young men waited for us to exit first, then followed us out.

Once they passed us, I giggled. "Wow, that was a bit much."

"They'll learn," Jamie said.

"Maybe we should say something to them?" We watched them from across the roof as they approached a table of women and were invited to join them.

"Looks like they're going to be all right tonight," Jamie said.

The heat and humidity weren't as oppressive as they had been earlier in the day, but our surroundings still felt like an almost-dry blanket straight from the dryer. I unbuttoned the second button on my shirt and rolled up my sleeves. The pants I had changed into were thankfully thin, and my open-toe shoes gave me some relief as well.

"See? It's not so bad."

I snorted and lifted an eyebrow at her. She gave me a huge smile. It was hard not to respond in kind. "It's better than it was at two this afternoon." I looked around to get my bearings and smiled at the charming atmosphere up on the rooftop. "Who's the band taking the stage? Have you heard of them before?"

Jamie pointed to the bass drum. "The American Alligators."

"That's a horrible name," I said.

"I've heard them before, and they're not bad. Besides, look around. It's not about the music, but the ambiance and definitely the company." The look she gave me told me she was interested.

I liked this bar. Colorful lanterns and white lights were strung above the crowd to provide light and just a fun atmosphere. As the band tuned their instruments, I returned my attention to Jamie. "Thank you for taking me here. You're right. It's not too hot, and I'm enjoying the company."

When the band started playing, Jamie scooted her chair closer to mine so we could still talk over the music. I ordered another lemon drop, my third and last of the night, but vowed to sip it slowly. My first meeting wasn't until ten, but I didn't want to show up puffy-eyed and smelling like vodka.

"See? It's not so bad," she said. I felt her warm breath against my neck when she leaned over to talk. Her fingertips brushed my shoulders as she put her arm on the back of my chair.

I automatically leaned closer. Surprisingly, her warmth was welcoming under the Texas heat. "This band isn't bad. I find line dancing fascinating."

Jamie stood and reached for my hand. "If you're in Texas, you have to line dance. It's a kind of initiation."

I shook my head. "No, I wouldn't even know what to do or how to do it."

She leaned closer so that she was inches from my face. "Do you trust me?"

"Our entire relationship has been built on trust." I slipped my hand into hers.

She placed a small kiss on my fingertips and pulled me up. "Then let's dance."

I followed her onto the floor, where she tucked us into a corner so we wouldn't mess up the entire flow of the dance floor.

"Watch the others and listen to me," Jamie said.

To say I was robotic was putting it nicely. I was so bad that Jamie stopped, turned me around, and shook my arms playfully. "Dancing is fun. Don't worry about being perfect. Follow my lead."

After a few quick moves, I was grooving with the entire group. I laughed and clapped my hands. When was the last time I'd had this much fun? Everyone around us was having a great time and forgave me when I bumped into them. And when the music slowed, I gladly allowed Jamie to take the lead. It was nice to be held, and she smelled wonderful.

"Thank you for making a crappy day not so bad," I said.

"Completely my pleasure. It's nice to save a girl and dance with her, too," she said. She gripped me a little tighter.

"I'm not complaining at all."

When the band broke for a quick break, we headed back to the table. Jamie caught me checking the time. "It's getting late."

"Big day tomorrow. I don't want leave since I'm having such a great time, but I should get some sleep."

"Okay, Cinderella. Let's get you back to the lobby."

Jamie settled our tab since I'd paid for dinner, and we waited for the elevator. I'm not sure when she grabbed my hand, but I was hyper-aware that our fingers were interlocked. She pulled me closer when we squeezed into the elevator. The hardness of her body wasn't lost on me. When the doors opened, I remained pressed against her for a few glorious seconds.

We said our good-byes outside the hotel in the quiet evening. Normally good-byes were awkward, but something told me this wasn't going to be the last time I saw Jamie.

"Good luck tomorrow. I know you'll wow them. It was nice spending the afternoon and evening with you." She pulled me close and brushed her lips across mine.

I don't think either one of us was ready for the sparks that ignited when our lips touched. I wanted to press against her and deepen the kiss, but I also had to be responsible. Regrettably, I pulled away. "Thank you for everything today."

"Keep in touch if you want to get together tomorrow, or the next time you're in town. I'm available to take you around." Jamie slipped her hands into her front pockets and smiled at me as she put space between us.

"Definitely," I said. I headed to my room, knowing that sleep wouldn't be easy after a day that had started off crappy but put a smile on my face by the end of it.

†

Andersen Enterprises was ten minutes away in traffic. I slipped into my black power suit and my heels, grabbed my messenger bag, and headed out to the new rental. The pep talk happened on the way to my first appointment. I pulled into a visitor spot in front of the two-story building, surprised we weren't doing more with them. They were a large corporation with over three hundred employees and a fat bank account, and I was going to do everything in my power to have a better relationship with them than Jim Beaumont ever did. I was meeting with Sasha Bowman and her staff about how our companies could work together profitably, and I planned to give them all the attention they needed. Jim didn't try to improve the business. He only traveled to Texas to visit family and friends and did a quick pop-in to

Andersen Enterprises and other companies in the Dallas area just to drop off bagels and yuck it up with the good ole' boys. Thankfully, they'd retired around the same time he did.

"Hi. Sidney Weston here to see Sasha Bowman." My confidence level was at an all-time high after last night's date. Was it a date? It felt like a date when I woke up with a smile on my face even though I didn't get enough sleep.

"Please have a seat, and I'll let Ms. Bowman know you are here. Can I get you some coffee or water?"

"No, thank you."

The receptionist quietly made a call and resumed her duties. I sat down in the lobby and pulled out my iPad to review several key points I wanted to discuss during the meeting. After five minutes, I was asked to follow the receptionist to the conference room, where five Andersen Enterprises employees stood the moment I arrived. I introduced myself and shook hands with each of them.

"Hi. I'm Sidney. I'm looking forward to working with your company."

"We were sad that Jim retired, but honestly, we welcome the transition," Mark Hargreaves, new vice-president of Andersen Enterprises, said.

"I want to do more with Andersen than Jim did. My ideas are fresh, profitable for both companies, and I want to open up a line of communication that remains open." I silently applauded my direct, honest opening.

"As soon as our CFO returns with our reports, we can get this meeting started. It shouldn't be much longer. In the meantime, how are you enjoying Dallas? Have you been here before?"

Right then, the door opened, and in walked Jamie, my hero from last night. She masked her look of surprise about as well as I did. "Um, I haven't been to Dallas before. It's a beautiful city. A lot bigger than Minneapolis or Kansas City." I kept glancing over at Jamie and watched as she coolly passed out her report and finally made eye contact with me.

Finance? I mouthed the word when our eyes met. She smirked and shrugged. If Jamie was CFO of Anderson Enterprises, she was more than just living a comfortable life. It was hard not to laugh aloud at this entire situation. She leaned over my shoulder and placed the report in front of me.

"Hi. I'm Jamie Wagner, chief financial officer of Andersen Enterprises. Very nice to meet you." She shook my hand and gave it a quick squeeze.

"Nice to meet you, Jamie."

"I look forward to hearing about our partnership." She sat down and stared at me so intensely that I looked away, only because last night's soft kiss flashed across my mind repeatedly and a wave of heat flushed my body and landed on my cheeks, my neck, and the soft folds between my legs. I shifted in my chair for relief, but the pressure only mounted.

I reached for the bottle of water that was in front of me to cool down.

I should have won an academy award for my performance. After a slightly shaky start, I was able to focus on our meeting and the numbers we both wanted to achieve. I answered all questions swiftly, informatively, and with a confidence I was surprised I conjured up, given that Jamie sat six feet away and stared at me for two hours straight. By the end of the meeting, we had reached an agreement that promised to be profitable for all as long as my bosses at Paxton backed me. I would ensure that they did.

Mark turned to Jamie after handing her the signed paperwork. "Right before we started, Sidney told us this is her first time to Dallas." When he stood, signaling the end of the meeting, the entire room stood, but nobody left. The room had turned casual since the contracts were signed.

Jamie looked at me with that adorable crooked smile on her face again. "Oh? How are you liking our city so far?" Jamie asked.

"The city is beautiful and very busy all the time."

The whole table chuckled. "Sidney, since you're from the very northern state of Minnesota, what do you think about our weather?" Mark asked.

I looked at him but then locked eyes with Jamie. "It's ridiculously hot, but I think I can handle this kind of heat."

LURED TO THE ROCKS

BARBARA ANN WRIGHT

Fragments of memory were all Sophia had of her life before the island, and they were of how she'd gotten here. She remembered shivering in someone's arms in a boat that had creaked, packed with bodies, and the oars had screeched in the locks as the sailors rowed. The world had become water, filled to the horizon with lashing wind and cracking thunder.

With all that water, how had the large ship behind them become an inferno?

Another fact lost to history.

Sophia had clung to the arms around her, but a great boom had torn her from her protector and flung her far into the air. One scream had risen above the others as the boat had capsized, "Sophia!"

Then the salty waves had closed over her head, and the sea had stolen her.

"You weren't lost for long," Auntie said in her mind. "We found you."

Sophia shook off the hypnotic haze of Auntie's magic, the only way she could relive her past. Yes, the sirens had found her, claimed her, taken care of her. But nothing she'd felt from them rivaled those precious minutes she'd been cradled in someone's arms. The sirens had never shown the depth of feeling she'd heard in that anguished cry of her name.

"Will you show me again, please?"

Bubbles rose to the surface of the cave's inlet. As they popped, Auntie's gurgling sigh echoed in Sophia's head. "Why relive it again and again? What more can you glean from a babe's memories?"

Sophia didn't speak. She'd become good at not answering. Auntie and the others couldn't casually see into her mind anymore. Sixteen years was a long time to learn how to hide her thoughts.

"If it's stories you want," Auntie said, "I can oblige. Now in the old days…"

Sophia rolled her eyes and let her mind wander away from Auntie's voice. She'd heard all the old stories, tales of sailors lured and eaten, laments about those who'd gotten away. She wondered again what it would be like if a passing ship managed to get to her before the sirens got to them.

No, the ships fast enough to reach her passed the island before they had a chance to even see Sophia. Auntie had said the sirens had moved halfway around the world to this location, which was off the coast of continents unheard of in their youth, in order to find easier pickings. They'd done well here, but every year brought more steamships among the sailing vessels, vessels fast enough to leave the sirens behind.

To leave Sophia behind, too.

Before she could become too maudlin, Mama called in her mind, "It's time."

Another ship. Sophia considered staying in the cave to pout, but it wasn't wise to disobey Mama. And to survive, the sirens needed to eat. She owed them; they'd saved her. They loved her. In their way.

She took a deep breath and dove into the sea. As they swam out of the cave, streaks of sunlight danced along Auntie's body, highlighting the giant, transparent sack in pinks and purples. The protruding sail on the end of her body cut through the waves as she propelled herself with long tentacles, and the purple and pink veins running through her bulbous body stood out like constellations. Auntie had said that humans would call her true form a jellyfish or bluebottle or man o' war, only the sirens were far larger.

Auntie kept her distance as they swam. Sophia had too many memories of those tentacles wrapped around prey, paralyzing, poisoning. It was an agonizing death she preferred not to watch anymore, and one she definitely didn't want to experience.

When Auntie floated to the surface, Sophia followed, blinking in the sunlight. Mama and Sister waited by the rocks, their nearly transparent bodies bobbing with the waves.

Despite what Sophia called them, they weren't her family. She used to ask why she was different, all skin and hair and teeth. The sirens could look like her if they shifted, but only Sister could make that change with any success now, and the process seemed painful. She could no longer sing and hold her humanlike form at the same time. Sophia thought again of the arms that had once been around her in that long-ago boat. Maybe if Sister shifted more and held her, she wouldn't feel so...

She didn't have a word. Strange when she had so many words for other things. She could call for help in almost any language. When she'd been younger, she'd been proud of that, before she'd really thought about death, before she'd started imagining arms around her all the time.

Sometimes, for more than just comfort.

Sophia clambered onto the luring rock, a barren hill in the middle of the sea. Just behind her, the island waited, not big enough for settlement but with trees and bushes. A place someone could survive alone, or so it seemed.

Sophia caught sight of white sails. What would they think when they spotted her? That she was lucky to have survived a shipwreck? That everything would be all right for her now? She thought of a passing steamship she'd once glimpsed, of a woman in a long dress with pale hair. Sophia still imagined what it would be like to stand beside her at the rail, gazing at the water far below, bound for Texas or Mexico or any of the exotic names the sirens gleaned from their prey.

Sophia's heart picked up speed. This was a sailing ship, not a steam one, and the sirens would catch it with her help. One of Sister's tentacles flopped a wet dress onto the rock. Sophia's hands shook as she slipped the sopping garment over her head. A dead woman's dress.

"Get ready," Mama said.

The ship came closer. Sophia could feel the sirens' fear. They often thought of steamships, too. They needed to eat to live. They'd saved her. She owed them.

Sophia flapped her arms and cried out. Auntie had torn the dress in places, showing more of her body in a tantalizing fashion. She'd said it worked almost as well as the ancient songs. And it *was* easier to accept the death of those sailors who stared as if the only reason for rescuing Sophia was because they wanted her body.

Even if their screams still haunted her.

She clenched a fist. It was too late to think such thoughts.

"They're flying an American flag," Sister said.

"And it's a brigantine," Mama said. "At last, a small crew, easily overwhelmed."

Auntie laughed. "But still enough to fill us up."

Sophia cried, "Help! Please, save me," in English.

The sailors spotted her and waved. Some scrambled into a smaller boat while the brigantine turned and slowed.

Sister and Auntie moved away. "We've got the ship."

"I have the lifeboat," Mama said.

Sophia cried, feigning happiness. One sailor raised a hand and called out. Sophia had no idea what he said, but his tone was soothing, questioning, probably about her safety.

Oh, that hurt. It *was* much easier when they leered.

†

Sophia watched the ship until it sank out of sight, lost in dark blue depths. She swam to the island and tried to block out the slurping, crunching sounds around her. When she kicked into her cave and climbed up the sandy shore, she spied a fish on the bank. One of the sirens had gotten her lunch while they'd been enjoying theirs, proof of their affection.

Sophia cooked it on a rock in her fire pit, then ate it while staring at the water in her cave. She tried to shake off the depression that had settled on her shoulders like a heavy cloak, but it wouldn't leave her. The sailors in the lifeboat and their cries for help replayed in her head. She stripped off the heavy dress but still felt its weight, and the image of the woman on the steamship kept coming back to her. Had her dress been weighing her down, too? Did she wait eagerly for those times when she could strip it off and be naked and free?

A warm sensation coursed through Sophia at the thought, and little tingles passed through her, collecting at her core.

"Is the fish all right?" Mama asked in her mind.

Sophia jumped and shook any rebellious thoughts away. The sirens couldn't easily pry, but if Mama really tried... "It's good. Thank you."

"Auntie dug into your memory again this morning."

With a sigh, Sophia closed her eyes, knowing what was coming, her fear giving way to irritation. "I only wanted to see—"

"Did you recall the part where I saw you drowning and saved you?"

"No, I just—"

But it was too late. Mama's magic enveloped her, taking her back to cruel grey waves under an angry sky, to the sea closing over her head again and again until a pounding wave pushed her down into a suffocating world of swirling shadows. Only a memory, but she had to fight to breathe.

Then, light, golden and warm. A woman floated toward her, larger than any human. She was like the sun, bringing life into darkness as she carried Sophia to the surface.

Gratitude and shame filled Sophia like fresh water permeated with grit.

"I transformed for you that day, though it hurt me dearly," Mama said.

"Thank you," Sophia whispered.

"We saved you."

"I know. Thank you." She shuddered and tried to breathe through her emotions, but tears dribbled down her cheeks. She scrubbed at them with the heels of her hands, struggling to hold on to the fact that she had a right to anger. It wouldn't keep coming back if it wasn't justified.

But she couldn't forget gratitude, either. Mama had plucked her from the sea. Auntie had made her laugh. Sister had cradled her. She owed them. They loved her.

Didn't gifts like the fish prove that?

"I'm sorry, Mama. I'm just feeling…" She searched for a word. She couldn't be lonely as she wasn't alone. "Lost?"

Mama didn't answer, but Sophia sensed her move away, probably to speak with the others about their irritating human. She left the cave to walk along the sand, relishing the breeze on her skin and drinking water from one of clay jars the sirens had stolen from a ship. The water of the dead.

"Sophia?" Sister's voice, faint, no doubt coming from the cave.

Sophia again considered not going, but she liked Sister and wanted to heed her call out of affection rather than fear. Inside the cave, she stopped in shock. Sister sat on a rock in human form, golden legs kicking the water, beautiful face alight with a smile.

"What are you doing?"

Sister laughed, and the sound called to mind warm summer breezes. She held out her arms. "I thought you missed me like this."

Sophia shuddered, tears gathering again as she climbed into Sister's strong arms. "Does it hurt?"

"Only a little."

"Change back," Sophia said, choking on the words, but she didn't want Sister to be in pain for her sake. She forced herself to stand again, away from skin that never felt warm enough, for arms that were too strong, too weighty.

"Then I couldn't give you my present."

Sophia frowned. "I don't want any human trinkets. They won't make me feel any better."

"This one will." Her golden curls moved like her tentacles around her shoulders. She was slipping back toward her true form. Quickly, she stood and pulled something from the shadows of the cave.

Sophia's stomach dropped to her knees.

A woman dangled from Sister's grip, her body limp. She wore a blue dress that covered her from neck to ankle, and dark hair cascaded around her like a veil.

"What have you done?" Sophia whispered, her emotions clanging like thunder and lightning.

"She's for you."

The woman moaned and moved. She kicked her legs until she stood on her own, though Sister still held her by the back of the dress. The woman pawed at her curtain of hair, and a pretty face emerged, large brown eyes wide at the sight of Sophia. When she looked up at Sister, she screamed.

"She's very lively," Sister said as the woman thrashed. Sister's hair moved like sea snakes when the woman's small fists banged into her, but Sister only laughed. The woman might as well have been fighting the cave. "Do you want to keep her?"

"Keep her?" Sophia asked. "As what? A friend? A pet?"

Sister shrugged. "Or a lover."

The same tingles as before passed through Sophia, but she shook her head. She couldn't even consider such a thing after seeing the fear on the woman's face. The woman had gone quiet, panting, still trying to pull away, her head whipping back and forth between them as they spoke.

"If you don't want her, I'll throw her to Auntie," Sister said.

"Yes, please." Auntie said. They were all three listening, watching.

"No," Sophia said, certain she didn't want that. "I'll...keep her." Keep her alive, if nothing else.

Sister let go, and the woman scampered away, muttering as she pressed herself into the cave wall.

Sister dove into the water, blurring as she returned to her true form.

The woman stared at the pool, at the light coming from the cave opening, and then at Sophia, fear shining in her eyes. Sister floated in the water, blocking that way out. The woman wiped her tears with the back of her hand and spoke a few words.

Sophia shook her head, one of the human gestures she'd picked up. Her few words of English wouldn't help now. "I can't understand you." She laid a hand on her chest. "Sophia."

After a moment, the woman licked her lips and said, "Christine."

She had dark circles under her eyes. Her hair was long and tangled. Sophia regularly cut hers with a knife and now she smoothed it down, wondering what it looked like, what this woman thought of her. She had so many questions but couldn't ask any. Christine said a few words, then repeated them, gesturing at Sophia's body.

Right. All the humans Sophia had ever seen had been wearing clothes. She moved to the side of the cave where she kept her things. She considered the ripped dress, but it itched, and it was hot. She pulled some dead sailor's clothes out of the pile that was her bed and slipped them on.

Christine gawked, then looked to her own sodden dress as if considering.

"What are you going to do with her?" Auntie asked.

Sophia shrugged. "What am I supposed to do?"

Auntie's chuckle bubbled to the surface. "I used to mate with the odd human from time to time, ages ago, when I could transform."

Is that all they could think of? Still, the same thrill traveled through Sophia's body. She'd never felt this drawn to the sailors, and the thought of the woman on the steamship caused her heart to race now and again.

"If you want to try, Sophia," Auntie said. "I'll talk you through it."

By the look on Christine's face, mating was the still last thing on her mind.

"Only if she wants to, and it doesn't look like she does." Sophia gathered more sailor's clothes and held them out, but Christine leaned away. Sophia set them on the ground. "Here. These are for you." She pushed the clothing forward.

Christine snatched them up but still stared, her eyes fearful. She glanced at the water and said something in a low tone of voice. Sophia caught the words, "Help me," but didn't know how to respond. She gestured to the clothes and then to Christine's dress.

Christine reached for her buttons, then paused, her cheeks turning pink.

"Humans like privacy," Auntie said.

Sophia's own face felt hot as she hurried out of the cave and into the sunshine. After a moment, Christine staggered into the daylight wearing the sailor's clothes and looking cooler if not more at ease. She'd tied her long brown hair up with a scrap of cloth and laid her bulky dress in the sun on a rock.

After she gave Sophia a hesitant smile, she stared at the island as if she'd never seen trees and rocks and sand before. Sophia gave her one of the clay jugs, and Christine drank from it like a dying woman. After a deep breath, she glanced at Sophia again, then stepped into the bushes and broke into a run.

Sophia sighed. She should have expected that. Ah well, Christine would tire soon enough, and maybe while she was gone, Sophia could figure out what to do with her. It was hard to follow her instincts when they were all over the place.

Christine stumbled back a few hours later. Sophia had built up her fire, even though it was already warm. Christine sat close to the flames. She hugged her knees, and her eyes were swollen from crying.

Sophia sighed. "She wants to go home."

"I hope she's a good swimmer," Auntie said. "Even the closest port at Galveston is several days away, and that's at our speed."

Sophia shook her head. She used to love when Auntie spoke of anything outside their little home, but now it seemed cruel. "I'm sorry," Sophia said to Christine. She sighed deeply. "Maybe it would have been kinder if you'd eaten her."

"I still could."

Sophia shuddered but couldn't help imagining it. All she'd have to do was get Christine close to the water, and Auntie's tentacles would take care of the rest.

No, Christine's pain would be over eventually if the sirens got her, but those last few moments…

Sophia pressed on her forehead, willing the memory of screams to go away. They seemed much louder with Christine here.

"It'll be all right." Sophia tried to sound soothing, and Christine looked at her with something that might have been gratitude. When she grabbed Sophia's hand, Sophia went stiff, managing not to jerk away. After her fear passed, she thought it a nice feeling, soft, warm, right.

"We have another one," Mama called, making Sophia jump and filling her with dread.

"Another ship?" Auntie asked. "Our lucky day!"

Oh no. Was this a companion to the first ship? If Christine knew the people, she'd have to watch…

"Stay here," Sophia said.

Christine cried out when Sophia dashed back into the cave and dove into the water.

"Another American ship," Sister said. "Maybe an entire fleet will go by."

All Sophia could think of was Christine's frightened face. So these *were* Americans, too. Christine really might know them. Sophia slowed. Maybe she could *accidentally* be late to the luring rock? She'd had a busy day, and she was tired.

What would the sirens do if they didn't believe her?

What would Mama do?

Cries echoed from the island. Sophia stopped and turned, treading water. Christine had climbed up the outside the cave onto a short bluff. She screamed and waved her arms.

"The fool," Sister said, her voice angry. "They might see her."

She was too far from the water for the sirens to reach. Sophia couldn't help a smile at the show of rebellion. Guilt tried to grab her at her traitorous thoughts, but the sirens had already eaten that day. Missing this meal wouldn't hurt them.

"Who cares if she brings the ship?" Auntie asked. "Whatever gets them to stop."

Hmm. Sophia hadn't considered that. "Should I get her down?"

The American ship came closer, sailors clustering along the rail.

"Get to the rock, Sophia," Mama said. "Two lures are better than one."

Something odd in her voice drove Sophia forward, but she could already tell she wouldn't make the rock before the sailors were in striking distance. She swam anyway. Perhaps the ship would see her in the water, perhaps not, and Mama couldn't get angry if Sophia tried to do as she was told.

Mama wouldn't have to get angry. She didn't need Sophia if she had a captive who would do her bidding without being asked.

And the sirens could reach Sophia just fine.

She gritted her teeth, fighting through the fear that wanted to paralyze her limbs. She should have taken off these clothes. They weighed her down too much.

With the ship closer, Christine seemed to redouble her efforts, shouting louder, but she didn't wave the ship in. She waved as if throwing the ship away and held her arms straight out, palms up. She cried out several words over and over, and Sophia caught, "Smallpox!"

The American sailors ceased gawking and swarmed over their sails, turning the ship.

"What is that idiot doing?" Auntie cried.

"Can you catch the ship, Sister?" Mama asked.

Sister streaked away, but the new ship caught the wind and seemed to surge forward.

"Sophia, get to the luring rock now," Mama said.

She'd never make it, and if the sailors thought the island wasn't safe, they might not pick her up anyway. When she clambered onto the rock, the ship was already far out to sea.

Sophia closed her lips on a happy yell and fought to keep her mental guard up. Christine had sacrificed herself to save this crew, a group of people she might not even know. And she'd been smart enough to know the sailors might not believe in giant jellyfish that turned into people—as these sirens were the last in the world—so she'd yelled about a disease. Auntie had once told Sophia that smallpox had driven them from their last home. It made the meat taste foul.

Sophia watched until she could no longer tell the departing sails from the horizon. If they told others the island was unsafe, everyone would give it a wide berth.

Guilt really did attack her, then.

"Bring that woman down to the cave," Mama said, her mental voice as hard as limpet shells.

Sophia swam back slowly, her emotions warring yet again. Curious how one day could change so much, even inside her. She felt even more tired than when she'd swum out, as if she'd aged more in this day than any other, the events wrapping around her like kelp. She climbed onto the island with no idea how to wrestle Christine down to the shore. Sophia didn't want to hurt her, didn't want to add to the agony before her death.

Christine grinned, her arms crossed as if she were proud of herself. "Smallpox," she said again.

Sophia couldn't help but smile back. "They want you dead now." She bit her lip and looked over the edge, hoping the sirens wouldn't be able to hear her.

"What if she doesn't want to go?"

Mama's voice was faint by clear. "Push her over the edge."

Christine edged closer, looking between the water and Sophia as if curious. She gasped and leaned even farther out, and Sophia bet she'd seen all three sirens floating on the surface. She grabbed Sophia's hand and tried to pull her away from the edge. "Sophia." She shook her head, tugging harder.

"You want to save me?" Sophia asked. An ache built in her chest that she tried to fight. Of course Christine wanted to protect her. Without Sophia, Christine would be all alone. She might die here. It was in her best interest that Sophia remain alive, just like with the sirens.

"Sophia," Christine said. She shook her head again, and there was fear in her dark eyes, but also something else, probably the same something that had made her chase her potential rescuers away.

Sophia had another flash of memory, this one coming on its own. Those arms were around her in the little boat again, and she'd looked up, just for a moment to see someone looking down at her, their eyes shining like Christine's now.

Christine...cared about her? So quickly? How could someone care if a person they'd just met lived or died?

Sophia breathed out slowly, already knowing the answer because she felt it, too. Maybe it was about loneliness or need. Maybe it was just…human.

"Sophia," Mama asked, "what's going on?"

Sophia let the guilt wash away. The sirens had saved her. She owed them. They loved her, but not like this.

"She's running off into the island," Sophia said, still grasping Christine's hand. "I'll try to catch her." She led Christine into the trees, far from the beach where the sirens might not hear them, and Sophia would have time to think.

Christine could hide. Sophia could claim not to have found her. Maybe the sirens would believe she'd tried to swim and drowned. Sophia could sneak her food and water.

And continue to lure in ships? How much had Christine figured out about Sophia's role in the sirens' diet? How much could she forgive?

No, Christine had to escape. Sophia couldn't bear her hatred.

The woman on the steamship leapt into Sophia's head again, but she stamped on that thought. She had to get Christine away first.

"Sophia," someone cried, and it echoed, a spoken voice. Sister.

"Run," Sophia said. She tugged Christine into flight. But where could they go? In circles forever? No, better to turn Sister away, give them room to breathe. Sophia pushed Christine into some bushes and headed toward Sister's voice.

Sister's golden face broke into a smile. Standing, she loomed, but her form seemed fuzzy around the edges, her transformation imperfect. "Where is she?"

"I don't know. Hiding?"

Sister stared, her eyes unreadable even with her smile. "Ah well. She has to eat sometime, and that will mean going toward your cave or the water. Then we'll have her."

Sophia bit her lip. Maybe with Sister alone, she could argue for more time. Then she could make a proper plan. "You said I could have her."

"I'm sorry, Sophia. Mama says no."

"What if, after I find her, I keep her away from the bluff? Whenever a ship comes, I'll—"

"You couldn't get her down the first time." Sister rested a large hand on Sophia's shoulder, and the contact seemed to tingle through the shirt. "Don't worry. When the next ship comes, we'll get you a smaller one, easier to manage."

As if Christine was a toy or a pet. What did that make Sophia? "I don't want another one."

Sister's smile fell, her face seeming to match her eyes at last. For the first time, Sophia noticed how Sister had changed over the years, becoming harder as she ceased to shift her form, becoming less human.

More like Mama.

Sister's grip tightened, and the tingle became a spear of pain. When Sophia sucked in a breath, Sister released her, blinking as if realizing she couldn't be so rough. Sophia had to swallow the urge to bolt. Sister wasn't Mama and neither was Auntie. Sophia could persuade them to listen. "Sister—"

"Sophia," Sister said, her hair moving on its own. She tried another smile, but it was still nowhere near as vibrant as Christine's. "We love you. You know that."

In their way.

It wasn't enough.

Tears welled inside Sophia, her emotions clashing together like a storm. "Please, Sister."

"Come on." Sister started toward the beach. "Tell it to Mama."

A good threat for an unruly child, but Sophia shook her head now.

Sister's form wobbled. Sophia stepped toward her out of fear. Her true form couldn't survive on land.

"Go," Sophia said, pointing behind her. "Run for the water."

"Not without you." Sister started toward Sophia, but something arced through the air and whacked her in the head. She stumbled, hissing, her features blurring.

Sophia spun to see Christine digging around in the undergrowth until she found something else to throw.

Sister roared and stepped toward Christine, but Sophia cried, "No, Sister, I can see through you. Run!" She grabbed Sister's arm, but a mammoth hand smacked her in the head, sending pain clanging through her and pitching her into the undergrowth.

Sophia held her head as she sat up. Sister was hurrying away or trying to. Her legs looked like blobs, tiny lines marking them and her arms where her tentacles would reform. Her face melted, and the top of her head held the beginnings of the purple fin.

With a groan, Sophia got to her feet, but she couldn't touch Sister now, couldn't help her. "No!"

Sister collapsed into her true form, so graceless and flat on land. "So…phi…a."

Sophia knelt at her side. "Why did you hit me?" she asked, sobbing. To hurt her or protect her from the poison in those tentacles? "I could have helped you. I'm sorry, Sister. I'm so—"

Sister shuddered once before going still, her mental voice falling silent.

Sophia curled around her knees and wept. When someone touched her shoulder, she almost leapt out of her skin. Christine stood behind her.

"You killed her," Sophia shouted. She sprang to her feet. "You killed…" She lapsed into tears again. Christine's arms went around her. When Sophia tried to pull away, Christine held on, murmuring soothing words. Sophia wept into her shoulder. Her tears stilled soon, and she could admit she liked the feel of those arms. After them, the memory of Sister's warmth felt false, an imagined heat, another part of their glamor.

"Christine?"

"Sophia?"

"How can I keep you and the rest of them alive?"

Christine's reply sounded tired, and Sophia didn't understand a word of it, but she imagined they felt the same sort of fatigue, a human depth.

Now what could they do? Hide on the island forever? They couldn't eat without going near the water. More than that, Sophia wanted to tell Auntie and Mama what had happened. She owed them that much.

Christine stayed with her. Sophia tried to shoo her back in the forest, but she seemed determined to die. It seemed sensible at the moment, anything to stop the feelings swirling within.

The closer Sophia came to the shore, the clearer she could hear Mama and Auntie's cries. Christine stopped just shy of the water, but Sophia waded in to her knees, hoping the sirens would feel her anguish as well as hear her words.

"What happened?" Mama asked.

Sophia took a great, shuddering breath. "Sister shifted to her true form on land."

Horrified silence reigned for a few moments before Auntie asked, "Why?"

"She was tired," Sophia said. "And she couldn't—"

"Because of something that woman did," Mama said.

Sophia felt pressure behind her eyeballs as if Auntie was sorting through her memories, but this was Mama's tremendous power. Sophia fell to one knee as the thoughts were ripped from her head. "Mama, please!"

"Because of both of you," Mama cried. She continued her onslaught, wringing out every word. Sophia relived the crack against Sister's head, the feel of her strike, the salt smell of her gelatinous body, and the sight of that last shudder.

"We saved you." Mama's words came as a harsh rumble, the fierce power of unarguable currents. "Ungrateful brat."

Sophia cried so hard she choked. "I'm sorry, Mama."

"One pitiful human life can't pay for the death of a siren." Mama's tentacles rose from the sea. "But it will be a good start."

"Wait," Auntie cried. "It's Sophia. You can't!" She pounced on Mama, forcing her back.

Christine dragged Sophia back on shore. Sophia sobbed, trying to think, but her head was screaming, and her face felt hot and sticky. Her hand came away bloody when she touched her nose. Everything had changed so quickly, too quickly. She'd been stubborn and angry and sad that morning, but now her insides were a churned-up mess. There had to be a way for everyone to have what they needed.

Everyone but Sister.

"Sophia," Auntie said, her mental voice breathless. "What happened? Why—"

"She wants to leave," Mama said. "She's killed Sister and now she wants to abandon us to die."

Immense pressure filled Sophia's head again, and she sank to her knees in the sand, Christine chattering helplessly by her side.

"Go," Auntie said.

Sophia tried to get to her feet, but Auntie hefted Mama's bulk, pushing her out to sea. "Calm down. I'll speak to her. Go!"

With one final snarl, Mama surged away, heading for deeper water.

Sophia sat in the sand. Christine sank next to her. Auntie floated a few feet from shore. Her transparent body barely threw a shadow, but the light reflecting inside her made her glow.

"I'm not giving Christine to you," Sophia said, wiping at the blood under her nose again.

Bubbles floated to the surface as Auntie laughed. "I know. I've been alive a long time. I know those feelings going through your head even if I've never experienced them myself."

Sophia fought to keep her lip from wobbling. "Oh, Auntie, I never meant to hurt Sister."

"I know that, you little fool." She sighed. "If you're going to leave, you need a plan."

"A plan for what?"

"To catch Mama off guard."

Sophia drew in a breath. "But…if we both leave, you'll…"

"Ah, Sophia. Our kindred are all dead, and it's past time we joined them. I knew this day would come."

Guilt clawed inside Sophia like a wild thing. Auntie might have been tired of living, but she could have swum far out to sea and starved if that was all she cared about. She cared for Sophia, too. In her own way, but it was still a form of love, real if different. "I'm sorry, Auntie."

"Everything ends, girl." One of her tentacles rose from the water and threw a fish onto the shore. "Eat. You'll need your strength."

†

For two days, Sophia and Christine stayed close the center of the island, sneaking to the shore to collect water from the cave and food from Auntie while Mama was distracted.

Even with Christine by Sophia's side, those seemed like lonely days. They sat close by the fire, resting their heads on each other's shoulders or holding hands, being human together.

As much as Sophia had thought of leaving before, it had never felt so real. She *could* be like that woman on the steamship. Christine had made longing explode into hope, and Sophia had to fight to keep from blaming her along with celebrating her. Christine hadn't asked for this, just as Sophia hadn't. And the sirens couldn't help being what they were. She supposed it was like a storm: no one was to blame.

And life could go on.

On the third morning, Auntie called, "Quick, come to the shore. I see sails on the horizon. I told Mama you were trying to wave the ship away, so she's watching near the cave. You can make it to the luring rock if you're quick."

Sophia didn't think. She grabbed Christine's arm and dashed for the water. There, sails in the distance. Christine gasped when she saw them and started toward the cave, but Sophia tugged her into the water.

Christine shook her head. "Sophia…" She babbled a few more words, looking at the water in horror.

Sophia pulled at her again, knowing she was looking for the sirens. She pointed to the ship and gestured, trying to seem as if she was putting something on board. Christine bit her lip but followed Sophia into the water. She didn't seem to want to go in above her waist, her eyes wide with fear.

"Forgive me." Sophia yanked on Christine's arm, pulling her off her feet. Christine gasped, sputtering, and Sophia turned her around to float face up while Sophia swam for both of them.

Sophia's heart pounded. They weren't fast enough. She imagined Mama coming for them, her poisonous tentacles wrapping around them, dragging them toward the terrible mouth that waited in the center. But she kept swimming, ignoring the tinny noise in her ears. When they reached the luring rock, she couldn't help making little panicked sounds as she helped Christine up. Christine collapsed, gasping and coughing. Sophia stood and shaded her eyes from the sun. They weren't out of danger yet. Mama could still reach them, but Sophia had to trust in Auntie. She waved at the ship, another American vessel, maybe the same one.

"Help me! Please, save me," she called in English, meaning the words for the first time. Christine gawked at her and babbled, but Sophia pointed her toward the ship.

It came closer, the sailors at the rail. She could put Christine aboard and stay on the island. She could keep Mama and Auntie alive. They'd saved her life. How could she be certain she didn't owe them her life in return, even after everything?

"Auntie." Tears streamed down Sophia's face as she turned, searching. "What will you and Mama do without me?"

"We'll live, or we won't." Her bulbous body floated between them and the shore. "Just get on the damn boat, Sophia."

Through her tears, Sophia laughed. It was the best blessing she could have hoped for. She turned to look at her island one last time and spotted a ripple in the chop. "Mama," she whispered.

"Thankless human trash!" Mama shrieked.

Sophia grabbed her head and fell to her knees, encased in blinding pain. Beside her, Christine doubled over. The agony lessened enough for Sophia to see Mama and Auntie wrestling, tentacles flailing, but the lash of their minds did the most damage, with screams that rattled through Sophia's brain and threatened to tear her skull apart.

"See what you've done," Mama cried. "Killed Sister and turned Auntie against me."

"I'm sorry, Mama," Sophia yelled, anything to get the pain to stop.

"Leave her alone," Auntie said. "Let her go."

"She never wanted to be free until that other human came along." One of Mama's tentacles whipped toward Christine. Sophia dragged her down and caught the end of the lash against her own back. She screamed as pain rolled through her, a thousand needles stabbing her flesh. Her shoulder struck the edge of the rock, and she tumbled down to slap into the water.

Her body went numb, and the blood roared in her ears as she faced the deep. Purple blobs floated into her vision, Mama and Auntie, tangled together and sinking. "Get away, Sophia," Auntie said. They didn't like going deep, but Auntie forced Mama past the rocks of the island and toward the fading light below.

As Sophia's lungs began to burn, Mama's shape trembled and blurred. "I'll find you," Mama said, so softly Sophia might have imagined it. Almost engulfed in deep blue, Mama blurred and reached out one golden arm, her mouth open in a silent cry as Auntie dragged her into darkness.

Sophia's body went light, and brightness flooded her eyes. Was this what dying felt like? Then Christine's face blocked out the sun, her eyes wide and fearful. She babbled some words and smoothed a hand over Sophia's brow.

Sophia took a small breath, all she could manage. The tentacle had barely touched her; she tried to hold on to that thought as the sailors hauled her and Christine on board. She wanted to weep but couldn't, not yet in control of herself. That seemed a blessing, as she had no room for fear, either.

Christine talked to one of the crew, who gestured to something in the distance. She caught the word Texas. It sounded like paradise. No more fragments. She'd have real human memories from now on.

HORSE PLAY

DENA BLAKE

"Do you have any large sponges?"

The smooth, familiar voice drew Jen from the prescription she was filling. She glanced up to find Beckett, the most infuriating woman in Coke County, staring up at her from across the counter.

"Did you say sponges?"

"Yes. The large kind, like for washing a car."

She let the pills slide from the counting tray into the bottle before she glanced up again. "There might be some on aisle five in the front with the rest of the automotive items." Beckett never failed to come looking for the strangest things. She *had* to be the only reason the store stocked so many odd items.

As usual, Beckett was dressed in a brightly colored T-shirt, Levi's that seemed to be hanging on for dear life, and Justin boots. The woman had legs for days. Jen always enjoyed the view when she came in—until she opened her mouth. She went back to her work, and then after a few minutes, Beckett's voice pulled her from her work again.

"How about gauze pads and latex gloves? You got any of those?"

She glanced up and found the most gorgeous blue eyes staring up at her. It was amazing how Beckett's short silver hair set them off perfectly. Jen blinked and shook the jolt from her system. She pointed to the area where the items were shelved before she glanced at her daughter, who was sitting next to the pharmacy counter playing a game on her phone.

"Aubrey, can you show Mrs. Beckett where the gauze and gloves are?"

"Sure." Aubrey popped out of the chair and headed to the aisle where they were located. "They're right over here, Mrs. Beckett."

"Drop the Mrs. It's just Beckett." Beckett took a few boxes of each item from the shelves. "Thank you kindly."

Jen watched the interaction between them out of the corner of her eye as she tried to focus on her work. Watching Aubrey was an unwanted habit she'd had to force herself to adopt even before they left Dallas.

Aubrey glanced up to see if her mom was watching. "You're the lady with the horses, right? I'm Aubrey."

"Nice to meet you, Aubrey." Beckett held out her hand. "I have a few horses on my ranch. Some of my own and some I board for other people."

"I love horses. They're so beautiful." Aubrey's voice was soft, almost dreamy. Not something Jen had heard lately.

"You interested in working a little?" Beckett tilted her head. "I can't pay you much, but you can ride whenever you want."

"That'd be awesome." Aubrey's voice rose. "I've never ridden a horse."

Jen couldn't let this conversation continue. "Absolutely not." She wasn't about to let Aubrey get on a horse. She twisted the top tightly on the prescription bottle.

"What the hell, Mom?" Aubrey scrunched her eyebrows together. "I want to learn to ride."

"Watch your mouth." She avoided Beckett's stare as long as she could. Accompanied by flattened lips and a raised eyebrow, her steel-blue eyes were still hard to escape.

"I'd be happy to teach her." Beckett smiled as she set her items on the counter. "I have plenty of horses for beginners at the ranch."

"I'm sure your schedule is booked." She scanned Beckett's items and placed them in a bag.

Beckett handed her a twenty. "I can make time. She can come out after school. Plus, I could use an extra hand around the place."

"She has homework to do after school." Jen slid the twenty under the register clip, fished out the change, and handed it to Beckett.

"She could probably use some extracurricular activities rather than sitting in the corner here, playing games on her phone."

Beckett didn't seem to be getting the message. She narrowed her eyes. "Why don't you just take care of your horses, and I'll take care of my daughter?" Hopefully that would make her decision clear.

"Don't you think it would be good for her to get outside?"

"She gets outside plenty."

"Sure doesn't look like it to me." Beckett slipped her bag over her hand and whispered to Aubrey, "Let me know if you change your mind."

"I heard that."

"You're welcome to come along with her." Beckett glanced up at her, and Jen felt like she was getting the once-over. "I can probably teach you a few things, too."

What exactly was that? An invitation? An insult? She wasn't sure.

"If you ever get off of that high horse you're on." Beckett threw up her hand in a wave as she went down the aisle.

That remark sealed it. She wasn't going anywhere close to Beckett's ranch, and neither was Aubrey.

†

After Beckett left the pharmacy, she went to the post office, the last place on her errand list, to pick up the colic medicine she'd had shipped Priority Mail to her post-office box. She'd run out because Barley was still having stomach issues. She hadn't been feeding him anything different, which had her puzzled and concerned about the horse's condition. She hoped the stomach issues resolved soon, or she'd have to call the veterinarian, which came with a huge bill she didn't have in this month's budget.

Her visit with the postmaster was much more pleasant than the one with Jen. As was usual after an encounter with Jen, she couldn't get her out of her head. Deep-green eyes and long auburn hair captured her thoughts. Jen was definitely beautiful—stunning, to be more accurate—but the aesthetics had worn off quickly after Beckett had engaged her in conversation. Jen seemed to have an opinion about everything, and it always seemed to be on the opposite side of the fence from Beckett. The woman was infuriating—had been since she'd come to town last year. She'd totally avoid Jen if she didn't work at the only general store in town. She refused to let one woman push her to drive extra miles to get her supplies elsewhere.

Beckett climbed into the driver's seat of her Crew Cab truck and headed home. Hearing a noise in the backseat, she glanced in her rearview mirror. Nothing. She must be hearing things. She flipped on the radio to listen to the news, then flipped it off again after a few minutes. Too depressing. Another noise from the backseat. She adjusted the rearview mirror for a better look and saw a wisp of brown hair peeking out from beneath the horse blanket that was lying across the seat. Her heart raced—who the hell had gotten into her car? She tried to remain calm as she took the next corner hard and watched as a small hand poked out from beneath the blanket to grip the seat. It seemed she had a teenage stowaway.

When she reached the house, she parked in front of the stables, got out, and pulled open the back door. "Come on out." No movement, so she tugged the blanket loose. "I have a gun, you know." Probably not the best tack.

Aubrey peeked from underneath the blanket. "It's just me." She had the same color green eyes as her mother. The resemblance was striking.

Beckett had to hold back a laugh. "You could've ridden up front with me. Does your mother know you're here?"

Aubrey nodded. "I sent her a text. She's going to pick me up after work."

After Jen's reaction earlier, she wasn't sure Aubrey was telling the truth and didn't dare probe further. There was probably more to this story than Aubrey was telling. Later, she would find out one way or another.

"I didn't know if you'd let me come with you. It's not like you and Mom get along."

"Your mom and I get along just fine, and I can always use help with the horses." *No matter how irritating Jen is.* "You can help me brush them."

After unloading the horses from the trailer, Beckett headed into the barn with Aubrey following her. She took a horse out of the stall and tied him to one of the hooks located on the outside of the gate. "This is Barley. He's one of my gentlest horses."

Beckett filled a bucket with a curry comb, a stiff-bristled body brush, a soft-bristled finishing brush, and a plastic mane and tail comb. She handed the bucket to Aubrey. "Barley is a good one for you start with."

Barley nuzzled her just like he knew her. "Follow my lead, starting on the left side, which is called the nearside."

"Why is it called the nearside?"

"Because that's the side of the horse you mount him on."

"Why?"

"That goes back to when men with swords rode them. They mounted from the left so the sword didn't damage places they wanted to protect." She took the curry comb from her grooming box and held it up. "This is a curry comb. You'll use it to loosen the dirt in your horse's coat. We want to remove any mud, grit, dust, and other debris before trying to put a real shine on the horse's coat."

Aubrey stroked the brush across Barley's midsection.

"Not straight across. Brush him in a circular motion, like this." She brushed the horse's hindquarter and watched as Aubrey did the same. "Now, while you're brushing him, check him over for injuries and skin irritations." She continued to curry the horse. "Let me know if you find any."

"When did you first start riding?" Aubrey kept on brushing the horse.

"Oh, I was probably around five or six. Maybe younger."

"Wow. That young?"

"When you grow up on a ranch you learn quick." She worked her way around to the off side of the horse. "People have lots of different responsibilities on the ranch, but everyone works the horses."

Aubrey moved around to the off side soon after she did. "Will you teach me to ride?"

She nodded. "If your mother approves."

Aubrey shook her head. "She won't."

"Why not?"

"She's afraid of them. My grandpa has horses, too, and she was bucked off when she was a kid."

Jen's attitude made sense now. At least regarding the horses. Parents should know better than to put a rider on a horse before they were ready. "Where do your grandparents live?"

"Here." She continued brushing.

She pulled her eyebrows together. "What do you mean, here?"

"At the Double T Ranch."

"Bob and Dorothy are your grandparents?" Why hadn't she made that connection before?

Aubrey nodded. "Yeah. I can see your horses in the pasture from the back porch." She dropped the brush in the bucket and took the sponge from Beckett's bucket. "What do we do with this?"

"We use it to wipe the dust off." She took the sponge from Aubrey, dropped it back into the bucket, and handed her the mane and tail comb. "You can see my horses from their house?"

"Yeah. I sneak out and pet them sometimes. Give them apples from the trees in the field." Aubrey glanced at her, giving her a wary look. "Is that okay?"

Now it all made sense. Nothing seriously wrong with Barley. It had to be the apples. "You're welcome to pet them anytime, but I need you to stop feeding them." She reached over and put her hand on Barley's belly. "Feel how hard that is?"

Aubrey felt his belly. "Why is it like that?"

"Too many apples give horses colic—stomach pain."

"Oh, God. I'm sorry. I didn't know."

"He'll be fine, now that I know what happened." She continued to curry the horse. "I'll talk to your mom. Maybe convince her to let you ride old Barley there. He's a quarter horse with a steady and calm temperament—good for riding the trails." She used to ride him frequently herself until she fell in love with Pearl, her Tennessee walking horse. Pearl was a bit stockier, but still elegant, and moved with the speed of the Texas wind when she was ready to go.

"What about your dad? What does he think?"

Aubrey shook her head. "No dad, just Mom. She used to have a girlfriend, but she didn't move with us. They fought a lot."

This was new information. She'd just assumed a beautiful woman like Jen had a significant other in her life. "I thought I saw a ring on her finger." A large diamond ring. She'd noticed it the first time they'd met, while she was picking up something in the store.

"That was her grandma's. Mom says she wears it to fend off the weirdos."

Beckett laughed. "I totally understand." More than one man who thought she needed help around the ranch had approached her. Occasionally she hired one or two people to help, but she had only one steady employee on the ranch to help clean the stalls and keep the fences maintained.

"Maybe you can teach Mom to ride, too." Aubrey seemed excited at the possibility.

"That'll be up to her as well." She had more horses like Barley but doubted Jen would take kindly to being taught anything. Helping her up onto a horse might be pleasurable, but considering most of her interactions with Jen, it would probably be more trouble than it was worth.

†

Jen slid the roller door down in front of the counter and locked it into place before she punched in the alarm code and pushed open the pharmacy door. "Aubrey." She slid her key into the door and locked the deadbolt before she glanced toward the chair where her daughter usually sat waiting for her. Not there. She made her way to the front of the store, checking the aisles as she went, but didn't see her. She stopped at the checkout counter where the clerk was sitting, reading something on her phone.

"Have you seen Aubrey?"

"She left a while ago."

"How long is a while?"

The clerk scrunched her eyebrows together as she looked up from her phone. "Maybe an hour?"

"Thanks." She went through the automatic glass door and scanned the sidewalk. Not there either. She spun around and checked the other side of the street, then up and down the pavement. She'd been inside just fifteen minutes before, hadn't she? Maybe it was longer. She walked across the street to the local diner. They'd discussed having dinner there, but it wasn't like Aubrey not to wait for her. She opened the door and scanned the restaurant.

"Who ya lookin' for, Jen?" Mabel rushed past her to deliver food to a couple sitting in one of the old-fashioned vinyl booths that lined the windows.

"Aubrey. Is she here?"

"Nope. Haven't seen her in here." Mabel was never free with her information. You always had to pry it from her, which was odd for the town gossip.

"Did you see her anywhere else?"

"Saw her out there in the street earlier, pettin' the horses in Beckett's trailer while Beckett went down to the post office."

"Thanks." She took out her cell phone, hit the button for Aubrey, and headed back outside. No answer. Panic rushed through her as she ran across the street and got into her car. "Aubrey. Call me back right now." She knew she wouldn't. Texting was her only method of communication. She fumbled to find the letters to form a message on her phone.

Where are you? I'm worried.

No response, so she hit the call button for her parents. Her mother answered on the third ring.

"Is Aubrey there?"

"Well, hello to you too."

"Sorry. Hello, Mother. Is Aubrey at the house with you?"

"I thought she was with you?"

"She was, but—"

"You lost your own daughter. Should've tightened the reins on that girl a long time ago. If I'd tightened them with you sooner then—"

"Then what, Mother?"

"Then you wouldn't be looking for your daughter right now."

"Don't ever insinuate that Aubrey was a mistake. If you ever say that to her, you will *never* see me or her again." There was silence on the line. "Understand?"

"I'll see you when you get home." The line went dead.

Having Aubrey at such a young age hadn't been easy, but she was the most precious gift Jen could've ever received. The responsibility certainly made her take a different path than she'd planned, but she wouldn't trade any of the experience to raise such a beautiful girl for anything. The joy Aubrey brought into her life outweighed the work a thousand times over.

She checked her text messages again. Nothing. She was beginning to type another message, when the bubbles appeared on the screen.

I'm at Beckett's house. She's showing me how to brush the horses.

Unbelievable. So many things went through her head as she typed her response.

How did you get there?

The bubbles appeared and Aubrey's response was quick.

Rode with her from town.

She was so furious she could barely hit the right letters.

Stay there. I'm on my way.

Who the hell did Beckett think she was, just picking up her daughter and taking her home? *After* she'd told her no when Beckett had been in the store earlier. She didn't really know Beckett all that well and didn't feel the need to explain her decision to her—to clue her in on the back story and reason for it—why she wasn't ready to give Aubrey the kind of unsupervised freedom that going to Beckett's ranch might provide. Not yet anyway.

†

Beckett heard the gravel crunching louder as a car raced down her gravel drive. Whoever it was needed to let up on the gas, or they might find themselves in one of the drainage ditches that lined the road. She walked out of the barn just as the car fishtailed and came to a stop in front of the house. *Jen.* Now she was sure there was more to Aubrey's story. She watched her get out of her car, rush to the porch, and pound on the door. Jen wasn't much taller than Aubrey. More petite than she'd imagined. Probably due to the fact she never saw Jen standing anywhere other than on the elevated pharmacy platform at the store. She strolled across the yard.

"Over here."

"Where is she?" Jen launched off the porch and sped toward her.

She jerked her head toward the barn. "In with the horses."

Dressed in skinny jeans and a pale-yellow, button-down shirt, the curves and swells Jen kept hidden under her pharmacy coat were surprisingly pleasant. In fact, if she lost the attitude, Jen would be very attractive. She was a lot of fire for such a small package.

Jen brushed past her. "I can't believe you brought her out here without my permission—after I said no."

Aubrey had lied to her mother. She followed Jen into the barn. "She wanted to learn how to care for the horses." She pinched her lips together. She'd take the heat for now. Wait and see if Aubrey fessed up.

"That's my call, not yours." Jen's anger was clear.

"Look, Mom. Isn't he beautiful?" Aubrey ran the brush across the horse's back. Her smile was so wide, no one would get the impression that she knew she'd been caught in a lie. Maybe it was a habit that didn't bother her.

"Let's go." Jen didn't seem to care about Aubrey's excitement and wasn't having any part of it.

Aubrey continued brushing the horse. "After I finish."

Beckett leaned against the barn door opening and waited for Aubrey to volunteer how she'd really ended up here at the ranch. It wasn't any surprise that she didn't.

"Absolutely not. You shouldn't be here in the first place." Jen plucked the brush from Aubrey's hand and dropped it into the bucket.

"You can't lock me up forever." Aubrey rushed past Beckett.

"Come back anytime, Aubrey."

"She's not coming back." Jen followed Aubrey. "You did *not* have my permission to bring her here in the first place." She spun around on her way to her car. "I'll call the police if you ever do this again."

"No. Mom. *Don't.*" Aubrey's eyebrows rose. "She didn't do anything wrong."

"*You*, get in the car. We'll talk about this when we get home." Jen yanked open the door, climbed into the car, and tore out of the driveway onto the road.

Beckett stood in the drive and watched the dust trail rise on the road. The car was long gone by the time the cloud dissipated. She hadn't expected such an eventful afternoon. She shook her head as she headed back into the barn to finish grooming the horses, confused. Which had impacted her more? The news that Jen was gay and single or the fact that she didn't take the time to listen to what anyone else had to say? How could a woman be so gorgeous and so infuriating at the same time?

†

Jen was furious as she glanced in her rear-view mirror. Seeing Beckett standing by the barn with her hands on her hips made the heat on her neck burn. She glanced over at Aubrey sitting in the passenger seat with her arms crossed tightly across her chest. The silence was more uncomfortable than she'd anticipated. She never was one to not talk things out—something her mother always hated and did her best to avoid.

"So, what do you have to say about this? You know better than to go off with strangers."

"She's not a stranger. She comes into the store all the time." Aubrey shifted in her seat. "You didn't have to yell at her like that."

"Okay. She's not a stranger, but she should've asked me—you both should've asked."

"It's not her fault. I hid in the backseat of her truck."

She yanked the car to the side of the road. "You did what?"

"She didn't know I was there until we got to her ranch."

Her stomach dropped. She closed her eyes momentarily and took in a breath. She'd just reamed out Beckett for taking Aubrey to her ranch, and none of what happened had been her doing. "Why?"

"I just wanted to see the horses, and I knew you wouldn't let me go."

She flipped the car around and hit the gas pedal hard.

Aubrey clutched the oh shit handle above the door. "We're going back?"

"Damn straight we are. We both have apologies to make." She might be strong-willed, but unlike her own mother, she knew how to admit when she was wrong.

"What?" Aubrey scrunched her eyebrows together. "What'd I do?"

"You let her take the blame."

Jen raced down the gravel drive, and came to a sliding stop, just as she had a little while ago. She didn't see Beckett anywhere in sight, but she was probably still in the barn. Aubrey didn't budge as she got out of the car. "Come on."

"But—"

"No excuses. People respect you more when you own up to your mistakes."

Aubrey got out of the car and walked slowly into the barn with her eyes glued to the ground. Jen followed close behind.

"Aubrey told me she got into your truck without your knowledge."

"Good. I hoped she would." Beckett gave her a soft smile. She wasn't even being smug about it.

Jen glanced at Aubrey. "Go ahead."

"I'm sorry. I shouldn't have hidden in your truck."

"And?" Jen prompted her.

"I'm sorry that I let my mom think you brought me here."

"Apology accepted." She pointed to the horse Aubrey had been grooming. "I'm just about done. Why don't you finish him up while your mom and I visit for a minute."

Aubrey looked at Jen for approval. Jen nodded, and Aubrey smiled widely and rushed to the horse. She didn't get those smiles very often and wanted more of them.

"I'm sorry as well." She slipped her hands into her pockets. "I shouldn't have jumped to conclusions."

Beckett tilted her head. "Didn't think you knew how to say those words."

"I've said them plenty. Just didn't think I'd ever say them to you."

"That's an accomplishment that calls for celebration." Beckett's face broke into the most beautiful grin, and Jen couldn't believe the zap that coursed through her. "I've got a roast in the crock pot. Stay for dinner?"

"I'm sure you weren't planning on company."

"You're right. I wasn't, but there's plenty. Maybe we can talk about Aubrey and the horses a little more."

Jen had no intention of discussing the subject of Aubrey helping with the horse any further. She was going to avoid that conversation as much as she could, especially in front of Aubrey.

†

Beckett grabbed a shirt from the back of a chair as she entered the house and tossed it into the laundry room. For some reason she was nervous about Jen's opinion of her house. She glanced around her kitchen as they entered, checking to make sure it wasn't too much of a mess. She lived alone, so she kept everything clean most of the time, but she always picked up a little more when she was having company.

"Dinner smells wonderful." Jen's stomach growled. "Sorry. I haven't eaten since eleven."

Beckett took a bag of rolls from the counter, poured them onto a pan, and slid it into the oven. "I hope you don't mind store-bought."

"Nope. We're not particular." Jen smiled. "Just thankful for the meal."

"Spoon or fork?" She fumbled with the silverware in the drawer. The nicer Jen was, the more nervous she became. Beckett had always known where she stood with her before—each on opposite sides of the fence.

"Spoon."

She set the table in three places. "Have a seat." She went to the refrigerator and took out the bag of lettuce she'd cleaned earlier in the day. "I'll throw together a salad to keep your stomach quiet."

"That's not necessary, unless you were already planning on it."

She wasn't, but it wasn't any trouble. "Every night." She turned to the counter and rolled her eyes at herself. "Tomato okay?"

"Absolutely." Jen's voice rose. "We love tomatoes."

She didn't dare turn around to see the smile that went along with Jen's voice. She took a tomato from the counter, chunked it, and dropped it into the salad. After she mixed it with a set of tongs, she slid the salad and several bowls onto the table.

"This looks delicious." Jen picked up the tongs and began filling the bowls. "Homegrown tomato?"

"The best kind." Beckett reached into the refrigerator and took out the ranch and Italian dressings. Hopefully those would do, since she didn't have anything else.

Aubrey immediately swiped the ranch, doused her salad, then jumped up, went to the silverware drawer, and brought forks to the table. "I'm starving." She dug into her salad.

Aubrey knew how to make herself at home.

"I've got tea, lemonade, and..." Beckett rummaged around in the refrigerator. "I think there's a beer or two in here."

"Lemonade for me, please," Jen said. She hadn't dug into her salad yet. She seemed to be waiting for her.

"One lemonade. Aubrey?" She held up the containers.

"Beer for me." Aubrey grinned.

"Lemonade all around." Beckett plucked a couple of glasses from the cabinet and set them on the table as she sat down. She and Jen went for the Italian dressing at the same time, and when their fingers touched, they both bolted back like they'd stuck a screwdriver in the same electrical socket.

"You first." Jen picked up the dressing and set it in front of Beckett.

She pushed it back across the table. "No. You."

"Please. You go ahead." Jen pushed it back. "I'm truly grateful you've asked us to stay for dinner."

Beckett picked it up and planted it on the table in front of Jen. "You're my guest. I insist." What the hell was going on? Were they actually having an awkward battle of manners?

Jen grinned as she picked up the dressing, shook it, and poured a modest amount on her salad. "May I?" She raised her eyebrows as she held the tilted bottle over Beckett's salad.

She nodded and felt the odd tingle in her belly once more. In an attempt to ignore it, Beckett looked at her salad and dug in. As they ate, the silence was weirdly uncomfortable. The lettuce crunching in her ears was magnified a thousand times. The buzzer on the oven rang, giving her a reprieve from the awkwardness. She sprang from her seat and took the rolls out of the oven, let them slide into a basket, and set it on the table.

"Help yourself to a piece of bread while I dip the roast up."

Beckett took in a deep breath as she dipped an ample amount of roast, potatoes, and carrots into each bowl. She was having a hard time grasping why this woman who usually irritated her like dry fingers on a microfiber cloth was making her so unsure of herself. She carried the bowls to the table and sat.

"So how did you end up here from Dallas?" she asked while scooping a bite of pot roast onto her spoon.

Jen seemed to be contemplating her response as she chewed the spoonful of pot roast she'd just forked and put into her mouth.

"Mom doesn't like my friends, so we moved," Aubrey explained. "We're staying with grandparents."

Jen swallowed and set down her spoon and wiped her mouth. It seemed she'd waited one second too long. "I like your friends just fine. What I don't like is the trouble you get into when you're with them." She took a sip of lemonade.

Beckett patted Aubrey's hand. "Your mom is probably treating you the same as your grandma did her."

"Not even close—don't compare me to her." Jen's eyebrows rose before she focused on her food again, pushing a piece of roast across her bowl and spearing a carrot instead.

She hadn't expected such a strong answer for such a simple statement. "It sounds like you did the right thing."

Jen didn't look up. "I did, and I don't need anyone's approval."

Apparently, she'd hit some kind of nerve and would leave it be for now. "More lemonade?" She held up the bottle.

Jen nodded, dropped her spoon, and held up her glass. "Thanks."

"Do you have a partner, Beckett?" Aubrey didn't seem to have a filter.

Jen reached for her napkin as she choked on the bite she'd just taken. "Aubrey, mind your manners."

"What?" Aubrey stared at Beckett. "You're gay, aren't you?"

She nodded and pulled her lip up to one side. "I am."

"So, why don't you have a partner?"

"Aubrey, that's enough." Jen held up her hand. "You don't come into someone's house and start grilling them."

"It's okay." Beckett set down her spoon and wiped her mouth. "I lost my wife a little over ten years ago."

Jen's face stilled. "I'm so sorry."

"Thanks. We had a good run." She smiled as Brandy's face popped into her head. "Aubrey tells me your partner is in Dallas."

"Seems you had a lot of time for discussion this afternoon." She shook her head. "I don't have any strings in Dallas." Jen stood and took her dishes to the sink. "Let's help Beckett clean up and then get on our way." She glanced at Beckett. "I'm sure you have things to do."

She shook her head. "Nope." She smiled at Aubrey. "Want some ice cream?"

"What flavor?"

She stood, went to the refrigerator, and pulled open the freezer door. Aubrey's eyes widened at the array of ice cream. Chocolate, vanilla, coffee, butter brickle, chocolate-chip cookie dough, peanut-butter chocolate, and several flavors of sherbet.

"You *really* like ice cream." Jen laughed and shook her head. "If that was in our freezer, it would be gone in a day."

The grin on Jen's face made her stomach flip-flop. "It's my guilty pleasure." She glanced at Aubrey as she went to the cabinet and took out some large bowls. "Pick as many as you want."

Aubrey followed her to the counter with three different flavors.

"Is that all?"

Aubrey glanced at Jen, looking for permission.

Jen flipped her hand toward the freezer. "Go ahead."

"What about you?" She raised eyebrows and waited for an answer.

Jen pulled open the freezer door and seemed to be searching for a certain flavor. "You have something against strawberry?"

"Nope. Love it." Beckett went into the garage and came back with a brand-new quart of strawberry ice cream. "I have a full deep freeze too."

†

Jen finished the last bite of her three scoops of ice cream and relaxed into the chair. "I haven't eaten that much food in ages." She felt like she was going to pop. "I think I might just have to roll myself out to the car."

"Mom, you *never* eat ice cream."

Beckett raised an eyebrow. "Really?"

"It's not something I buy regularly." Jen stood, collected all the bowls, carried them to the sink, and rinsed them before she loaded them in the dishwasher.

"She never does dishes at home either." Aubrey's filter seemed to have totally disappeared.

"She cooks, and you clean up. That's only fair." Beckett came to her defense, which was unnecessary.

"She hasn't cooked since we got here." Aubrey sucked on her spoon. "Grandma does all the cooking."

"Only because she insists."

"And your mother works all day, too."

She smiled at Beckett's persistence. "It's okay. She'll figure it out some day when she has kids of her own."

"Do you have any kids?" Aubrey again with the questions.

Beckett shook her head. "No. Somehow I never got that pleasure."

"Too bad. Then I'd at least have someone to hang out with when I come see the horses."

"What's wrong with me?"

Aubrey grinned. "Nothing. You're kinda cool, actually. Isn't she, Mom?"

"I can't disagree." Her cheeks heated as she held eye contact for a moment.

Beckett's smile widened and her cheeks reddened. "Wow. Cool status. I'm flattered."

Seeing Beckett smile like that was a new experience, and her stomach swarmed like it was loaded with fireflies. Things were happening tonight with Beckett that she'd never expected, and she wasn't quite sure how to deal with what she was feeling. She cleared her throat. "We should go." She was reluctant to let the feelings pass without explanation but would let them settle to see if they remained after the night was over.

"I'm sure you have your hands full with your job and Aubrey, but you're both welcome to come back to see the horses or just to have ice cream anytime."

"*Every day.*" Aubrey's voice rose.

It was nice seeing Aubrey happy. Maybe the horses would help her acclimate to living here. Jen was ashamed at how she'd judged Beckett before truly getting to know her. It seemed she was just a woman trying to make it in the world with what she had. More than she could say for herself at times.

"Go on out to the car. I'll be there in a minute." For some reason Jen felt she needed to explain about the way she'd acted before. Apologize, even. "Sorry for the rudeness earlier. I have mom issues and don't like being told what to do."

"That's pretty evident." Beckett moved closer. "To be clear, I didn't invite you to stay tonight because I'm interested in being your mother."

Beckett touched her hand, and heat spun up though her arm to her chest, then straight down to areas she hadn't expected. Beckett leaned—she leaned, and when their lips met her mind clouded. She deepened the kiss, and sweet Lord, she was in heaven. When they finally parted, Jen had to steady herself on the porch railing. "That was…"

"Very nice." Beckett smiled. "Dinner tomorrow?"

She nodded. "I'll come alone."

50 BY 50

RENEE MACKENZIE

The drive from the airport to the hotel has me more than a little frazzled. In all my research leading up to this trip, I ignored the comments about the Austin traffic patterns and traffic in general. Next time I need to pay closer attention.

I have to accept the fact that I am not good at making my own travel arrangements. Dara always decided where we would go on our vacations, always made the reservations, and always did the driving when we were in an unfamiliar place. Recently single, I plan to get much better at traveling alone.

The hotel room is small but will do. The subdued color palette is pleasing to my otherwise overwhelmed senses.

After I place my laptop bag and carry-all onto the desk (never on the cloth-covered chairs or love seat!), I wipe down surfaces with the Clorox wipes I always travel with.

My laptop gets powered up, my 50-by-50 Word document is opened, and I scroll down to the "Eat a Meal in Every State" section to copy and paste the bright red checkmark next to Texas. I don't even try to temper the big, goofy smile that splits my face.

I save the document, then make a quick parenthetical comment next to my checkmark exclaiming "the best burrito ever" before saving it again. I'm glad I stopped on the way to the hotel to eat lunch so I could check off Texas. I am not counting any state I went to with Dara or with my family as a child. This list is just about me. So, thirteen states down.

I peruse the document and make a separate, mental list of the other items I hope to check off over the weekend.

One item in the activities section is to partake in the Austin Music Scene. This I will do tonight. I've researched venues and have come up with a few options.

I may even have the chance to add to my ongoing tally toward hiking 1000 trail miles. I need to check my browser history to see which of the places I've looked into are easily accessible from the hotel since I am still shell-shocked after the drive from the airport. How in the world did I manage to get lost so many times?

Maybe I will see a new life bird—I have heard there are Crested Cara Cara in this area! Or better yet, see the bats I've heard so much about.

Then there are the flowers I'd like to take pictures of— the bluebonnets and Indian paintbrushes top the list. And as a bonus, the bluebonnets are the state flower of Texas. I briefly entertain the idea of adding "Take photos of state birds and flowers" to my list, then realize I would have to start over with the "Every state" section if I add to the goal of eating in every one of them. Never mind.

My pulse quickens as my gaze drifts farther down the Activities section of my list. Of the fifteen items on this part, five are sexual in nature. Nothing has been checked off yet. There is only one on the list that I consider possible for this weekend trip to Austin: Have a one-night stand. Possible, but I won't rush into it just for the sake of checking something off my list.

How I ever managed to get to forty-five years old without having a one-night stand flabbergasts me. Okay, maybe it doesn't. I've spent so much of my life trying to be a "good girl" that the sex part of my list of hopeful, first-time activities could be the entire fifty things I want to do before I turn fifty years old. But I had narrowed it down to only five so that I could leave room for all the places and activities of a nonsexual nature that I deemed more important.

Okay, maybe not more important, but I stand by my choices of the thirty-five places and ten *other* activities I have placed on my list.

†

I pull out my phone as I step away from my Uber driver's car. The ride share is necessary because I plan to drink tonight. And I might drink a lot. I punch the amount for a generous tip into the app on my phone, then look up to see the line forming outside of T's. I'm happy to see that the reviews online were right about the clientele being mostly women.

I join the queue and am pleased that the line moves quickly down the long hallway. The two women directly in front of me are in leather mini-skirts. Behind me is a woman in tight jeans, a black tank top, and clunky motorcycle boots. I glance down at my own tight jeans and flower-patterned, sleeveless, button-down shirt and decide I don't look too out of place.

When I turn forward again and follow the flow of the line down the hallway, my eyes linger on the ass of the woman to the right. Without the short, black, high-heeled boots I wear, I would still be at least an inch taller. Before I can stop myself, I imagine running my hands up her legs, under her skirt, and into enough wetness to coat my hand.

I am shaking off the image when I find myself at the front of the line, being asked for my ID and the cover charge. Once done paying, I scan the interior for the restrooms. I want my bladder empty and lipstick freshened before the band takes the stage. Ry's Beat, as far as I've been able to see online, has a classic rock sound infused with a bit of R&B.

I am in and out of one of the restrooms, making a mental note that they are both unisex. A lot of places in the South have been slow to follow this trend. I even know of owners of places in my part of Virginia who would like to go unisex, but hold out so as not to be perceived as "caving to the queers" in the eyes of their staunchly conservative patrons. I no longer give my business to those places.

I scan the room for a place to sit just as the lights are lowered. A woman jumps off a barstool to make a beeline for the stage and I slip onto the vacated seat. The bartender who approaches is pretty, and quite hot. We flirt a bit, she gets me my glass of wine, I give her a good tip for her attention.

I am aware that many of the women here are much younger than I am. I am not uncomfortable with this knowledge, not really, because I know most people have a hard time believing I am forty-five. I have taken very good care of myself my entire life, and can say without conceit that it shows.

As the band warms up on stage, I sneak quick peeks at the bartender and think about my list. Once the band starts playing, I can officially check the Austin Music Scene off my 50-by-50 list, but now I am wondering about the One-Night-Stand option of that list. My face warms as I catch a quick glimpse of the bartender again before she is off to the other end of the bar to serve another woman.

The first soft words of the song that comes from the stage cause me to spin my barstool around to face away from the bar. My gaze scans up and down the length of the tall, lean singer as the words begin to come out faster and louder.

Tight, black jeans cover thin legs and a black-leather vest hides the breast area. The muscles of the arms holding the guitar in front of the singer grow taut and are covered in tattoos. Dark, shaggy hair falls across the forehead of an angular face.

My gaze moves to the guitar and I feel heat growing everywhere on my body as I watch the undulating movement of the hips against the back of the guitar. I am wet and don't know if it is a man or a woman making me that way.

Ry, I gather, is the singer based on the way the women cry out the name all around the room. It appears I am not the only one swooning.

When Ry throws her–his–their head from side to side to the beat, sweat is thrown out in all directions.

Wetness settles more prominently between my legs and I feel a roiling in my stomach. Shame? Confusion? I am a firm believer in the value of the entire alphabet—LGBTQA+— but have never had any reason to believe any letter but the L applies to me. This is going to take some processing; of this I am certain.

Ry finishes a particularly rocking song and the applause thunders around me. When Ry places the guitar on a stand to the left and stands center stage behind a microphone, my gaze goes there—yes, my eyes go right to Ry's crotch—and I see the slight bulge there.

I squirm on the barstool. Either Ry is packing, or for the first time in my life, I am lusting after a man. As much as this surprises me, the fact that it doesn't actually bother me is an even bigger surprise.

I bring my focus away from Ry's crotch and when I look in the singer's eyes, I see lust reflected right back at me. My breath catches in my chest. I am all but panting as Ry sings a hauntingly beautiful ballad. His eyes are closed now. Some notes make me reconsider my conclusion about his sex, but mostly I just watch and listen, and feel the heat washing over and over my body.

Ry's Beat plays some original music interspersed with covers of other bands. They do a wonderful job on all, but I am particularly impressed with their version of Maroon 5's "Memories" and "Chasing Cars" by Snow Patrol. Well, I can say "they" when talking about the band, but my attention is riveted on Ry the entire time they are on the stage.

I am so aroused by the end of the final set that I start looking around for someone to bring back to my hotel room. Every man and woman in the club will be vying for Ry's attention, so I decide to find a woman as aroused as I am for some consolation fucking. Why not? It will check an item off my list.

I chuckle to myself as I realize several people have already started to partner-up. A few couples, people who didn't actually come in together, if I remember correctly, are groping between each other's legs already.

I take a big sip of the water I have been nursing for the last hour and try to cool down. I am no longer truly entertaining the idea of hooking up with any of the other women hungrily scanning the club for someone to ease the ache of wanting. I don't want to be with someone just for the sake of getting off and checking the activity off my list. I decide that I will only do the one-night thing with someone I desire beyond reason. I am relieved by this decision.

I catch a glimpse of Ry's tall, lean body in my peripheral vision and turn to face the singer. I can't keep my eyes from tracking the entire length of that divine, sweaty body. At the end of the second pass of my gaze, my eyes are captured by Ry's.

I'm barely breathing as Ry approaches, stopping a foot or so away from me. Close up, I can tell Ry is probably mid-thirties. Faint crow's feet extend from the outer corners of the dark, smoldering eyes.

"Hi," Ry says, voice gravely from use and still not identifiable as male or female.

Dark eyes bore into mine.

Hello letter B...or Q, I think, no longer worried about which sex this hot person is. *Really,* I ask myself, *what the hell is up with the labels anyway?*

"Enjoying yourself?" Ry asks.

"Immensely." I am shocked at how smooth my voice is, not giving away the tension that has been building inside me since I first saw Ry on stage. "You were amazing."

Ry smiles, big and open, before chuckling and saying, "Thank you."

I can feel eyes on us as people wanting to catch Ry's attention watch us. Goose flesh erupts on my arms and I can feel my nipples pressing against my floral, cotton shirt.

Ry looks at the line for the rest rooms and my gaze follows.

"I need to throw some cold water on my face. There is an employees' restroom in the back. Come with?"

I nod my head slowly and feel my teeth biting my lower lip.

Ry takes my hand and leads me to the back.

I go in the single-stalled bathroom with Ry and watch as the door is shut and locked behind us. Ry freshens up in the sink, then turns to face me, leaning against the countertop.

"What's your name?"

"Megan."

"Megan. I like that."

My blood pounds in my head, heat consumes my body.

"I liked the way you watched me on stage. Did you like what you were seeing?"

"Yes." The word barely makes it out of my mouth.

I jump when there is a knock at the door.

"Come back later," Ry calls out. Turning back to me, Ry then says, "Is that okay? Do you want to stay in here with me for a little while?"

I nod.

"Can I kiss you?"

Another nod.

Ry leans in and I reach out to touch a smooth, soft face. Her face. I know the second our lips touch that Ry is a woman and I hesitate when I realize I am a little disappointed. But am I? Having a one-night stand is on my 50-by-50 list, not having sex with someone of the opposite sex. But I had wanted this person with no regard to their sex, hadn't I?

She slowly pulls out of the kiss and I trail a fingertip over the inked images on her left shoulder. A pocket watch, compass, and interlocking gears cover her flesh in shades of black and gray ink. Below the elbow a more colorful, nautical theme plays out on the ropy muscles of her arm.

"You okay?" Ry's question is gentle.

"Yes," I hiss. "Much more than okay." I raise my eyes to meet hers.

Ry presses against me and I can feel the bulge in her crotch press against my sex. It is exciting and I want Ry to take me in this bathroom. I want her to take me hard and fast. I can't make myself say the words, but I do move to unfasten my belt.

She understands and helps me with my belt before unbuttoning and unzipping my jeans. Together we push my jeans down to my knees. She growls as she pushes the crotch of my panties aside.

Ry's mouth finds my neck at the same time her fingers find the wetness between my legs. We moan in unison.

The raw, heated scent of my desire and Ry's sweat fill my senses.

She pushes what feels like two fingers inside me at the same time that she rocks her hips into me. My body responds with another gush of wetness. She starts a steady rhythm inside me as the fingers of her left hand find one of my nipples through my shirt. She pinches my nipple and I gasp. The rougher she gets with me the wetter I grow.

Within minutes she is thrusting deeper inside me than anyone—including myself—has ever been. My hands slip under her leather vest and I grab at her back, my fingers digging into her flesh. Orgasm rips through me and she barely keeps me from sliding onto the floor.

"I got you," Ry says into my ear.

I catch my breath and reach for her belt buckle. She removes my hand and leans closer, whispering in my ear. "Come home with me."

I nod and stand there dumbly as she pulls up my jeans and refastens them.

Ry tells me to wait for her just inside the back door while she goes for her guitar. We are on the way out of the club when Ry asks about my car. I mumble the word "Uber." and she changes our trajectory about forty-fives degrees and leads me to a gray Honda Civic. The small car is not what I was expecting, but there is something about its simplicity that turns me on. I'm pretty sure every little thing about Ry will turn me on.

Ry puts the guitar case in the trunk and holds the passenger-side door open for me. When she climbs into the driver's seat and starts the engine, my heart pounds harder and harder. I am really doing this. I really just had sex in a bathroom with a stranger and am going home with her.

"What brings you to Austin?" Ry asks me.

I cock my head and she quickly adds, "You don't sound like a Texan."

"Oh," I say. "I'm from Virginia." When her gaze flicks back and forth between me and the road, I add, "I'm here on vacation. A long weekend."

"Cool," she says. "Check anything off your list yet?"

My head snaps around and I stare at her. "My list?" I choke out the question. My head starts to spin and I am confused by her knowledge of my list.

"Don't most tourists have a list of things they want to do on vacation?"

"Yeah—yeah, I guess they do." I relax a little.

She laughs. "Have you, then?"

"Burrito and live music," I say, flustered.

"You had a burrito on your must-do-in-Austin list?"

"No, it's on my Eat-a-Meal-in-Every-State list." I cannot believe I have said that out loud to a stranger. She's going to think I'm insane.

She is sneaking glimpses of me as she drives. "Can't say I saw that one coming."

I laugh. When I see the corner of her mouth twitching upward, I laugh even harder.

"How many states so far?"

"Thirteen."

"Is it always a burrito?"

I bark out another laugh. "No. Sometimes it's sushi, or BBQ, or tacos."

"Oh, thank goodness." She wipes imaginary sweat from her forehead. "Because eating a burrito in every state would be a little weird."

"You have something against burritos?" I tease.

"No, that just feels way too rigid." She flips on her blinker, a move that surprises me from this rock god. When she turns onto a side road and then immediately onto a long driveway, I grow nervous. She parks and turns in her seat to face me. "How long have you been working on this list?"

"A little over a year." I try to hold her gaze but her dark eyes are so intense I have to look away.

"Feels like there is a story there."

I nod my head but don't offer any further insights. My friends and family know that Dara left me one day after our ten-year anniversary, but I haven't told anyone that I had also just started treatment on precancerous lesions in my bladder. The health scare combined with being newly single made me reevaluate my life, at which time I started my 50-by-50 list, and a keen desire to live my life for me and only me from then on.

We go inside and Ry pours two glasses of water. We each take a sip before she takes mine from me and places both on the kitchen counter. Without another word, she pulls me into a small bedroom halfway down the hall. She strips me, then herself, and I find my eyes going to her discarded briefs and lingering on the packing cock she'd worn in her pants during the show. Heat grows on my face and neck.

Her hands and mouth are all over my torso and hips, then land on my shoulders and start directing me down onto my knees. I gently run my fingers over the smooth skin of her thighs as I settle into a kneeling position in front of her. When my mouth finds her heat, I am amazed by how very wet she is.

I dig my fingers into her firm ass and start working her with my face and tongue. Her moans and the pressure of her hands in my hair keep me close. I lose myself in the scent and taste of her.

†

I pull the covers over my head as I stretch, then pull them down to look through one semi-opened eye. I am not in the hotel room. The night before comes rushing at me and I sit up. I am alone in Ry's bed. I look around and find my clothing folded on a small dresser I hadn't noticed earlier. Maybe Ry has left the house and I can get dressed and out the door without having to see her.

The slight soreness between my legs is a reminder that Ry and I were up until the early hours fucking. A pleased sigh escapes me as I replay an image of Ry hovering over me as she slammed her fingers into me over and over. I'm pretty sure I had never come as hard as I did last night. Or as often.

Smiling, I mentally check off One-Night Stand on my 50-by-50 list. Then I hurriedly get up and throw on my clothes, all but my boots.

I am quietly trying to find my way out of the house when a voice behind me says, "Good morning, Megan. Do you have time to stay for an omelet?"

I turn and the sight of Ry in boxers and a faded T-shirt sends heat throughout my body.

"Oh." I swallow hard. "Good morning."

She looks me up and down, then stares at my boots that I am gripping in my right hand as I shove my phone into my back pocket with my left hand. I place my boots on the floor by the front door, sneak a feel to my front pocket to ensure

104

driver's license, credit card, and hotel key card are still in my possession.

She smiles and I melt a little.

"It's just breakfast," she says with a smirk.

"Okay. Thank you."

"Spinach, caramelized onions, and goat cheese okay in your omelet?"

I almost say yes, but stop after reminding myself that I don't do things I don't want to do anymore. "No onions, please." I give a little shrug. "Reflux."

She nods and pushes the onion away from the cutting board.

I watch her crack open the eggs and become enthralled by the movement of her hands. Between her guitar playing and our late-night activities both in the restroom at the club and here at her home, I am not surprised that her hands work so beautifully in the kitchen as well.

I catch Ry stealing glimpses at me from across the table as we eat our omelets and toast. I quirk up an eyebrow. Amazing myself with my boldness, I ask in a cocky voice, "Yes?"

Her gaze quickly leaves mine, skirts around the room a few times, then comes back to me. "What can you tell me about your list of 50 things?" she asks.

"Oh, it's just some places I want to see, things I want to do."

She puts down her fork and stares at me, a glint in her dark eyes. "Anything I can help you with?"

After almost inhaling my final bite of toast, I catch my breath and take a sip of water.

"Have I already?" she asks, eyes wide and smile wider.

"Live music–you were a part of that." I hold her stare as I add, "And have a one-night stand."

She blinks a few times, then stands and clears the dishes from the table. When I find her at the sink, I lean against the countertop, a few inches from her.

"Breakfast was wonderful," I say.

"Glad you liked it." She stops fidgeting with the dishes, but doesn't look at me. "So, two things down, how many other items on your list will you get to while you're in Austin?"

"My goal is to see bluebonnets, bats, and maybe some new birds." I elbow her gently. "How about you, do you have any big plans for today?"

She shrugs. "I might take my Z out."

"Z?"

"My 2011 370Z Roadster Convertible. I don't drive her every day, just on weekends when I want to let the wind blow in my hair."

"Nice. Where do you usually go on weekend drives?"

"I like to cruise the hill country just west of here." She turns away from the sink and looks at me. "If it doesn't go against your bucket list–"

"50-by-50 list," I correct her. "Bucket list sounds like the person plans on dying when it's done."

She smiles. "What does happen when you finish your 50-by-50 list?"

"I start another one, I suppose."

"So, if it doesn't go against your 50-by-50 list to spend more time with me, I could take you on my drive to see some wildflowers."

"I would like that." I place my hand over hers where it rests on the edge of the sink. "Convertibles are hot."

"Anything about them on your list?" she asks with a lopsided grin.

"No, but I am not a slave to the 50-by-50 thing." I actually had planned to be, but am seriously rethinking that strategy.

She hurriedly washes up the dishes and excuses herself to get dressed for our drive. I shove my feet into my boots and wait for her to return.

†

"Here is my girl," Ry says as she opens the garage door.

Ry's *girl* is a work of art. At first look, I think the sports car is black, but quickly realize it's more of a black cherry. The red soft top perfectly accents the car's color, but it's the wine-colored leather seats nestled into the black interior that leave my mouth hanging open.

"She's beautiful," I whisper.

Ry's smile tells me my response was perfect. We get in and with a push of a button the car purrs to life. Ry holds down another button and the windows go down, then the top retracts, shifts, and disappears into the back of the car.

I don't even attempt to figure out the route Ry takes us; I just sink into the comfort of the seat that hugs my back. Only occasionally do I pay attention to the looks the Z gets as Ry weaves her way out of Austin and toward the hill country to the west. All I can tell from the signs is that we are heading toward Fredericksburg.

"Do you have any kind of list?" I ask.

"Not really. I mean, there are a lot of places I would love to gig either with the band or alone, but it's not really a list like yours."

"Where are some of the places you'd like to play?"

Ry glances at me, then back at the road. "Santa Fe, for starters."

"That's supposed to be very cool."

She changes lanes and speeds up. "Sedona and Seattle. Oh, and San Diego."

I am pleased with the amount of joy I hear in her voice. "There are a lot of S's on your list," I tease.

She shifts in her seat. "It's not planned. Strictly coincidental. And not the only places on my list either."

"Thank goodness, because that would be as weird as having to eat a burrito in every state."

She reaches over and takes my hand in hers. At first, I tense, but she doesn't let go and within seconds I am relaxing into her touch enough to run one finger across a series of musical notes tattooed onto her right arm. There is so much variety tattooed onto her arms that I think I could get lost in the images for hours and never see it all adequately.

"When will you start checking off some of those cities on your list?" I ask.

She shrugs and releases my hand.

"What towns have you gigged in outside of Austin?"

"Not many. Houston and Dallas. San Antonio."

She leaves the highway and we travel onto a two-lane road. I cock my head and look at her for a long moment. "Nowhere outside of Texas?"

"I really hate airplanes, so that has been a bit of an issue. I don't think I would travel well alone, either."

"What about your band?"

She shrugs. "They are mostly happy to just play in Austin. They're all settled down and have full-time jobs."

Ry leaves one road for another and I close my eyes, letting the wind stroke my face and tousle my hair.

"Do you work another job?" I ask.

"I do. I cook during the week at a restaurant downtown." She runs her fingertips along the leather-wrapped steering wheel. "How about you, what do you do?"

"I freelance. Graphic design."

"Oh, that's cool. So, you can work from anywhere?"

"Mostly."

"That should help with conquering your 50-by-50 list."

She squeezes my hand before releasing it to hold the steering wheel with both hands and leaving the paved road for a two-lane farm road. She takes the road quite slowly and I hope it isn't too rough on the little sports car.

I start to say as much, but lose my words as we round a bend and the wildflowers come into view. I glance at a No Trespassing sign and Ry says, "As long as we don't trample the wildflowers it will be fine."

Ry pulls the Z to the edge of the road. The blanket of flowers spreading out in front of us is breathtaking. It is blue as far as I can see, with some orange and yellow sprinkled in.

Ry opens the driver's side door and gets out. She is opening my door and staring down at me within moments. When she offers her hand, I take it and she helps me out of the low-sitting car. She pulls me against her for a quick embrace once I'm on my feet.

I miss the warmth of her as soon as she steps away from me. We exchange smiles before I crouch near the edge of the flowers and pull out my cell phone to take some pictures.

"Here," Ry says from behind me. "Let me see your phone. I'll take a few pictures of you with the flowers in the background."

I do as she asks and she takes several photos.

"Selfie?" I ask, hoping she won't find the request too...too what? Forward? We have already had sex—earth-shattering, multi-orgasmic sex—how could a picture together be too forward?

She pulls me into her arms, my back to her chest, and takes a selfie of us smiling into the camera. Then she turns to kiss my cheek and takes another.

"Beautiful," I say as I stare into the mass of bluebonnets.

"Yes," she says. "You are."

I hold my breath for a moment, then she turns me in her arms and kisses me. This kiss is nothing like the peck on my cheek. This kiss is searing and full of desire.

We break the kiss after a minute, but don't pull away from one another.

"I like showing you new things," Ry whispers.

"Oh yeah? What else would you like to show me?" I ask, my throat thick with want.

"Is there something else on that list of yours I can help with?"

I stare into her eyes and I know without a doubt she's talking about sex.

"Oh, wait," she says. "If we have sex again, you won't be able to check One-night Stand off your list?"

I think about what Ry said about eating a burrito in every state being too rigid. I don't want to be rigid; I want to be happy. And I know without a doubt that more sex with Ry would make me happy.

"I'm going to change One-night Stand to Sex in Semi-public," I announce.

"You can do that?"

"It's my list." I kiss her gently on the lips. "I can do whatever I want with it."

"Ready to get out of here?" she asks, her voice low and raspy.

We are walking back to the car when I see an interesting rock. I pick up the green mottled stone and hold it up for a better look.

"Serpentine," Ry says. When I just shrug, she adds, "It's a healing mineral. It will help clear your heart chakra."

"That's–well, that's more new agey than I would have pegged you for."

Ry laughs. "What? I just know because serpentine is a big deal in this area. There's an old mine not too far from here."

"Oh?"

"Is mining on your list?" Ry teases.

"No, but it sounds interesting."

She pulls a necklace from beneath her shirt and holds it up for me to see. "It doesn't polish up as slickly as some stones, but it's got this cool, waxy translucence about it."

I touch the stone in her necklace and look at the one I'm holding. The rough stone is a lighter shade of green than the one she's wearing.

I look from the rock in my hand to her, and back to the rock again, silently asking the question.

"Yes, you can take it." She pushes it into my front pocket, her fingers lingering with a soft touch that sends a shiver through me.

†

We are in the shower, rinsing off, when Ry says into my ear, "I'm happy to help you with anything else on your list."

"Oh, you're interested in roller derby? Spelunking?"

"Yes, actually I am, but I was referring to those items that are sexual in nature." She runs her tongue along my jaw line. "What else is there? How many of the fifty things on your list are about sex?"

"Ah, well—"

"Come on," she says, running her thumbs across my nipples. "Tell me more about your list."

I take a shuddering breath at her touch. "Thirty-five places, fifteen activities, five of which are sexual," I blurt.

"How many of the five are left?"

"Four."

"Sex in semi-public is the only one checked off?"

I nod my head.

"Tell me the others." Now she is stroking between my legs. "Tell me, baby."

In my mind I say, *Strap-on, bondage, anal, and a sex party*. But to her, I say, "Wouldn't it be more interesting to have the items present themselves more...I don't know, organically?"

"Trying to guess could be fun," she says as she grabs my ass.

I am so wet after her words, so swollen and ready to let her do it all.

"Unless you want to do things with different people, not just me."

"There is no rule about doing more than one thing with one person. And if there were, I would gladly break it." I press against her, trying to get friction between my legs. "I would break it," I repeat.

She pulls back from me and I groan my disappointment.

"Let's getting moving. I can't wait to organically check off any and every possible thing on your list."

My disappointment is quickly replaced with excitement.

†

The airport is bustling around me, but I am not paying attention, I am fiddling with the new necklace around my neck and concentrating on the sound of Ry's clear, passionate voice in my earbuds. I downloaded her band's only record before starting the stressful drive to the airport earlier this morning.

The sound of her voice gives me goose bumps. Low with desire one moment and richly smooth the next, Ry's voice reminds me of all the ways she brought me joy over the last couple of days, the least of which was sexually. Wait, what? It was all about sex, nothing else, right?

I shut my eyes and give in to the realization that, although sex with Ry was amazing, it was more than just that. I am leaving Austin with a new friendship to enjoy, even if we are never in the same state again.

Suddenly that idea seems unbearable. I turn off the music and think for only a second before I pull up the texting app on my phone and type as fast as I can.

Want to go to Santa Fe with me next month? I could fly in and we could drive together from here. I'll make travel arrangements if you find the venue to gig.

Within seconds, her reply is on my screen. *Yes.*

I quickly type, *I'll call you tonight and we can discuss dates?*

Again, instantaneously, *Yes.*

My fingers caress the smooth serpentine stone pendant that Ry traded me for the rough rock I found on the flower-edged country road. She told me I should wear her serpentine necklace while she polishes up the stone that I found. Then, she'd said that I can decide which one I want when she's done. I hadn't let myself register that she obviously planned to see me again.

I smile and another text comes in. *Safe travels. Let's add some sexy things to your list when you come back out here.*

Now my response is quick and short. *Yes.*

RAINSTORM

ANNETTE MORI

When I was a kid one of my favorite things to do was walk in the rain during one of the famous summer rainstorms in Houston. It was like taking an outdoor shower. I shouldn't have done that when I moved to Amarillo where the rain is freezing cold, even in July. It hadn't stopped me from trying.

Like a horse returning to its corral, I saw the rain and I wanted to dance and sing in it. I wanted to reinvent the scene from *Singing in the Rain*. I needed to be silly again. Act like a child and simply enjoy those simple pleasures before the reality of adulthood completely overtook my body and soul. Thank goodness I still danced in the rain, even as I eased into adulthood. If I hadn't, I would have never met my wife.

I'm old now as I watch the rain splatter against the pane of the window in my hospital bed. I lift my head an inch above the pillow and stretch to see the fat wet drops splatter against the clear glass. My wife is holding my hand and smiling at me. Her hair frames her face. She was never one to follow the rules and decided there was nothing wrong with shoulder length hair on an old woman. No cropped silver hairdo for her. I'd given up on long hair years ago, finding a short haircut a lot easier, especially after I became ill.

"Can we?" I ask.

She shakes her head and that sad, indulging smile appears. "They would never let me take you outside."

"Please."

She knows it won't be long and I see her resolve start to wane. The mischievous smile appears, and I know I've won this last request. Her head turns to the right and left and then it lands on the wheelchair beside the bed. I know I won't get to dance in the rain on my own two feet, but I can still sing. My wife will twist and turn with me in the wheelchair and we'll do a modified dance in the rain.

"Okay," she agrees, and her silver hair moves with her laughter. "We'll have to time this so Nurse Ratchet doesn't catch us." She's still quite the jokester.

I giggle. My mind takes me back to the day we danced in the rain for the very first time.

†

Henry was droning on and on about some unimportant financial statistic as the clouds rolled in, and I knew a rainstorm was imminent. He was trying to impress the new Director of Marketing. She was hot. Everyone was trying to impress her, including me. The drizzle began as I glanced out the window and I couldn't help myself; I started to zone off. My report was next. I'd missed the cue to begin because I was watching the drizzle increase and become a full-on rainstorm. I was itching to run outside and play.

At the time, we worked in Port Lavaca where the summer rainstorms felt like a caress on my skin, both invigorating and calming. I'd always wondered how it was possible to be both exhilarating and soothing, but later my wife would remind me that making love was a lot like the rainstorms and then she would give me "the look." The one that said, "well duh," making love with the right woman was always revitalizing and comforting. Perhaps not at the exact moment, but the whole encounter encompassed both experiences.

"Sarah? Sarah? Are you still with us?" Jim asked. He was the CEO and a kind old gentleman. He'd hired both of us and later told me it was the two best hiring decisions he'd ever made. At the time of hire, I hadn't yet shared my particular quirk with rainstorms. When I did share my affinity to the special storms, he rolled with it like the wonderful boss he turned out to be. Some of my colleagues would take cigarette breaks, I would take rain breaks. I considered them a lot healthier and so did Jim.

I turned my head toward Jim. "Yes, sorry, but I need a minute. Can we take a break?"

"Sure, sure. I'd like some coffee myself." He grinned and his face transformed into one of a little boy on Christmas morning. I knew the cookies were calling Jim, just like the rain was calling me. The coffee was an excuse to grab two chocolate chip cookies that the catering department had prepared for the meeting.

The minute Jim lifted his large frame from the chair to make the trek to the cookies, I ran outside. I was too excited about the rain to remember to grab my rain jacket. Not that I really ever bothered to do that when the rain appeared. As I lifted my face to catch the raindrops and began to twirl, I heard her voice.

"What are you doing? You'll catch your death in this weather. I have your umbrella." She offered me one of those compact, black nylon umbrellas that everyone carried on rainy days. Except, it wasn't mine, because I hadn't carried one since childhood.

Funny how a traumatic experience as a child turned into my fascination for the rain. I couldn't have been older than six when I walked home one blustery day in the rain, holding the large umbrella tightly against my tiny body. When a gust of wind flipped my umbrella upside down, I thought I had broken it. After managing to fold it back into shape to hide my mistake, I realized the rain was warm, and let the swollen droplets fall. I snuck quietly into our trailer. I didn't want to admit to breaking the cheap umbrella. I knew an expensive rain suit and boots were luxuries we couldn't afford. I tucked the evidence into my closet and religiously took it with me on subsequent rainy days, but I never flipped it open again.

Smiling, I turned my attention back to the beautiful new Marketing Director. I laughed and maybe it sounded maniacal to her. I don't know because I never asked. "I am dancing in the rain and in two seconds I'm about to start singing. It opens a person up to the wonders of the world. You should try it. Besides, I think you just stole Henry's umbrella. That's not mine. I never carry one."

She smiled at me, set down both umbrellas, and lifted her own face to the clouds and rain. As she began to spin, I started singing. She didn't know all the words, but managed to follow along. After we finished the song, we both laughed, squeezed the excess water from our hair and walked back inside to return to the board meeting.

Jim held out a towel for me. "Sorry, I only have one. You'll have to share." He winked at me. Henry was grumbling something like, "Batshit crazy." He might have asked about his umbrella. I wasn't paying attention. My focus was lasered on the water trailing down my partner in crime's face from her wet hair, darkened to almost black from the rain.

I gently towel dried my future wife's hair and asked, "Do you want to grab dinner after the meeting?"

"I'd love to. Somewhere with a fireplace because I am drenched." She laughed.

Prior to meeting the love of my life, I had zero ability to determine whether a woman might be open to a relationship with another woman. She made it so easy to figure out. She was always front and center with everything. There was never a coming out for her, she simply accepted the fact that she loved women and thought everyone else should follow without any consternation. I loved that about her. I don't honestly believe she was ignorant of the whispers behind our backs, she simply did not give a thought to them. At all.

†

By the time we left for the restaurant after the board meeting, the rain had subsided. Fate had smiled on me again after I learned she'd caught a ride with a colleague because her ancient MG Midget was on the fritz again. I could not only offer her a ride to the restaurant, but I'd get to escort her home and perhaps receive an invitation for coffee. Coffee was the code for something else entirely. I didn't always accept that offer, but tonight I would if extended to me.

I took the long way to the restaurant so I could pass by my favorite field of bluebonnets, vast and colorful after all the spring rains fed the tiny blossoms. Like the riddle of what came first, the chicken or the egg, I wasn't sure if my two favorite colors were blue and green because of my love for our state flower, or if the love of this particular flowering variety was a result of my favorite colors. I've never been the type of person to select just one, with the exception of my wife. I have multiple favorite foods, favorite books, songs, and numerous other wonders of the world. Life is vast and must be lived to the fullest, ignoring a society's need to make us choose just one.

The tiny petals that resemble the old-fashioned bonnet of pioneer women never ceased to bring a smile to my face. I glanced over at the beautiful woman sitting in the passenger seat and saw the same look of awe on her face. That was the defining moment for me. The moment I knew that love at first sight was not a fluke. Not only did she dance in the rain with me, but I could tell she worshipped the bluebonnets with the same vigor. We were truly a match made in heaven.

"They're breathtaking, aren't they? No matter what, I don't think I could ever move from Texas. I'd miss them too much."

"You could always visit," I suggested.

"Not the same thing as having them literally in my back yard. My house might be as dilapidated as my unreliable

MG, but with five acres, including my own personal field of bluebonnets, I have heaven at my doorstep."

"I'm looking forward to taking you home. I hope I'll still be able to see them in the dark. Maybe the clouds will clear and the moon will shine bright enough to catch a glimpse."

"Or, if you're really good, you can see them in the morning."

I resisted the urge to pump my fist in the air. She was feeling the crackle in the air and I was sure it wasn't as a result of the rainstorm. That was the third sign to cement my absolute belief that I would ask this woman to be my wife before the end of the year. And I did. When it is right, there is nothing that will get in the way. Of course, it wasn't legal back then, but I didn't care. I had absolute faith that the politicians would pull their heads out of their asses and somehow, before I died, it would be legal. I'd run down that aisle a second time for sure.

"I'd like that. If you have breakfast fixings, I can whip up something that will endear you to me even more than dinner and drinks."

"I'll hold you to that." She winked and my stomach fluttered in anticipation of our first date. When her hand pushed through the still wet strands of her long, dark hair, I felt the familiar stirring of arousal that I would need to tamp down for the next several hours. The anticipation was all a part of the full experience of love and lust.

"So, Marjorie, that's not a very common name." I began the inane chitchat required for a first date.

She chuckled. "Marjie. I hate Marjorie. When I was in grade school, Tommy Jones tried to give me the nickname Margarine. And yes, that really was his name. Believe me, he was not even close to Tom Jones who I happened to like as a kid. Don't judge."

"And," I prompted. I could tell there was more to the story.

"Well, I can tell you I am no margarine because I am the real deal. Soft and creamy just like butter and I told him that."

I laughed. "That stopped him from calling you Margarine?"

"Nope the punch in the nose stopped him. No one ever tried to give me a nickname after that. I told them all they could call me Marjie, and from that point forward nobody has ever called me Marjorie."

"Feisty. I like it." I put my hands up in supplication. "Any other rules I shouldn't break? I'd hate to receive a punch in the nose for inadvertently doing something wrong."

"Like I said. I am the real deal. I'll never be a second-rate substitute for anything." She narrowed her eyes. "If we become an item and you ever partake in margarine on the side, you won't like my reaction any better than Tommy Jones."

"Now why would I ever choose margarine over butter? Soft and creamy sounds divine to me."

"Good answer."

After that exchange we never devolved to small talk and I found out how utterly charming and intelligent Marjie really was. She had a grasp of the arts, politics, philosophy. You name it, she could hold her own in a conversation. And yet, those attributes were simply the icing on the cake. It was Marjie's passion for life and love that cemented our relationship. Sometimes her passion caused knock-down drag-out fights when we would disagree, but I always preferred that over the milquetoast conversations with women who lacked passion. No opinion irked me more than anything else.

After dinner I took Marjie home and because I am a gentlewoman I'll never confirm or deny if we made love on our first date. But I will confess to never making love to another woman after taking Marjie to dinner. I'd have married her the next day if it was legal, but unfortunately at that time, it was barely acceptable to my small, inner circle of friends.

I give enormous credit to Jim, the CEO of our small critical access hospital. He recognized the spark between Marjie and I right from the start and was forever in our corner, even after the word leaked out that we were together. A few of the more conservative board members had an entirely different reaction, but they knew if Jim left, they were screwed since he'd been the one to basically save the hospital from financial ruin. Henry, on the other hand, pissed me off until the day I retired.

†

I'm not afraid to die. Luck, fate, good karma, I'm not sure what has shined upon me, but something always has. I met my wife at a time when I wasn't completely led by my vajayjay. Oh sure, it tugged at me quite a bit. My wife is a beautiful woman, even to this day. She is and was a total package of complexity and perfection, not just something to make my drawers dampen with excitement. Mind you, there is nothing wrong with that, but there is also a lot more to a marriage than exhilaration between the sheets.

Music is playing on the portable Bluetooth player. My wife bought the small cylindrical device to keep music playing whenever I needed a boost of good energy. Music, like my beloved rain, always seems to cheer me up. I smile when the song, *Ironic* by Alanis Morrisette comes on. Marjie blesses me with one of her famous grins.

"Turn it up," I say.

"It's already at nearly the top, you're going to get me in trouble with the nurses again," she says and then proceeds to crank it up as she glances at the open door in the room.

I squeeze her hand as much as I can in my weakened state and she smiles at me. "Thank you."

"Only you could have the power to summon the rain on our wedding day," she says as she gets that faraway look in her eyes. I know she is remembering our wedding day.

I am convinced she knows that I also want to think about our special day. We'd always laughed at the oddity that for us, rain on our wedding day was not ironic at all, but rather perfect. I close my eyes and the whole movie that was our wedding spirals through my mind as if it were yesterday. My body might have turned against me, but my mind never did. I thank the universe for that. I cannot have imagined a greater travesty than forgetting Marjie and all of our years together.

While sipping my first cup of coffee, I looked out on our expansive back yard and smiled when I saw the dark clouds rolling in. The ends of the white tablecloths were fluttering in the breeze, even though the folding chairs were pushed against the tables. I thought it was a good thing we ordered the canopies to cover the area where the caterers would be preparing the meal.

"What are you grinning about?" she asks.

"It's going to rain today." I was giddy with excitement.

"You know that most sane individuals would not pray for rain on their wedding day. Our guests will not be amused when they realize we did not rent tents for the ceremony." Marjie shook her head.

"They'll thank us for the unique experience."

"No, they won't. People gussie up for a wedding." Her arms were crossed as she propped her tea on her forearm.

She appeared to survey the back yard and the path leading to where we were going to recite our vows. None of that was covered.

I began laughing deep in my belly. "Gussie up? What are you, eighty-five? Besides, the eating area is covered."

"That is a perfectly acceptable expression and the canopies won't help during the ceremony." Marjie sipped from her tea. "Do you think we've jinxed the day by sleeping together last night?" She waggled her eyebrows.

I waved my hand in the air as if I was swatting away any negative vibes. "Nope, I don't believe in all that superstitious hooey. Besides, look at those glorious rain clouds. As I always say, the rain decided to wash our souls today. It'll be perfect."

She shook her head again. "Nutball. I believe the correct saying is that the sun decided to shine upon us, but that certainly is not happening."

I held out my hand. "Shall we go upstairs and start primping for this thing. Unless…that's another superstition you feel queasy about."

Margie laughed. "Nope, we've already demolished the big one, several times last night, I might add." She winked.

That was my gal. She could roll with the best of them.

†

We'd been together a long time by the day of the wedding. Legal marriages were now available to us and that's why we wanted to tie the knot. Yet, we weren't going to follow any tradition for our marriage and we certainly weren't going to have anyone give us away like we were a piece of prime meat. Walking hand in hand down the grass path in our backyard, listening to Brandi Carlile's, *The Story*, I felt the first droplet of rain. I was hoping for a lot more than a drizzle. As I looked at the faces of the small group of friends and family, I could tell they did not share my secret wish.

Fortunately for everyone the ceremony was short. The minute the officiate pronounced, "You may kiss one another," the sky opened up like the petals on a rose, slow and full. As we experienced the joy of our first kiss as a married couple, the warm rain flowed and bathed us in magic. We stood soaking in ambrosia from heaven and began twirling while our wimpy guests ran for cover. My sister noted that we were completely mad as she dashed for the large tents, not more than twenty feet from the house, where the caterers were working hard to create a masterful presentation of food.

The long white dress clung to Marjie and I could see her nipples poking through the silk fabric. My linen suit didn't offer as much to Marjie and she complained loudly of that once we had the opportunity to change.

"How'd you do it?" Marjie asked.

"Do what?" I grinned at her while removing my wet tunic.

"Arrange for the rain at the perfect moment. It's not like you're on a first name basis with the guy or gal upstairs. Have you ever even set foot in a church?" She pointed to the back of her dress.

I moved behind her and tugged on the zipper. "Don't be intolerant, I know you're more worldly than that. When we put our wishes out to the universe, the universe always answers."

She let the dress fall to the floor and then draped it over a chair in our bedroom. "Okay, then I'm going to ask the universe for rain on our honeymoon when we walk onto the balcony in our silky skivvies." She turned to face me, then winked. "The ones I already packed. I'm gonna ogle your breasts when your nipples stand at attention like mine did today."

Marjie brushed her hand over my still wet bra and she got a preview of what did occur on our honeymoon. We were blessed that year with two opportune rainstorms. One in Texas where we were married and one in Mexico where we honeymooned. Over our long life together we enjoyed many storms and the calm that happened before and after. Like our marriage, storms and passion raged throughout. There were good times and bad, but through it all we endured, even relished those storms. We gave them the proper perspective and respect they deserved.

†

Not only did the rain mark the joyous events in our lives, but somehow it followed us around for the less than blissful times. Fortunately for us, the water refreshes a person and rejuvenates their soul, and it has a tendency to put out a raging fire, even when the rain is warm.

Our first knock-down, drag-out fight came not long after I moved into her house. Honestly, I don't even recall what caused such a row, but I remember the feelings of pure panic as my new girlfriend raised her voice like I'd never heard before. It wasn't like I was afraid of her since she was 120 pounds soaking wet. I feared losing her. Would she walk out on me? The reality set in that I'd never had a relationship with someone who could hold their own. I'd always dominated. This woman was going to challenge me in ways I'd never known before.

I do recall her yelling, "You are the most stubborn woman I've ever known. I wish you'd stop being so pig-headed and narrow-minded."

Well, that was like a red cape to a bull. I fancied myself as the most open-minded person in our conservative town. How dare she call me narrow-minded? I matched the decibel in her voice and added a new level. I was not one to let anyone get the better of me. The yelling became a screaming match until we heard the boom of thunder that undoubtedly punctuated the end of one of our sentences. We looked at one another and she grinned first, extending her hand.

The clouds were dark and angry, matching the atmosphere a mere minute before the loud boom. You'd think that would only serve to stoke the raging inferno, but it always had the opposite effect on us.

Running outside, we danced in the rain and let the water cool the fires ignited by irritation over something we both knew was inconsequential. Since she'd offered the first olive branch, I mumbled the first apology. Then I did something so uncharacteristic, it surprised both of us.

I mumbled into her neck, "Please don't ever leave me or kick me to the curb."

She pulled back and looked into my eyes. "Now why would I ever do that, you stubborn fool? Not one single person on this planet argues better than you. You, love, will always keep me on my toes. If I can't handle a little disagreement now and again, I have no business entering into any relationship."

I quirked my eyebrow. "Little disagreement?"

"Okay, maybe it was a full-on scream fest, but don't you feel alive? Isn't it better than always agreeing? It is always the couples that agree on everything who fall out of love because their life is so boring and placid. I don't understand how anyone can be shocked when the inevitable divorce happens. No passion, no love. You, darling, have passion."

"As do you." I pulled her closer against my wet body.

"I'm sorry for yelling so loud that we almost missed this rainstorm, but I'm not sorry for disagreeing with you," she whispered in my ear.

I pulled back to look her in the eyes. "Was that an apology?"

"Yup, get used to it because that is as far as I will ever go." She pulled me close again.

"You know you hurt my feelings saying I was narrow-minded." My mouth was close to her ear again as I said these words quietly.

"I know and I meant every word at the time." She stepped back and gently kissed my nose. "I am sorry for hurting you and not clarifying that what you said was narrow-minded, not who you fundamentally are as a person. We're going to hurt one another from time to time; it is inevitable. I'm sorry I can't promise never to hurt you. I can promise never to leave you because I'm madly in love with your stubborn ass."

"I think I've met my match." I brushed her wet locks aside and looked into those mesmerizing eyes that had captured me when I first met Marjie.

"You certainly have," she responded, then captured my lips in a searing kiss.

When we returned to our dry house, we began ripping at each other's soaking wet clothes. I learned something that made our fights a lot more palatable during this first major quarrel—our love making rose to a whole new level.

†

The song, *Ironic*, ends and I look into the lined face of my beautiful wife and nod that it is time. The wheels on the chair bump along the rough sidewalk and jostle my old, worn body. The pain would have been excruciating, but the cold, clean rain is refreshing and just enough of a distraction to keep me settled. It should feel uncomfortable, but it doesn't. I was sure my wife would get in trouble for wheeling me out into the frigid, Amarillo rain, but why should they care? I am dying. It isn't like I will catch my death in the rain. I'd already caught something else and it wasn't a measly cold.

"Remind me why we moved to Amarillo?" my old voice croaks.

"I wanted to be closer to family as we got older. I needed the help when…" Her voice trails off.

Marjie is still a feisty old broad at eighty-six, but she is eighty-six and these last few years were getting to be too much. I knew it and she knew it. It is unfair of me to remind her of this, especially since that argument was the last knock-down drag-out fight we'd engaged in. I no longer had any fight left in me after that. We both knew what agreeing to move meant for us.

"I'm sorry. I like Amarillo. I do. It's just that I miss the warm rain."

"I know, love, I know. I do too."

"A person can get used to anything, though. I'm starting to enjoy this refreshing rain." I smile at her.

She strokes my shoulder. "Liar."

"No, honest. I never thought I would, but I really do. Cold rain, warm rain. It makes no difference. It has always been about cleansing one's soul. Letting Mother Nature caress and love you. You always got that. All these years we've been singing in the rain together were the very definition of perfection."

Marjie pats my shoulder again. "I think you may have forgotten the times we disagreed. Vehemently, I might add. I think we scared your nephew when he walked into one."

I chuckle. "That was my favorite dish you broke into a thousand pieces. What did that sink ever do to you?"

"I didn't throw it at your head like he thought," she defends.

"Oh my goodness. Do you remember the look on his face?"

"Sure do. I thought he was going to convince you to divorce me."

"Nah, if anyone understands passion, it's him. He told me once that if he were ever fortunate enough to find someone like you, he'd never let her go. And he didn't. I caught him and his wife once in one of their epic arguments and I do believe they learned from the best."

"Love and passion were never a problem for us. I wonder if it might have been better for either of us to find a partner who was a bit more Zen about things."

I don't know how I feel the warm droplet on my cheek in the midst of the cold rain, but I do. I see the tears drop from my wife's eyes. We both know this will be the last time we dance and sing in the rain together. The end is near.

As she spins the chair in the rain, I hear her clear voice sing with mine the Whitney Houston classic, *I Will Always Love You*. And I will always love her, even as my soul makes its way to the other world, I will take that love with me.

PINS AND NEEDLES

JULIE CANNON

PROLOGUE

"Alright Dixon. You want it so bad, it's yours. But let me remind you, we said that a bank in some hick town is not going to survive. Sodbusters and cowboys don't have money."

Will took offense to the term sodbusters. She had grown up on a farm and even though no one at her place of employment knew that, nonetheless she was proud of the fact.

"That's why they need the bank. They can..." Will shut up when her boss held up his hand.

"You have what you've been begging for the past three years. Now go," her boss said, his tone full of disgust. If Will had a silver dollar for every time the old man said no, she would be the richest woman in the territory. But that wasn't what this was all about. Not at all.

CHAPTER ONE

The stagecoach rumbled through the center of town. The townspeople watched, interested in the occupants inside the carriage pulled by half a dozen large horses as it rattled down the dry dusty road.

Will coughed as the dust settled inside the coach when it stopped at the station. Her three fellow passengers held handkerchiefs to their mouths, their eyes watering. The two-day trek from the train station had been brutal. The rough ride of the carriage and the dust and heat had been almost unbearable. The cushions on the hard, wooden seats were worn and the curtains, designed to keep the dust out, only served to keep the heat in. She had untied her tie and opened the top button of her collar only three hours into the trip. Her coat stayed on, not out of propriety, but because she knew her sweat had soaked through her shirt risking exposure of the thick band of linen wrapped tightly around her chest.

The man seated beside her had introduced himself after he, his wife, and daughter boarded in Batestown. Ralph

Winston was a shopkeeper in Waco, their destination. According to Winston, Waco consisted of a large general store, blacksmith, livery, doctor, two cafes, a seamstress, newspaper, small hotel, and a school which doubled as a church on Sundays. A sawmill was about a half mile to the east of town, the big saw powered by the Brazos River nearby. Several farms were a fifteen-minute ride from the center of town and many more farther out.

Ralph's wife, Veronica, talked about the residents the entire two days, and Will had wondered how much of it was gossip and how much was, in fact, gospel. Veronica had talked so much, Will felt like she had lived in Waco her entire life.

During one of the stops at a transfer station, Ralph had told Will about the saloon in town. For twenty-five cents you could get a hot bath, and for $1 one of "Francine's girls." Flo was his favorite, he had whispered after double-checking that his wife wasn't nearby.

Will played along. She was used to pretending to be someone she wasn't. For the past eight years she'd played the role of Will Dixon, a tall, very thin man with short, dark brown hair and a smooth face. A man who kept his private life private despite the urging of coworkers and the mothers and fathers who had introduced her to their daughters. Little did they know that beneath the ill-fitting suit and trousers and starched white shirt, were the same curves and female attributes as their daughters, including the *woman's monthly*.

140

Wilhelmina Dixon, the youngest of eight girls and two boys had been born to Fred and Mabel Dixon twenty-five years ago. She watched her mother suffer and age under the strain of raising a pack of children and, from an early age, she wanted something much different. She loved her mother but could not envision a life anything even remotely like hers. When she was seventeen, she left a note for her mother near the stove and walked away. She'd sent several letters back home telling her mother that she was well. Will had not included a return address so she was not certain her mother had ever received them. It was a sacrifice she had to make for the life she wanted.

Bernice, Ralph and Veronica's daughter had stared at her with shrewd intent the minute they boarded the carriage in Batestown. As her mother droned on about the peculiarities of the residents of the town of Waco, the looks Bernice gave Will grew bolder, giving Will no doubt of her interest.

The door of the stagecoach opened and a plump man wearing spectacles, wrinkled trousers, a clean white shirt, and dusty boots greeted them.

"Welcome to Waco."

Will exited the coach first, followed by Ralph who helped his wife and daughter step out onto the hard dirt packed ground.

"You must be Dixon the banker," the man said, shaking Will's hand much too vigorously. "I'm Samuel Perkins, mayor of our fair town."

Perkins' hand was damp and after he finally let go, so as not to offend the mayor, Will put her hand in her pocket to wipe off the man's sweat.

"Yes, I am," Will replied. "Nice little town you have here. At least what I saw coming in."

"Thank you, we worked hard to have a nice little place where people can come in and have a drink at the saloon or a bite to eat at the diner. Miss Lucille makes the best biscuits and peach cobbler in the county," he said, patting his large girth. "Won first prize at the County Fair two years in a row," he boasted, obviously proud of Miss Lucille's contribution to his town.

Will didn't get a chance to reply. Her garment bag was tossed on the ground beside her, and two men were wrestling with her trunk and the four that belonged to Ralph and his family.

"Let me show you to the hotel," Perkins said and took off walking. "The boys will bring your trunk along shortly."

Perkins led them across the street avoiding the potholes and horse droppings common on every street in the territory. Will felt the eyes of several of the townspeople on her. She had gotten out of the habit of slouching when she left her home years earlier and assumed her new identity. Will had been taller than every girl and almost every boy in the small school in her hometown. As much as she hated to admit it, Will had succumbed to the pressures of being an outsider, and began slouching in an attempt to minimize her height.

She was teased constantly but now it was advantageous for the life she had worked so hard to create for herself.

CHAPTER TWO

"Ouch," Mary Alice said, but what she really wanted to do was curse.

"Are you alright, Mary Alice?" Caroline Brody asked.

Mary Alice was putting the final touches on Caroline's wedding dress. Saturday was the big day and everyone in town was invited. Caroline's father, Charles, was the owner of the largest cattle ranch in the territory, and with what he was paying Mary Alice for his daughter's wedding dress, she wouldn't have to worry about income for a while. That would be a relief.

Since taking over her great aunt's shop two years earlier, Mary Alice had worried almost every day about how she was going to pay the rent on the building that housed her shop. There was a small kitchen, parlor, and bedroom in the rear where she lived. Some months were so lean she was only able to have one meal a day. One month it was so bad she ate every other day. She had planted a garden behind the building, but it didn't yield as much as she had hoped, the bunnies and other critters taking their fill each night. She finally had enough spare money to buy fencing pickets and that had kept her nocturnal neighbors at bay.

What Mary Alice really wanted and was saving for was one of the new Singer Pedal Sewing Machines she saw in the catalog in Mr. Winston's general store. Mary Alice knew that if she had it, she would be able to make more dresses, and even the occasional suit, much faster than sewing everything by hand. Even as careful as she was, her fingers were often swollen and bleeding from being stuck by a needle or a wayward pin.

Maybe the new banker... Mary Alice thought, then frowned as her moment of hope plummeted. Banks didn't lend money to women.

An hour after Caroline left, Mary Alice was sitting in her kitchen when the bell over the front door jangled.

"Yoo-hoo, Mary Alice."

Mary Alice cringed at the familiar voice. Veronica Winston was the town gossip and Mary Alice hated gossip. She thought it rude and just plain not nice to talk about your neighbors the way Mrs. Winston did. It was one thing to share information it was another to do so the way Veronica did. She obviously prided herself on being in the know.

"Mary Alice?" Mrs. Winston repeated,

"Just a moment," Mary Alice said, pulling her tea kettle off the stove. If Mrs. Winston heard the kettle, she would invite herself for tea and be here for hours. Not only did

Mary Alice not want to listen to the woman talk nonstop, but it would put her behind schedule. If she had that pedal machine though...she banished the thought as she entered the front room.

"Hello, Mrs. Winston. Welcome back. How was your trip?" Mary Alice asked politely, even though she had little interest in listening to her brag endlessly about the trip she and her husband and daughter had taken to Austin.

Where Mrs. Winston was a gossip, her daughter Bernice was snippy, self-centered, pampered, privileged, and extremely judgmental. She often came in with several of her friends and they were often vindictive, mean, and ugly as they talked about the town residents.

"It was wonderful. The people were so friendly and welcoming."

Mary Alice half listened as Mrs. Winston extolled the highlights of her trip. When she stopped to take a breath, Mary Alice said, "Elijah brought your fabric by yesterday. It's beautiful." It was actually quite ugly and completely not practical, but Mrs. Winston didn't pay Mary Alice for her opinion. She paid her for her exquisite workmanship.

"It is, isn't it? I'd like one dress out of each as soon as possible."

Like Mary Alice had nothing else to do.

"The new banker was on the stage with us," Mrs. Winston said.

Mary Alice's interest in the conversation perked up.

"He's a tall, skinny, gangly fellow and doesn't even have a hint of whiskers. Very young too. I don't know if I trust him. How can someone so young know what to do with a lot of money?" That was her way of telling Mary Alice of her husband's financial position. Like everyone didn't already know by all the comments Mrs. Winston and her daughter often dropped around town in their conversation.

"He must know what he's doing if the bank sent him here," Mary Alice said, unsure why she was defending someone she had never met.

"That may be," Mrs. Winston said, her face scrunched up, her real opinion showing. "He said he was going to give loans to farmers and ranchers in the area. Can you imagine? Said something about the bank is for everyone with a dream, not just the wealthy." Mrs. Winston scoffed at her own statement.

Mary Alice's dashed hope sprang to life, but she did not comment. She didn't dare appear to be too interested. If Mrs. Winston had any idea, the entire town would be talking about how foolish Mary Alice was by the end of the day. Like they didn't talk about her enough.

Mary Alice was twenty-two and not married even after more than a dozen men had offered otherwise. Born smack dab in the middle of three girls and three boys, Mary Alice was always a step out of the crowd. When her sisters were playing with dolls and helping churn butter, she was in the field with her father and brothers. Before her brothers were old enough to help their father, Mary Alice could often be found in the fields or on a horse. As each brother was able to contribute more and more, she was relegated back in the house with her mother.

Her parents were aghast when, time after time, Mary Alice turned down the many young men who came calling. She'd found their manners nonexistent, their hygiene distasteful, and their clumsy kisses nothing short of disgusting. She didn't understand why she didn't have the same euphoric giddiness as her sisters and her friends when they talked about the boys in town. She never experienced the daydreams of marriage and babies and other domestic duties.

What Mary Alice did dream about was independence. Being on her own, making her own decisions, not expected to obey her father, and then her husband. Not knowing what to do with their nineteen-year-old, unmarried, rebellious daughter, her parents sent her to live with her mother's aunt, a widow seamstress in Waco. Three days and one long train ride later she found herself on her Great Aunt Wava's doorstep. Several years later, the old woman died, and Mary Alice took her place as the town's seamstress.

"His clothes are not at all respectable for a banker," Mrs. Winston commented, her voice dripping judgment. "Maybe you should visit him and sell him on your services."

The way Mrs. Winston said it made it sound like Mary Alice would be selling other "services" as well.

"Thank you, but I'm sure he'll come to see me as he sees fit. Now if you will excuse me, I'll get started on your dresses."

Mary Alice had never solicited for work and she certainly was not going to start with the banker. He would think her unable to meet her financial obligations, and he certainly would not loan her money for her sewing machine.

CHAPTER THREE

Will was tired of making small talk and mingling with the guests Mayor Samuels had invited to his home to meet the new banker. Even though it was a requirement for her job, Will was always uncomfortable spending more than a few minutes with someone. She was afraid they would see through her masquerade and run her out of town, or worse.

"Mr. Dixon?" The unforgettable voice of Mrs. Winston came from behind her. She braced for more gossip.

"Mrs. Winston, it's a pleasure to see you again. Are you enjoying the party?" Will half listened to the woman's answer, looking for a way out before she tried to match her up with her daughter.

"If I may say, Mr. Dixon, we have a fine seamstress in town."

Will forced herself not to fidget with her clothes. Tailors did not make suits for her body shape and she could not afford a handmade suit like her superiors in Austin.

"Her name is Mary Alice Walker and her shop is just a few doors down from the store. I know she would be happy to help and she's quite reasonable. No offense, Mr. Dixon, but you cannot dress like a vagabond and expect to get any respect in this town."

Will disliked the woman more every time she opened her mouth. Will did not share the woman's opinion of the people that she had met this first week in town. They were warm and welcoming and gracious. The farmers and ranchers she had been able to meet were polite and often invited her to stay for a meal.

Yesterday, Will had moved out of the boarding house and into the rear of the building that, after some minor remodeling, would be the Bank of Waco. In three weeks, funds would arrive from Austin and the bank would open. Doc Kenner signaled to her, and Will politely, yet quickly made her escape.

"It looked like you could use some rescuing," Doc Kenner said. Doc was one of the first to welcome her to WACO and she found him easy to talk to. With his greying hair and ever-present scruff of whiskers, it was hard to tell how old Doc was. He could be forty or sixty. Life on the prairie added years to a man's age. Doc had a very keen eye and Will was extra careful around him.

"Mrs. Winston can carry on a conversation," Will replied politely.

Doc laughed. "You are a smooth talker, Will."

Will didn't hear the rest of Doc's comments because her attention completely fixated on a woman who had just walked in. The chatter of the guests and the people around her faded in a haze and everything else around Will disappeared.

The woman handed her wrap to the maid at the door and she glided farther into the room. She greeted several of the town folks, and when she smiled, Will felt the breath leave her lungs. She had never had such a reaction to anyone before. Her heart was pounding in her chest so loud she thought for sure Doc would not need his scope to hear it.

"Will?"

It took Doc touching her arm to break the spell the woman had cast over her.

"I'm sorry, what did you say?"

Doc looked at her for so long Will started to get nervous. He looked between Will and the woman, then back at Will. Finally, he spoke.

"I asked if you've met Mary Alice Walker. She owns the tailor shop in town. It's amazing what she can do with a needle and thread in her hands."

A flush of heat ran through Will at the thought of other things she wanted Mary Alice Walker to do with her hands. Will suddenly felt a little lightheaded. She had never had these kinds of thoughts about someone before and certainly not a woman.

"Are you okay, Will?" Doc asked. "You're all flushed."

"Yes, I'm fine, not to worry. No, I have not met Miss Walker although Mrs. Winston speaks highly of her professional skills." Will tore her gaze away from Mary Alice to focus on Doc. "She went so far as to say I need to see her. I believe she said I was dressed like a vagabond."

"She can be very direct," Doc commented, smothering his smile by raising his glass to his mouth. "Let me introduce you. I think the two of you will have a lot in common."

CHAPTER FOUR

Will did not get a chance to ask Doc what he was referring to before she found herself looking into the most vivid blue eyes she had ever seen. They sparkled like the stars in a country night sky and Will's knees were suddenly weak.

"Mary Alice Walker, may I introduce you to our new banker, Will Dixon," Doc said. He turned to Mary Alice. "I was just telling Will that you are an outstanding seamstress."

"You're too kind, Doc." Mary Alice extended her hand toward Will. "Pleased to meet you, Mr. Dixon."

Will was mesmerized by her soft Texas accent and the way she had said her name. Doc nudged her and Will felt her face flush in embarrassment.

"Yes, pleased to meet you as well, Miss Walker."

Mary Alice's hand was warm, her fingers rough, probably from endless hours of sewing, Will surmised. She didn't seem to be embarrassed by their condition, her grip was strong and confident. Will suddenly wanted to feel them on her skin, touching her, caressing her breasts. Heat ran through her body. She knew there were women who loved women like men, and she had felt the stirrings of attraction to several women when she was in Austin. From the way men talked about women, she had some idea what to do if she dared get that far. One evening after returning from Houston, one of her coworkers, who had far too much to drink, told Will exactly what women did together. She had not been able to sleep well for weeks after.

Will had never let herself think that was possible for her. She could not risk everything she had worked for.

"Doc and Mrs. Winston have spoken words of praise for your skill with a needle," Will managed to say. It was Mary Alice who blushed this time.

"Thank you, I do the best I can," Mary Alice said modestly. "When did you arrive in town, Mr. Dixon?"

"A few days ago. The Winstons and I were on the stage together from Batesville."

"That must have been a very long ride." Mary Alice's eyes twinkled with mischief and Will found it hard to breathe. After a moment, something flickered in them that Will recognized as interest and, for the first time, she didn't want to run from it. She actually wanted to race toward it.

"I'm sorry, please forgive me," Will said, realizing she was still holding Mary Alice's hand. Doc slipped away after winking at her.

"It's alright, I completely understand, Mr. Dixon."

Mary Alice had noticed Mr. Dixon's interest reflected in his dark eyes. What surprised her was that she was not repulsed by it nor threatened in any way. She actually welcomed it. She inhaled sharply putting her hand on her suddenly jittery stomach.

"Are you all right, Miss Walker? May I get you some water?"

Will's concern appeared genuine.

"No thank you. Maybe some fresh air." Her legs quivered when she admitted to herself that what she really wanted was to be out from the prying eyes of the townsfolk and alone with Will.

"Certainly," Will said, stepping aside and escorting her through the double doors to the veranda.

The blast of cool evening air did nothing to dampen the heat that was racing through her veins. What was wrong with her? It was like she had never spoken to a man. Certainly not a man like Will. She already thought of him as Will and not the more formal Mr. Dixon.

The stars sparkled in the sky and the crickets chirped in the distance, and Mary Alice was completely aware of the man standing beside her. They had just been introduced, yet he was unlike any other man she had ever met. He was tall, and slight, but not a milquetoast in the way that other pampered, city men were. He was respectful, he smelled good, and he was well mannered. His clothes however were awful. They were far too big and hung on him like an old potato sack. With just a tuck here and there, he would be quite handsome. An odd surge of jealousy surged through Mary Alice. She didn't want any other woman to think him handsome.

"It's quite a beautiful night tonight," Will commented.

"Yes, it is. Spring is a wonderful time of year."

Mary Alice didn't want to mix business with pleasure with Will but, uncharacteristically, her mind had run out of things to say. She was used to making small talk while her clients stood in front of her getting fitted for their garments.

"I understand you intend to provide loans to some of the smaller ranchers and farmers," Mary Alice said, gambling that he would not be shocked by her interest in things that were traditionally not discussed by women.

Will looked at her, one eyebrow raised. Mary Alice's stomach fluttered.

"Good news travels fast," Mary Alice added, to hide what he surely thought was gossip.

"Yes, I do. Banks should not be just for those who have money. Banks are the lifeblood of a community. Sometimes all it takes is just a little help for a businessman or a rancher to become successful."

"Or a seamstress." Mary Alice held in a gasp. She had no idea she was going to say that, and she chastised herself. Her boldness might have just cost her any chance she had of getting her sewing machine.

Her heart raced as Will studied her for a long time. Finally he smiled and said, "Or a seamstress."

Mary Alice hid her reaction. It was too soon to rejoice. She calmed her nerves before saying, "Have you always wanted to come to Waco?"

"Yes. I've met some folks who had passed through here and they spoke very highly of it. And I wanted to get out of the city."

"Really? You don't see many city folks coming to the country."

"I was raised in a town very much like this."

"Near here?"

"No, it's too far away for anyone to have ever heard about it. How long have you been in Waco, Miss Walker?

"About four years. I came to live with my great aunt. She taught me everything she knew about sewing and tailoring." Mary Alice couldn't help but notice that Will had quickly changed the subject back to her. In her experience, men were more interested in talking about themselves than the woman they were talking to.

"Maybe I'll stop by. Mrs. Winston thinks I need some help," Will said, looking down at his clothing. "I'm beginning to think she's right."

Mary Alice laughed. "Don't let her know you said that." Mary Alice forgot what she was going to say when desire sparked in Will's eyes. It threatened to draw her in, and she did not want to stop it.

Laughter from two men stepping out on to the veranda brought Mary Alice back to her senses.

"I think it's time for me to go. I just stopped by to be polite with Mrs. Winston's invitation."

"I'll walk you back," Will said quickly.

"That's not necessary, Mr. Dixon. It's a short walk that I've been taking by myself for years." Mary Alice said. She was not sure what she would do if she allowed him to walk her home. She was so out of sorts she was afraid she just might kiss him. That would be scandalous and cause far more talk about her.

"My mama would whup me if she knew I didn't escort a lady home." Will's eyes twinkled as he teased. "So, I must insist."

Mary Alice's knees threatened to give way, but she could not make a fool of herself. Not when she needed him. She might want Will Dixon the man, but she needed Will Dixon the banker more.

"I think it's been some time since that happened, Mr. Dixon. You're all grown up into a nice fine man." Mary Alice gasped, shocked at her boldness.

Desire flared in Will's eyes, then a look of dark sadness flashed over his face, then was gone. Mary Alice was just about to ask if she had said something to offend him, but Will motioned towards the door.

They said their goodbyes to their hosts and walked down the wooden sidewalk. A million thoughts raced through

Mary Alice's mind, all of them troubling. What if she had offended him by her forward behavior? What if he would not loan her money to purchase the sewing machine? What if he had been repulsed by her brazen boldness?

She stumbled over the uneven sidewalk and Will grabbed her elbow. Heat seared up her arm, through her and settled between her legs. His touch was like a match to a flame. What was going on with her? Was this what it was like between a man and a woman?

"Best be careful," Will said, his voice breaking the silence as he slipped her hand into the crook of his arm. "You see, I was right. If I wasn't here, you might have fallen and torn your beautiful dress."

Mary Alice couldn't see but heard the smile in his voice. She felt the muscles in Will's arm quiver, and she had to take a few more steps before she was able to speak. "You might be right, Mr. Dixon. Thank you."

They chatted about the town and all too quickly they arrived at her door. Mary Alice didn't want the evening to end but she only had one chair on her porch. It would be too awkward for one of them to sit while the other stood. She certainly could not invite him in for tea. A man alone with her in her house after sunset? She pulled out a large key from her bag turned the lock, then turned around.

"Thank you again, Mr. Dixon. I enjoyed our conversation."

"As did I, Miss Walker. Though if I may be so bold to admit, I enjoyed our walk as well."

Will's face was cast in shadows, but Mary Alice heard the huskiness in his voice. Before she did something that would make him think her a brazen hussy, she said good night and closed the door behind her.

CHAPTER FIVE

Mary Alice's perfume hung in the air and Will had to force herself to turn and walk away. She was completely captivated by Mary Alice and that was very, very dangerous. She had not been aware of anyone else in the room and had been completely transfixed by how comfortable and outspoken she was. Most women, especially those in a small town like Waco, demurred to a man and never dared to say anything out of place. Mary Alice was definitely unlike any women she had ever met.

For the next two weeks, Will worked nonstop getting the bank ready. There was a myriad of details that filled her days and well into the evening, but Mary Alice was never very far from her mind. Will had seen Mary Alice several times, whether it was walking across the street to the café, or simply sitting outside on her porch, enjoying the cool afternoon, her mending in her lap. Twice Will was able to sit behind her in the small church. While others around her obeyed the preacher's command to stand and close their eyes in prayer, Will had an unobstructed view of Mary Alice's long neck, straight back, and thin waist tapering to her hips. She kept her hands in her pocket so as not to reach out and pull Mary Alice to her. She didn't chastise herself for such sinful thoughts in the house of the Lord.

Earlier this morning, Will was hanging up the new sign when Mary Alice walked by. When she greeted her, Will promptly struck her thumb with the hammer and almost fell off the ladder. She had to bite back a curse lest she be embarrassed.

It was five days before the bank opening when Will finally got up the courage to walk through Mary Alice's front door. The bell overhead rang when she opened the door and again when she closed it.

"Just a moment," Mary Alice called from another room.

Will glanced around the room. There were spools of yarn stacked neatly on a shelf, bobs of thread were lined up neatly on another shelf, and bolts of cloth stacked high on a table. Two handmade shapes of a woman's torso were on sticks as if standing sentry over the room. On one was a dress with pins in the hem, the other held cloth that Will assumed would eventually be another dress. Her hand shook as she removed her hat. Will had debated coming here and had talked herself out of it many, many, times. Before she had a chance to come to her senses and leave, Mary Alice stepped in the room.

"Good afternoon, Mr. Dixon."

Will's mouth went dry. The sound of Mary Alice's voice and the way she said her name made Will's insides quiver.

"Good afternoon, Miss Walker. I hope I'm not disturbing you."

"No not at all. I was just making some tea. Would you like to join me?"

Will hesitated, fighting the urge to say yes. She'd already spent way too much time with Mary Alice, and what she was doing here now was downright foolish, if not dangerous.

"No thank you. I've come to see if I may partake of your services." She held up a parcel wrapped in plain brown paper tied with twine. "I've brought one of my suits. Would you be able to help me with it? It's a bit big. Would you be able to do it by Monday?" Will knew she was probably rambling.

"It depends on what it needs," Mary Alice said reaching for her pin cushion and sliding it over her wrist. She motioned to the corner of the room where a curtain hung on a makeshift rod. "Why don't you put it on and let me see what needs to be done."

Will tried not to panic when the realization hit her that Mary Alice meant for her to take off her clothes and put on the suit. Then she would have to do it again when she was finished. That was two times she could be discovered, and Will almost backed out.

"Don't be embarrassed, Mr. Dixon. I'll step outside until you're finished."

"Um..." Will stammered.

"It's the only way I can see what needs to be done," she said patiently. "I'll have to pin it wherever it needs it and I can't do that if you're not wearing it. Don't worry, I won't stick you," she added teasingly.

"I'm not embarrassed, Miss Walker. It's your reputation I'm concerned with," Will lied. It was the discovery of what was underneath the material that was a problem.

Mary Alice waved her off. "Not to worry. People come in and take their clothes off all day." Mary Alice's hand flew to her mouth. "Oh, my goodness, that's not what I meant."

Will's eyes blazed and she held her breath. What would he do? Finally, she smiled uncomfortably.

"Not to worry, Miss Walker. I'll be just a minute."

Will's hands shook as she quickly stepped out of the trousers she was wearing and into the best trousers and jacket she owned. She took a deep breath and steadied herself before pulling the curtain back.

"Come over here into the light," Mary Alice said, pointing to a short stool by the window.

Will nervously stepped up and turned around to face her. Will couldn't speak as she felt the heat of Mary Alice's eyes on her. She scanned the coat and trousers with a professional eye, but Will detected she lingered a little too long in certain areas. She started to sweat.

"Mr. Dixon?"

Startled, Will almost stumbled off the stool

"Yes, sorry. What were you saying?"

"I asked if you had any specific adjustments in mind."

"Um, no. Whatever you think is necessary. I'm afraid I know nothing about choosing a suit." Little did anyone know she bought her suits from a catalog. She never risked entering a tailor shop. Until now. She was out of her mind.

"Well," Mary Alice began, lightly tugging on her jacket sleeve. "It doesn't need much," she said looking at the front of the coat. "Maybe a tuck here and there."

Will jumped back when Mary Alice ran her hands over the lapels on her coat.

"I'm sorry, Mr. Dixon. Did I do something wrong?" Mary Alice asked, flushed with embarrassment.

Wills chest heaved as she tried to catch her breath. Very few people had ever touched her, and no one had ever touched her *there*. Her breasts had sprung to life and her heart was racing.

"No, no, of course not," Will managed to say. "I've just never done this before. You surprised me that's all."

"Don't be concerned, Mr. Dixon. I have to move the fabric to pin it where it needs to be."

Will felt foolish and wished she had never come through the door. She was risking everything, to be acting so foolish. But she wanted to stay even more. She wanted to feel Mary Alice's hands on her, even if they were to move a pin or two. She wanted to feel the heat from her body as she stood close. Feel her eyes on her as she checked the lie of the fabric. She was in big, big trouble.

166

"Of course," Will managed to say. "Please continue. I apologize for my skittishness."

As Mary Alice pulled, straightened, and pinned, jolts of heat shot through Will's body where Mary Alice's hands skimmed her body. She clenched her jaw so tightly she thought she would break a tooth. Unusual wetness had pooled between her legs and she prayed Mary Alice could not detect it.

"Be careful, taking this off. The pins may stick you."

Will was sweating profusely as she as she donned her original trousers and coat and made sure everything was in place before she stepped out from behind the curtain. Mary Alice was on the front porch and came inside when she saw her.

"I'll have this ready for you at the end of the week. Will that be alright?"

"Yes of course, that will be fine."

"Is there anything else, Mr. Dixon?"

"Uh, no, thank you, Miss Walker. I'll see you in two days." Will wanted to say more. Wanted to stay and learn more about Mary Alice. Who was she fooling? She just wanted to be with her.

CHAPTER SIX

"Was that the banker I saw leaving the other day?" Francine asked after Mary Alice waved her into her kitchen.

"Francine, I've told you many times to use the front door."

"And I've told you many times I am not going to sully your reputation."

"You know I don't care about that."

"Well, you should."

It was a constant argument Mary Alice had with Francine. Francine Marks was the owner of the saloon and Mary Alice knew the women of Waco crossed to the other side of the street when Francine was out. The men did as well when walking with their wives, often hiding their faces behind their hats. The last thing a husband wanted was for his wife to know he was on first-name basis with the saloon owner or one of her girls.

Mary Alice didn't care what the townspeople thought of her friendship with Francine. She was a good friend and Mary Alice envied her freedom to make her own decisions.

Francine was a smart business owner, didn't water down the liquor, and made sure her girls were clean and not mistreated by the cowboys passing through. Francine and her girls were customers Mary Alice enjoyed when any of them came into her shop.

"Now answer me, child. Was that Mr. Dixon?"

"Yes, I'm doing some alterations for him."

"Quite a few if rumor is true. He's been over here several times."

"You know I don't listen to rumor, especially about my customers. And besides, how am I supposed to make alterations if he doesn't come by?"

"He's a handsome fellow. Very neat and clean."

That was quite a compliment considering it was Texas in the mid eighteen hundreds. Dirt and dust were everywhere and water scarce.

"You'd expect nothing less from a banker," Mary Alice replied.

"What do you think of him?" Francine asked. This was not the first time Francine had asked this question. She always brought Will's name up in conversation when they talked.

"What do you mean?" Mary Alice tried to keep her tone light. Francine saw everything.

"I mean what do you think of him? Is he as nice as everybody says he is? You spent quite a lot of time together at the Winstons' party a few weeks ago."

"We were just having polite conversation." But, as much as Mary Alice had relived each word more than a dozen times, it was much more than that.

"And were you just having polite conversation at the Hansons' barn raising? What about when he sat across from you at the church luncheon a few days ago?"

Francine's knowledge of everything that happened in town was even more complete than Mrs. Winston's. Mary Alice had maneuvered herself so that Will would have no choice but to talk to her on both of those occasions as well as several others. Since Will was not coming to her, she would go to him. She was downright brazen if anyone had suspected.

"Are you lying to me or yourself?" Francine asked, her eyes all knowing.

"What are you saying? I'm not lying to anyone." Even to Mary Alice her argument sounded weak.

Francine looked at her with disbelief. She had years of reading people and Mary Alice knew she didn't stand a chance of getting anything by her.

"I'm not really sure about him," Mary Alice said finally to fill the uncomfortable silence. "He's different than any man I've ever met, and I can't really say why." Mary Alice refilled their teacups. "We talk and have had tea, but it's as if he is hiding something or holding something back."

Francine chuckled. "He's only been here a few weeks. No one can know everything about someone in that short time." Francine leaned back in her chair and looked directly at her. "What I do know is that he hasn't been upstairs."

"Upstairs" was how Francine described the behind closed-door activities of her girls.

Mary Alice had long ago stopped blushing at Francine's frank talk. She had told Mary Alice stories that both shocked her and made her laugh so hard she had suck herself with a pin.

"I suppose he's been busy getting the bank ready to open," Mary Alice said, averting her eyes and defending Will.

"I suppose you're right. But I don't think that's it," Francine said grinning.

It took a moment for Mary Alice to understand what her friend wasn't saying.

"You can't mean he doesn't like women in that way?" She and Francine had had some interesting conversations about men and women together with their own kind. At first Mary Alice had been shocked, but who was she to judge another person's life?

"No, the way he was looking at you yesterday at the café, he is definitely interested."

Mary Alice hadn't known Will was in the café when she stopped by for lunch. Her body tingled at the thought that he was looking at her, and did much more than that when she looked at him.

171

"And the feeling is mutual," Francine added. She held up her hands to stop any comment. "Don't try to convince me otherwise. Your face is flushed and you're glowing just thinking about it. And it's about time," Francine added, reaching over and patting Mary Alice on her hand. "You're a good woman and you need someone in your life, but I'm concerned for you Mary Alice."

"Concerned? In what way?"

Francine leaned forward, placing both forearms on the table. "I'm very fond of you Mary Alice and I don't want to see you hurt."

Mary Alice was confused. She had no idea what Francine was talking about. She told her so.

"I have seen just about everything in my forty years, Mary Alice, and I am never wrong. Now I don't care what people do or who they do it with. What I do care about is that *everybody* knows the complete truth, including that which can only be seen behind closed doors. Or behind perfect manners, smooth talk, and ill-fitting clothes."

"What are you implying Francine?" A niggling thought that had been in the back of her brain grew louder.

"There is more to *Mister* Dixon than what you can see."

Mary Alice suddenly felt lightheaded. Could it be? She'd heard about women passing themselves off as men to fight in the war or run a ranch. Could Will be doing the same thing to run a bank?

Heat rose through Mary Alice just like it had every time she had fitted Will. Touching his clothes had felt like she was touching him. When she ran her hands across his shoulders to smooth out the material of his coat, she felt him twitch. Not able to stop herself, she had repeated the movement several more times, enjoying the way his muscles danced under her hands. And she wanted to do it again, and much, much more.

"So, what does that make me?" Mary Alice asked, afraid of the answer that felt so right.

"If you continue down this road, it makes you a woman who will live a difficult life. One shrouded in secrecy. Your secret is safe with me, Mary Alice. but others will not be as welcoming. There may come a day when you will be forced to leave, and it might not be pleasant."

A whirlwind of thoughts and emotions flooded Mary Alice. Shock, disbelief, and confusion warred with desire. She jumped up and paced around the small room. She couldn't speak for the lump that was in her throat.

"But what it will also do is make you happier than you ever thought imaginable. To share your love with someone who loves you just as much in return is priceless. But it may come at a cost and you need to be willing to accept that."

Mary Alice didn't know how long she sat in her kitchen after Francine left, but it was well past dark. A thousand thoughts and scenarios ran through her mind, including one that she kept coming back to. She was an independent woman and had always gone after what she wanted, public rebuke be damned. Why should now be any different?

CHAPTER SEVEN

Will was more than a little nervous when she returned to Mary Alice to pick up her clothes. She had made several trips to Mary Alice's, each time bringing with her additional clothes. Mary Alice did excellent work and several of the townspeople commented about how dapper Will looked recently.

Will had thought of nothing else but the way her body had reacted during her fittings. Will had worked hard to develop and maintain an air of calm confidence, but every time she thought of Mary Alice's hands on her clothes, detected the scent of her perfume, her hands started to shake and she had a hard time breathing. She felt like she could combust at any moment.

She had trouble sleeping and for the last few nights she had vivid dreams of herself and Mary Alice together. They were naked, lying in the middle of Will's bed, their bodies intertwined in passion. She woke up sweating, her body tingling, her heart racing out of her chest.

The thoughts Will was having about Mary Alice terrified her. For the first time in her life she wanted to go on long buggy rides through the countryside, Mary Alice beside her. Have a picnic by a stream, the sun shining on Mary Alice's face. She yearned to sit on the front porch with her and watch the fireflies dance in the dark. She wanted to learn everything about Mary Alice and share her dreams. She wanted to hear her laugh at funny stories of her childhood. But the most troubling were the thoughts she had when she closed her eyes at night.

Will envisioned waking up every morning in her arms after a night of lovemaking. Each day Mary Alice would make sure her tie was straight, and her suit ironed, before she kissed her and sent Will off to work. Will would come home to Mary Alice in the kitchen taking a loaf of fresh bread out of the oven, preparing a meal for them, or sitting in the parlor quietly waiting for her. Their evenings would be filled with conversation about their hopes and dreams for their life together until they retreated to their bedroom where they would share their love, often until they fell asleep from exhaustion.

Will hesitated in front of Mary Alice's shop door. She needed to remain completely unaffected, pay her for her services, and hightail it out of there. That is what she *should* do. What she *wanted* to do was spend the afternoon with Mary Alice, talking about everything and nothing, stay for supper, and kiss her before she left. Will wanted to do more than kiss Mary Alice and she did not want to leave. Will stepped inside, confident she would do what was right. She always did.

Mary Alice looked up from a bundle of fabric in her lap as Will stepped inside. Her face was drawn, dark circles under her eyes. She hurried over and knelt in front of Mary Alice, taking her hands in hers.

"Mary Alice, are you alright? Has something happened?" Will searched her eyes looking for any sign of the trouble that must be causing her such anguish. "Mary Alice?"

"It's nothing, Mr. Dixon," Mary Alice said, her voice tight with emotion.

"Mary Alice, if someone has hurt you or is threatening to…"

"No, that's not it," Mary Alice said quickly, pulling her hands away. Mary Alice stood and brushed her dress like she was brushing off whatever had her so upset. "Your jacket is finished if you'd like to try it on."

Will frowned as she removed her blue jacket and donned the black one. There was something very wrong, but Mary Alice was not going to share. Will had thought they had developed a friendship over the course of many fittings but obviously she was mistaken. Then it dawned on her. Mary Alice saw her as a man, and men and women were not friends. For the first time, Will wanted to be someone other than her carefully presented life.

"Turn around," Mary Alice said. "I had some trouble getting the correct lie on this one."

Will did as she was told, grateful Mary Alice would not see the anguish in her eyes. She tensed as Mary Alice's hands ran across her shoulders. She relished the feeling and wanted to lean into it. She never wanted to leave.

It took a moment for Will to realize that Mary Alice's hands were no longer smoothing the fabric. They were caressing her. Will didn't move. She didn't dare. If she did. she would never again feel Mary Alice touch her.

"Will?"

Mary Alice's voice penetrated the haze of desire that rattled Will's brain. She had called her by her first name, something she had never done.

"Yes?" she had managed to say.

"Why have you never come calling?"

Mary Alice's voice was soft and quivering. Will couldn't speak, the knot in her stomach had quickly traveled to her throat.

"Do you not find me attractive?"

Will spun around, Mary Alice's hands shifting to her chest. "Absolutely not. Mary Alice you are beautiful. Any man would be proud to come calling on you." Will knew she had said too much. She hated seeing the doubt in her eyes.

"I'm not right for you, Mary Alice."

Will's heart ached. After all her preparations, everything she had planned for, she had never expected this. She had never allowed herself to get this close to anyone. Until now. Until she stepped off the stage in the dirt town of Waco, Texas.

"I think you are."

Mary Alice's voice was firmer now, her eyes clear. She pinned Will with the sheer determination in them. Wills heart beat hard and she knew Mary Alice could feel it.

"No, I'm not."

"Why do you say that?"

How could Will explain? How could she tell this beautiful woman standing in front of her that she was a complete fraud? That everything Mary Alice knew about her was a lie? Mary Alice would never trust herself again. Will could not do that to her.

"Because I know myself better than you do. I could never give you what you want."

"How do you know what I want?"

"What every woman wants, marriage, children." *If only I could give that to you,* Will thought.

"What makes you think that's what I want?" Mary Alice asked seriously.

Will tried to step away, but Mary Alice grabbed the lapels on her jacket. "I'm not talking about this anymore, Mary Alice. I'm sorry if I've led you on or gave you a false impression."

Mary Alice looked at Will so long and with such intensity that Will thought she might break. The doubt and confusion and anguish on Mary Alice's face earlier drifted away and was replaced with determination.

"Will, I know who you are."

Will's stomach seized and she wanted to run. *Get out! Run!* Her feet were frozen and Will did nothing to change that.

"Of course, you do. I'm the banker," she said, trying to diffuse the tension between them.

"No. I mean I *know* who you are."

Will was stunned. Her carefully crafted costume had been exposed by a petite seamstress with golden hair, sky blue eyes, and who said what was on her mind. Will knew what came next would determine her fate in Waco. Everything that she had dreamed about and worked for could blow away in the next breath.

Mary Alice emphasized the word as she stepped closer and Will could not breathe. If she knew Will's secret, why was she moving closer? Why were her breasts pressed against hers? Why were her hands sliding up to wrap around her neck? Why was she pulling her head down? Why was she allowing their breath to mingle? Why was she...

"You are the one that I want, Will Dixon. *All* of you."

Will exploded in sensation when Mary Alice kissed her.

THE DEVIL'S BACKBONE

LACEY L. SCHMIDT

The beast never slays the hero, and yet. Show me a hero and I'll tell you the tragedy. This is the story about what happens between the beast and the hero's end. It is not often told. Maybe for a reason. You decide.

It started with a small, vaguely illegal curiosity. Or maybe it was the legality of the behavior that resulted from my curiosity...I know, who am I to judge the legality of my curiosity? After all this story has already started in the voice of the unreliable narrator. While I think I am reliable, I fully acknowledge I am the narrator, and you don't really know me yet...therefore, unreliable may be fair. Again, you decide.

I am a coder, a programmer, a loner. This is a modern fairy tale. I live in an old limestone cottage on Purgatory Road, by chance not far from the Devil's Backbone Tavern on the Devil's Backbone Scenic Drive. The road is billed as the most haunted stretch of Texas Highway. Bikers love to roar over its knobby blacktop spine to the tavern, pretending they are dragon slayers. Everyone wants to slay the beast. With Harleys mostly, but also some Hondas, an occasional Ducati, and a little Kawasaki even. At any rate, probably because of the tavern and all those bikers posting to social media about their prowess, Purgatory Road has stellar internet connections. I live in the Texas Hill Country, surrounded by beautiful rugged and rolling hills, with shaggy pecans and smoky mesquite trees dotting the valleys. I don't have to do people, except once or twice a week to check in with the suits in Austin (a.k.a. Little Silicon Valley). I warned you I was a code slinger.

Life was grand on Purgatory Road before my curiosity got the best of me. You see, there is this castle on a hill overlooking the bend on Highway 281 and FM32 (the hundred-degree left-handed bend of that Devil's Backbone drive). I don't mean a mansion. I mean an honest-to-God actual Greystone storybook castle. Who would build such a thing in Texas? Most of the too-wealthy-whack-jobs in Texas build a ranch-style mini-mansion à la JR Ewing in

Dallas or a largely tasteless hill country hunting lodge with enough large furniture to accommodate forty well-fed linebackers. I was torn. The castle owner could be cool. He could be an outsider with a staunch love of Monty Python's Holy Grail. Or he could be a douche bag with lots of money and a kingly ego. A small part of me fantasized that maybe this castle-owner was even a fellow reclusive lesbian coder who managed to procure a cool billion in bitcoins or something.

Long story short, there was an easy way for a coder with a slight hacking tendency to find out. I saddled up my 1967 Mustang (Pearl White of course, I am the doomed hero after all), and drove out to the Highway 281 rest stop near the castle with a few choice gadgets to hack the castle's Wi-Fi network. What I found was an eyeful of awful shit no human should ever have to endure. Videos, photos, diagrams of horrific murders. I won't describe what I still see nearly every night in my nightmares. If you want an idea you can just picture the goriest horror movie ever banned in this country…then multiply that by making the victims the most sympathetic and innocent assortment of man, woman, and child you can think of.

The castle had over 200 rooms, one for each of the fairy tales in Grimms' Fairy Tales plus some. In sixty-nine of those rooms, the castle's owner, Waylon Dorin Mills, had created a hellish interpretation of tales using mangled corpses. A dead diorama if you will. He had plans, too, to do all 200 tales. So many stories like Snow White, Little Red Riding Hood, Sleeping Beauty, Hansel and Gretel (even the corpse playing the witch made me cry) will never be the same again for me. I managed to download a tremendous amount of evidence despite my shaking hands. No one ever taught that fucking beast about firewalls, so I made sure to make it his Achilles heel.

I don't remember much about the drive to Austin after. My knuckles looked even whiter than the white of my steering wheel. There was a lot of traffic and every family in every car was a reminder of the victims the beast could still claim if I didn't hurry. I went directly to the Texas Highway Patrol's headquarters. I would have gone directly to some federal agency if I had known where one was, but I passed by the Patrol's HQ all the time on the way into those weekly work meetings. It took several hours of convincing, but once I got a few of them to look at the data I'd downloaded, things went quickly. I threw up in some guy's desk trash bin. Mostly bile as I hadn't eaten anything since dinner the night before. They gave me a bottle of water and a small black coffee in a shitty "recyclable" Styrofoam cup. I remember the fluorescent lighting and an odd number of men with boots, pot bellies, and mustaches. Then some guys in department-store suits who shaved and knew how to tie ties came in. Federal agents, I think. Anyway, I got to go into a tiny room with four men twice my size and no attorney. I wasn't being charged with anything, yet. That was my chance to cooperate, my chance to be a "hero" they said. If I agreed to turn over the evidence and a detailed written statement about how and why I'd found what I'd found, then they would let me remain anonymous and walk out again with no charges filed.

Part of the deal was that I never talk to the press about the case or my involvement. Of course, I think I am safe with you though, right? Anyway, this is technically a fiction anthology, not a news publication. I am not winking (wink, wink).

In the end the guys with the pot bellies and the badges got the glory. The girl with the keystrokes got to keep quiet. I tried to keep the nightmares at bay by counting the one hundred and thirty-one fairy tales that the beast did not complete. I tried avoiding the spontaneous recall of gruesome images by picturing the beast's face on the news as the court convicted him, but I also saw the faces of the victims' families. Family representatives frequently thanked law enforcement for the closure, but their eyes still said that justice was too little cold comfort too late.

My brilliant coding work suffered, of course. I started transposing lines of code. Acquired Dyslexia. I had a therapist. It didn't work out. He wore sweater vests. In Texas. He did mention that journaling could help me process. That wasn't so dumb apparently.

It was one of my suit bosses in Austin, Andrew, who had a strangely good recommendation. I mentioned that I was having trouble sleeping, even in the locked comfort of my own home, I just felt entombed. Andrew asked if I'd tried sleeping outside, specifically some place pretty with stars to look at. Apparently, he likes to photograph the stars and he said it is tough to stay awake with all the peace and quiet out there. A co-worker asked him about the wild animals. He just laughed and said we're the wild animals you have to worry about. No truer words than that.

I packed up the Mustang the next afternoon and headed to Enchanted Rock State Park. I didn't take a tent. I strung up a hammock in the car campground, no one else was camping on a Tuesday in February. I stared up through the stout, naked oak branches at the moon and stars, and found I could breathe deep and slow. My thoughts dissipated into pinpricks of winking stars and the quartz twinkling in the mighty, granite, rock bubble beyond my heels that the park is named after. Who knew camping, or at least sleeping outside, could be so relaxing?

I became an addict who camped out four or five nights of each week. I gained back the fifteen pounds I'd lost. Turns out cooking outdoors is relaxing, too, and inspires my appetite. Although, I'm strictly vegan these days. That post-beast acquired quirk is too hard to fight. The Acquired Dyslexia eased up. I coded well again. I socialized with my coworkers again some...well, at least as much as I ever did, and as much as a team of coders who work 90% virtually ever socialize outside of text chats.

Spoiler Alert. You're probably thinking this was the tragedy. My PTSD, and that the hero soldiered on just fine, but if that were so, why would I keep journaling at you for so many more pages? We're just getting to the tragedy. You can't have real tragedy without romance, and there hasn't been any romance yet. So, see? Spoiled my narrative. At least you probably expected it after that unreliable narrator chat, right?

My camping spree led me to camp out in just about every state park that year. My coworkers gave me a camera for my birthday in June, and I started taking some star photos (and random portraits of trees) with a little tutorial from Andrew. One thing led to another, and some of the photos were good, so I donated them to the parks to use for education or their social media accounts and stuff. I frequented Enchanted Rock the most and became friends with a ranger there named Mel. Mel is an Army veteran, former medic in Afghanistan. She has seen shit she would rather forget, too, and no. this isn't the romance yet. Falling in love with another battered soul who helped you heal wouldn't be tragic, would it?

But Mel's interest and mentoring would lead me to choose the tragic trail. She met me at my favorite campsite one night in November. She toed the ground with a hiking boot and I knew she was trying to find a way to tell me something she wasn't sure I would like. I offered her a cup of chamomile tea. I knew it was serious when she accepted some of my "herbal crap" to sip. Two swallows through pursed lips later she asked me if I would camp out on the deck of the Battleship Texas with her for a fundraiser. I didn't take time to think it through or ask questions about who else would be onboard. Mel was my friend. Of course, I said yes. I was at least certain she'd said on deck, not in confined indoor bunks, so all would be well.

For those of you who have never toured the iconic Battleship Texas, a little description is in order (skip ahead if you've visited before). The ship is berthed in San Jacinto State Park, which features an obelisk taller than the Washington DC monument (of course everything is bigger in Texas, even the monuments built by men with likely erectile dysfunction). The monument sits on the spot of the San Jacinto River where General Santa Anna surrendered to Sam Houston and Texas won its independence/rebellion against the Mexican government. You're thinking so good so far, I know, but peek at a map. The San Jacinto River becomes the Houston Ship Channel right about there. The park and the battleship are surrounded by refineries and freeways. Rushing rivers of light pollution and those wild, murderous animals, known as people. Mel had the good grace to wince and blush through a smile when I pointed out the details she'd left out. It was for a good cause after all. Her veterans' group had chosen to support the foundation raising money to preserve the Battleship Texas; and I was the only photographer of any sort she knew, let alone could recruit to attend for the price of a dinner catered by Subway and the rights to sleep on an old boat with a select group of history buffs willing to donate lots of money to the cause.

At least, we would be sleeping on the wooden deck and not entombed in the steel bunk rooms belowdecks. Those bunks and the steel needed to be renovated, hence the fundraiser, a night on deck under the stars. Or in the glow of the refinery lights. Same difference, and oh, could I please get some pictures of the stars with the battleship and if possible, the monument too in them? There may have been some Photoshop slaving necessary. Don't judge. Photoshop is just another part of the art process. If you wanted pictures of what was actually there, you'd take them with your own damn smartphone camera. I take photos of what it feels like to be there. Smartphone cameras may never be high definition enough to capture that.

What captured my attention most that evening before sunset was a striking brunette woman with soulful blue eyes, pert nose, and a bright impish smile. Her smile was tempered by something I couldn't define. Shyness? An old sadness? That light hint of mystery was the hook of tragedy.

It didn't occur to me when she introduced herself as Julie Weiss. The name sounded only barely familiar. The kind of familiar that a common name sounds. I called her Jules. I like to ruin my chances with beautiful women early but my nicknaming a stranger had the unintended effect of drawing her in. She smiled like a model in a toothpaste commercial and touched my elbow as she told me how good it was to hear someone call her that again. Apparently, that is what her father called her when he was alive. My elbow tingled for over half an hour. I'm not much of a mingler anyway, so I don't think people noticed I was being weird on the edges of the festivities.

Speeches were given. I even took photos of some people. Most of them happened to feature Jules somehow, but still, they got what they paid for from their photographer. The dozen donors were slated to camp out in a spot near the bow, with the monument looming above like a giant nightlight. Mel and I begged off to the stern, our heavens opened up to murky water, and the traffic light of ships passing in the night, but it was the most open skyview on board and I breathed easier, until Jules wandered over and asked if we minded one more bedroll along side. I could have said no. Mel vaguely nodded and looked to me for the final say. I found myself smiling and saying sure when I wasn't sure at all.

The city around us was noisy and so was Mel's snoring. The wooden deck, under the boat's big steel guns and looming shadows, was strange and uneven. We slept in a line, with me in the middle, Mel to my right, Jules to the left. The foam pads we all used beneath our sleeping bags were oddly firmer and less comforting on the long, wooden, deck planks than they were on raw earth. It was warm for December and too humid. We slept on top of our sleeping bags. I remember thinking that if I ever fell asleep, I would wake up dreading the dewy dampness that would be clinging to me everywhere by morning. Looking back, that is ironic. I watched the night sky grow so cloudy that it reflected only the orange glow of the refinery's mercury vapor lights. Around three in the morning, Jules gave a few sleep-strangled cries and mews like a cornered kitten, but the deck was still and silent. I started singing in my head, "three o'clock and all's well." Jules rolled over and flung an arm and a leg over me. I startled but it didn't wake her. She just snuggled her face into the side of my breast and clutched my ribs closer in with her fingertips. Her hair smelled like sunscreen and cinnamon. I decided I could live with it, she'd probably roll back over by morning anyway and it wasn't like I could sleep. Only, I did fall asleep.

I woke up to Mel gently toeing my right foot and I squinted at her in confusion as she held a finger to her lips and tilted her head toward my left arm, which felt oddly numb. Jules was still sleeping on it. I started again despite Mel's hands mimicking a "stay down, stay calm" pat in the air above me. My jerk and the dawn were enough to jolt Jules awake. It was almost like an old-fashioned cartoon. Maybe Fred Flintstone's Barney Rubble waking up to a bear in his bed? She smacked her lips a little and gave a muffled groan as she pulled her head up, sleepy eyes meeting mine for just an instant before she sprang up like a startled snake wearing an alarming coat of red paint to color its embarrassment. She issued at least a two-minute long litany of "Oh my God. I'm so sorry." Then there were tears as she slid down into a ball against the stern wall and buried her face in her arms while still mumbling something about how horrified and sorry she was to invade my space.

I tried telling her it was okay. No harm done. I was just glad to have slept a few hours. But she kept mumbling into her forearms, with her hair hanging over her eyes. I wasn't sure what was so wrong. I mean, sure, snuggling a relative stranger was a tad embarrassing, but it didn't seem like the kind of thing that would cause this sort of grief. I looked to Mel. She shrugged and gestured I should move closer. I crawled over to Jules and sat beside her. No touching, just nearby. She still didn't make eye contact, but I could make out a little more of what she was saying. She'd lost someone. She didn't sleep so well. Nightmares. No excuse. She was still so sorry. I glanced at Mel again, and she just cocked her head to one side and tapped a fingertip between her eyes. Our unspoken language for maybe she's seen shit she would rather have not, too. I gave the barest of nods.

Mel wandered away, so I asked Jules about it. Remember the part about me liking to ruin my chances with beautiful women early? Yeah, well, this stupid move didn't work as expected either. I guess it should have been apparent from the way Jules had nestled her nose into the side of my breast overnight that she needed a hug, but I was still shocked to find her crying in my arms. I tried murmuring reassuring things, but I'm not really the reassuring type. I ended up confessing I'd seen terrible things that I didn't like to talk about, but that I knew it helped some people to talk about the terrible things they'd seen, and I would listen to her do so if she wanted.

Jules nodded, and I gave her the handkerchief in my pocket for her tears. She smarted off about how, of course, the knight in shining armor had a handkerchief to offer on demand, and then laughed when I admitted I'd already worn it as a sweatband while taking photos once in the last twenty-four hours. I was willing to let her deflect as long as necessary, or even forever if she didn't really want to talk about it. Half an hour in of talking but not talking about whatever it was, Mel brought us both black coffees. Jules asked Mel to sit, too, and said something about wanting to give us an explanation, not because she needed to, but because we were the first people she felt okay explaining it to. I understood that. My truth was that I wanted to tell both her and Mel what I'd seen, why I was so weirded out in my own head even if I looked okay to others, but I didn't want to give them that burden of knowing, or imagining how it felt, or of ever having to worry about legalities associated with my deal with law enforcement.

I was looking Jules square in the eye, my heart on my sleeve, when she carefully told us that her wife had been murdered by the Fairy Tale Killer. I know all the blood drained from my face because Jules told me it did, and apologized profusely for not saying it right. It was like a bomb went off nearby for me. My head was ringing like a bell. I struggled through the loud numbness to tell Jules it was okay, she said it fine, that I was just so very sorry for her. I think Mel was smoother, but I was the one that Jules was imprinted on, the comforting arms she was more familiar with. I held her hands and their warmth broke through my own chill. I should have said something then, but I didn't. I remembered seeing Jules cry on TV in the background of a press conference after Mills was convicted. She'd been clutching a picture of a woman I thought resembled the one Mills cast as his raven-haired, eyes-hollowed-out, Snow White. I tried not to remember the video of the room just then. I kept my damn mouth shut against the ringing in my ears. It isn't like I knew any of Waylon Dorin Mills' victims personally. I'd just seen shit I shouldn't, and no one likes to hear about that. Especially not the spouse of one of his victims who believes no one else has unnecessarily seen the desecrated and defiled corpse of their loved one.

We exchanged phone numbers with Jules before leaving the ship. At first, Jules met both Mel and I some evenings at Enchanted Rock, but at some point, Jules and I started doing things together. Just the two of us meeting for Sunday brunch in Fredericksburg or in San Antonio to hear Jim Cullum's Jazz Band. We weren't dating. We were falling in love. I don't think either of us really registered that was happening until we met up to camp in Garner State Park one weekend to watch the Perseid Meteor shower and possibly wish upon a star. The site I'd reserved was smack up against the Frio River on a bend of tent-only spots so that it was possible not to notice the lights of other campers behind us, and the better to see the stars reflected on the dark river in front of us. We set ourselves up in camp chairs with a bottle of wine, red night lights nearby if we needed them, and waited in the dark with my camera. The waiting got long, and we got hot. The Frio river, clear and cool, is always inviting; but it was overwhelmingly enticing that night. A quick skinny dip sounded entirely reasonable until we were in the water. I poked my foot on a rock and slipped under with a yelp.

It was minor. There was no risk of me drowning right there. I was just surprised, and so was Jules. She grabbed me even as I was standing up again and held on tight. Her soft naked body pressed against mine, her breath hot and hard in my ear. I stood stock still. Unable to move. Nearly unable to breathe for god knows how long before I managed to tell her I was fine. I was stable standing there. She pulled back enough for me to see her face and her eyes flashed in the dim light before she kissed the hell right out of me. I know folks say that some kisses are like fireworks, but that doesn't suit this kiss. Fireworks are too short and too cold. This kiss was like a decades long supernova, thousands of degrees too hot even for tungsten. Months' worth of falling in love were wrapped up into one explosive moment when all we could do was cling to each other and hold on.

After that it all seemed so obvious, we felt stupid. Mel even barbecued tempeh and shared her home-brewed beer with us to celebrate the next weekend. The tempeh was for me. They ate Mel's famous Shiner beer-can chicken, and I wanted to tell them then, too. But I didn't. Not the proper timing in the tragic story arc of course.

Jules is a history teacher at a high school in Bulverde, a town about thirty miles west of Purgatory Road. Even dryer Texas Hill Country. The longer we were together, the more I took to staying at her place. Even sleeping inside more since there is a nice big skylight in her bedroom, and ten-foot ceilings. With her arm slung over my ribs, I didn't feel entombed, but rather cocooned. Safe at night. During the day though, I started to feel guilty. Maybe I'd saved lots of people, maybe even Jules, from the Fairy Tale Killer; but I didn't save Jules' beautiful dead wife, Rosa. No doubt from then on I knew Rosa Rangel was Waylon Dorin Mills' choice to play Snow White. Of course, Jules had a picture of Rosa with life in her beautiful dark eyes, bounces in her black, silky-looking ringlet curls. Rosa looked like an angel. Like that old Radiohead song, "Creep," her skin looked so perfect in the photo that it could make me cry, and I was the creep living Rosa's promised life, loving Jules, being loved by Jules in her stead.

I pleaded a big software project due and sequestered myself for a week back in my cottage on Purgatory Road. In between coding, I ran simulation after simulation in my head of just telling Jules the truth, trying to calculate all the possible outcomes and figure out which, if any, were in my favor. Zero compute. By week's end I hadn't showered or eaten enough, and I had neglected to hear the phone ring a few too many times. I was drooling at the screen, looking for the same damn syntax error for the third hour in a row, when Jules busted in with her key. She looked relieved to see me actually sitting at my desk in cartoon-sheep pajama pants and a Dr. Pepper T-shirt, gamey and coding as promised. She spun my chair around to face her, kissed the top of my head, and settled on her knees in front of me, hands on my thighs. She started to say something about mandating a break and a shower before our eyes met. Whatever she saw there in my eyes inspired a flinch and the whisper, "Oh, honey, what is it? What's wrong?"

There is the tragic arc. There I was facing the woman of my dreams in stinky clothes with greasy hair and bags under my eyes the size of a major league baseball team's bat bag. Then and there is where and when I finally told her the whole sordid extent of the tale from my character's eyes. I was so stupid. I waited so long, until I was about as unhuggable as a person can get, and didn't even ask for a hug first, for what I knew was likely to be the last time Jules would even want to look at me. Her last image of me would be as a stinky, lying by cowardly omission, corrupted hobbit like Gollum crying, "My Precious, My Precious..." as she slammed the door and ran far, far away.

I was stupid.

And as it turns out, overly dramatic. Jules did cry, because I was crying, and then she did strip my pajamas and toss me in my shower. However, she did not run away. Not even a little. She wrapped a towel around me and held me close as she asked a few gentle questions. Then she made me a tofu scramble and curled around me while we slept. The next morning she asked me to move in with her full-time, to just leave Purgatory Cabin behind for a while, so we could see if we could really build a future together as well as share this abominable and strange intersection of our pasts.

I said "hell yes" faster than I can convey here, and seven months later she said "hell yes" she would marry her hero before I could even finish asking the question. I once saw a quote or a meme, something, along the lines of real heroes being all around us uncelebrated. Ordinary people who rise to the occasion and then quietly slip away. I believe that. Jules is a hero. Her strength of spirit is heroic. Her love saved me even after my heroics left me convinced I was destined to become a freaked-out beast.

You're probably a hero waiting to happen, too. You just don't call yourself that, and so you think you'll escape the tragedy. You won't. Not if you want to love or be loved.

The tragedy? The Fairy Tale Killer and all the darkness associated with that beast made love possible for me and Jules. It's tragic how much shit any one of us might have to go through to find our soul mate. Out of the worst things, the most impossibly horrible things, came the best thing that ever happened to me. This is a cautionary tale. Don't lose hope. Suffer your turn at being a hero, and maybe you can tell the tragedy of finding love in the ashes after pulling the devil's backbone from the very beast. Even heroes must die one day. However, there is time to ride off into the sunset with the girl of your dreams in a Pearl White '67 Mustang. I think this is very reliable advice from an unreliable narrator, but you decide.

TAKE ME ALL THE WAY

MJ WILLIAMZ

The night was so electrically charged, I swore I could see the sound waves bouncing off the crowd of people gathered on Rainey Street. Musical waves were carried on the night air and I followed them, drawn by the allure of the beat, the rhythm. Like another's heartbeat, it called to me.

I'd spent the night wandering from stage to stage, feeling alive thanks to the assortment of music I'd heard. Something different was calling to me though. I could feel the air pulsating with the beat. I followed it, slowly though, as it wasn't easy to fight my way through the crowds.

And what crowds there were. As I pushed through them, I was acutely aware of their hearts beating, their arteries pulsating with the music. I longed to drink from someone, anyone. But I stayed strong. I followed the beat until the whole sky lit up with the most amazing laser show I'd ever seen.

Lasers of all colors shot out over the crowd. I looked up, watching the lights. They were mesmerizing. The sights and sounds were captivating, and I wanted more. The music had a distinct beat and, as I tore my focus from the lights to the people, I noticed young men and women, half naked, jumping up and down by the stage. Was this the way people danced nowadays? But, even as I wondered at its oddity, I couldn't resist the pull to join them.

And, once in the center of them, I noticed most of them wearing jewelry, necklaces and bracelets that lit up. The brightness against the backdrop of the night reminded me of black lights of the seventies.

I started jumping up and down to the music and was soon lost in the moment. I felt a tap on my shoulder and an androgynous being smiled at me. He or she handed me a bright-red blinking necklace. Grateful, I smiled back and put it on. Now I was one of them.

Though I wasn't. Not really. For one thing, I was fully clothed. I was dressed in black skinny jeans and a tight black

T-shirt. For another, though I looked to be in my late twenties, I was several hundred years older.

Their hearts pounded as they jumped and danced. And sang and shouted. I was suddenly dizzy. Not from the music and the lights and the jumping, but from a need, a carnal need to satisfy something so deeply rooted in me it was a part of my very existence.

I needed to get out of there, though I was loathe to leave. I could take one of the party goers. Easily. But I couldn't. These youngsters were just starting their lives. And I couldn't hurt them.

Blinded by the demand my body felt, I struggled to get through the throng of people. It was nearly impossible. For every two steps forward, the crowd crushed me back another ten. The music was merely a buzzing now and it was growing annoying.

And then I heard something besides the music. I heard screaming. It was coming from far away. My preternatural hearing picked up on it though, and I lost all pretense of being civilized. I used my unnatural strength and pushed through the crowd.

I was back on the street in a minute. The screaming was louder, and I followed the sound of it. I turned onto Davis Street and then the screams were muffled, but I could still hear them. The sounds led me to Willow, and at the end of the street, on the bike path, was a darkly clothed figure laying on top of someone who was clearly struggling.

I took a deep breath and approached. The figure on the bottom, a woman, was fighting for her life, but the man who had her pinned didn't care. He was fumbling with his zipper when I grabbed him, pulling him off her and holding him as he fought to get free.

"You're not going anywhere," I said.

I half carried, half dragged him off the beaten path and out of sight of the woman. The man's anger turned to fear as I unsheathed my fangs and sunk them into his carotid artery. I drank until his heart stopped beating. Satisfied he'd never hurt another woman, I licked the wounds and the punctures closed. I let him drop and hurried back to the woman.

She was crumpled on the ground in the same place I'd left her. Her sobs reached inside of me, to a place I hadn't realized still existed. I squatted next to her.

"Are you okay?" I asked.

She nodded, apparently unable to speak.

"What happened?"

"I was walking the path…"

"At this hour?"

"I figured everyone would be at South by Southwest," she said.

"Okay." I nodded.

"Anyway, he jumped out from behind a tree and attacked me." She looked up and, for the first time, made eye contact. "You saved my life."

I stared into her emerald eyes, red rimmed and still teary. They showed fear and gratitude.

"I just happened to be in the right place and the right time," I said.

"Well, thank you. Is there some way I can repay you?"

"That's not necessary." I offered my hand and she took it. She stood tall, an inch or two taller than myself.

"I must insist," she said.

"Let's get you home first. Your dress is filthy, and I doubt you'll want to wear it again."

"You're right. Come on. My apartment isn't far."

"You want me to come with you?"

"Yes. I need a bodyguard. Which, by the way, how did you get so strong? You handled him like he was a ragdoll."

"Adrenaline," I said.

She nodded and didn't say another word until we got to her place. It was a nice apartment on Red River. I stood in her spacious living room, decorated in black and white. I felt quite comfortable there.

"Have a seat," she said. "I'll be right out."

I sat on her black leather couch and checked out her big screen TV. I wondered what she watched. Sports? Cooking shows? Mysteries? Comedies? I had no idea and didn't even know why I cared. I'd leave her apartment and never see her again. As soon as I was sure she'd be okay.

She emerged from her bedroom wearing gray skinny jeans and a charcoal sweater. She looked amazing. She had obviously brushed the hell out of her blond hair as it shone.

"You feel better?" I said.

"Much. I took a shower and scrubbed that asshole off me. I feel wonderful. Thank you."

I shrugged.

"I'm just happy I happened along at the right time."

"Mm. Me too."

"Okay then." I stood. "I'll leave you to it. Just be careful, okay?"

"Please let me buy you a drink. I don't want to be alone. I'm sorry. I know you've already done so much. I don't mean to take advantage of you..." The words poured out on top of each other, seemingly racing to get out of her mouth.

"Sh." I placed my hands on her shoulders. "Calm down. If you're not ready to be alone, I'll gladly go somewhere with you. Just relax, okay?"

She took a deep, shaky breath.

"I'll try."

"Good." I smiled at her. And she smiled back. And I knew, deep down, that she was going to be fine. "So, where to?"

"I know a small, quiet bar. It's not for dancing or watching sports or anything like that. There's no live music. It's just a place to go for drinks and unwinding."

"That sounds great. Lead the way."

We walked a couple blocks and she kept looking over her shoulder.

"Relax," I said. "No one is going to hurt you while I'm around."

"Am I that obvious?"

"It's understandable. I just need you to know I'm not going to let anyone hurt you."

"Thank you." She bumped me with her hip.

"You're welcome."

She stopped in front of a tall building and opened the door. I stepped into a room that was full of chrome and glass. It was clean and spacious and empty with the exception of a bored looking bartender.

"Tanya," he said as he looked up.

"Hi, Todd."

"What can I get you?"

"I'll have a hot toddy." She turned to me. "And you?"

I exhaled slowly. I had no idea. It had been years since I'd drunk alcohol.

"Um… I'll have a hot toddy, too, I guess."

She laughed. It was a magical sound.

"You're original."

"I have no idea what I want."

"What do you like?" Todd said. "Chocolate? Caramel? Rum, vodka, tequila?"

"All of the above." I laughed. "Though admittedly I do love me some vodka."

"How about a mudslide?" Todd said.

"People still drink those?"

"Sure do. Choose a booth. I'll bring your drinks to you."

Tanya chose a red leather booth in the far corner of the establishment.

"For privacy," she said. I nodded my understanding. "So you know my name. Now, what's yours?"

"Severina," I said. "Though you can call me Rina."

"Rina. I like that. And obviously, you can call me Tanya."

"Thanks, Tanya. And nice to meet you."

I extended my hand and she placed hers in it. Her skin was soft, supple, and inappropriate thoughts entered my mind. I pushed them away. That was the last thing I needed to be thinking of with a woman who was almost raped less than an hour ago.

"Tell me about yourself, Rina. Where are you from? Your features are so dark, and you have a slight accent, though I can't quite place it."

"I'm originally from Italy," I said.

"How fun." Her whole face lit up. "I've never been to Italy though it's on my bucket list. Tell me all about it. Where are you from?"

"Venice," I told her. And it wasn't a lie. I'd been born in Venice and turned on the Piazza San Marco. That had been four hundred years ago, though I wasn't about to tell her that.

"Is it magical? Oh please, say it is."

"It is." I smiled. "It's magical, and mesmerizing, and romantic, and historical."

Tanya sat back against the booth.

"I knew it," she said. "I've got to get there. I've wanted to since I was a child."

"A worthy aspiration."

We sipped our drinks and chatted about inconsequential things. After our second cocktail, there was a lull in the conversation. I should have offered to walk her home then, but I still wanted to hang out with her. There was something different about Tanya. She was a unique individual to be sure.

"So, what do you do here in Austin?" I said.

"I'm a dentist." She laughed. "Not the most glorious of occupations, but I like it."

I was grateful that I had been born with nice teeth. And that I'd been turned while I still had them all.

"May I ask you a question?" she asked.

"Of course. Anything."

"How is it you happened upon me tonight?"

"I was catching my breath, simply taking a stroll, when I heard you."

She nodded slowly.

"How fortunate for me."

I shrugged again.

"I'm just happy I was there."

"Me, too. What were you catching your breath from?"

"I'd been at this incredible show. You know, South by Southwest. But it was so highly charged that I needed to step away."

"South by Southwest. Ah yes. I haven't actually gone to a show this year. Though I can open a window in my apartment and hear it all."

"It's amazing," I said. "The music actually comes alive. This is my first experience and I'm hooked."

"What concert were you at?"

"What?"

"When you had to step away?"

"I'm not sure. Some sort of electronic dance music. I believe they call it drum and bass? I don't know but the lasers, the beat, the dancers." I shook my head. "It just got to be too much for me."

She threw her head back and laughed.

"Ah yes. That is my favorite."

"Really?"

"Used to be. I was a candy kid."

"I'm not sure I understand?"

"I used to go to raves," she said. "All over the country. Listening to that kind of music. I love it."

"Raves?" I was confused and didn't mind showing it.

"Festivals. It was wonderful being young."

I laughed.

"It's not like you're old now," I said.

"I'm in my thirties. And you? How old are you, Rina?"

Four hundred and seventy-two years.

"I'm twenty-seven."

She nodded as if approving somehow. Of what I wasn't sure.

We finished our drinks just as Todd announced last call. I went to the bar and handed him a hundred dollar bill.

"Thank you." I turned before he could give me any change and walked to the front door. Tanya joined me and we walked back to her complex.

"I suppose this is good night," I said.

"Please. Walk me to my door. I'm still a little gun shy."

"Of course. No worries. I'm here."

She unlocked her door and turned to me. I handed her my phone.

"What?" she said.

"Please enter your number. I'd like to see you again."

She entered her number.

"I'd like that. Can I see you tomorrow?"

"Sure. What time and where?"

"I don't know. Come by my apartment say…"

"Eight o'clock? I can take you to dinner and maybe we can go dancing?"

"Not at South by Southwest though, okay? I know of a women's club."

I smiled, intrigued.

"Sounds wonderful," I said. "I'll be here at eight."

The night was still young when I left Tanya. I still had several hours until sun up, but I had no desire to do anything. I didn't want to submerse myself in crowds. I wanted to be alone with my thoughts. So I made my way back to Evergreen Cemetery where I was staying.

I pushed aside the heavy slab of granite covering my grave of choice and climbed in.

As soon as the sun set that evening, my eyes opened wide and I was ready for the night ahead. Another night with Tanya. Tanya. I smiled to myself. I couldn't wait to see how the night played out.

I dressed in black skinny jeans again and a black cashmere sweater with a V-neck. The night was chillier than the previous night, and I felt the cold more prominently now. I didn't want to be uncomfortable. I wanted all my focus to be on Tanya.

At precisely eight o'clock, I knocked on her door. Tanya looked stunning in her black skinny jeans and a thin green sweater that really brought out the color in her eyes.

"Where's your green?" She looked me up and down.

"Green?" I had no idea what she was talking about.

"It's Saint Patrick's Day, silly. You need to wear green, so you don't get pinched."

"I guess I'll be getting pinched then."

"Nonsense. Let's swing by your hotel and you can put on something green."

"No." I panicked. How would I explain I didn't have a hotel? I certainly wasn't going back to the cemetery. "Surely you have a button or something?"

"I do." She laughed. She went into her room and emerged with a button that said, "Kiss me. I'm Irish."

"But I'm not Irish."

"Everyone is Irish on Saint Patrick's Day," she said.

I put the button on, and she smiled at me.

"Happy?"

"Very. And now I have a confession to make."

"What's that?"

"I had a huge lunch of corned beef and cabbage and I'm so not hungry for dinner."

I was relieved. I couldn't eat. It was impossible. My body couldn't process food. So I would have had to come up with an excuse myself for not eating dinner if I took her out.

"That's fine," I said. "And it's a little early to go dancing so let's go back to that bar you took me to last night. We'll have a few drinks before we head to the club."

"I can't drive if I've had a few drinks," she argued.

"We'll catch an Uber."

"Sounds good."

The bar had green and white streamers hanging from the ceiling, and Irish music emanated from the speakers. It was nice, I thought, though Tanya was thrilled. Her whole face lit up as she looked around the small bar.

"The place looks amazing," she told Todd.

"Thanks. We're expecting a crowd tonight."

"I'm glad we got here early then. We'll take a couple bottles of Guinness."

"Guinness?" I arched an eyebrow.

"Sure and begorrah. We're all Irish tonight."

I laughed. Tanya was a fun woman and I really enjoyed spending time with her. We made our way to the back booth again and she raised her glass.

"To new friends," she said.

"To new beginnings."

We each took a sip and I all but chewed the thick liquid.

"Do you not like it?" she said.

"I do," I lied. "It's just not my absolute favorite."

"Well, you can choose the next drink. But it has to be Irish."

"Fair enough."

I got us each a Jameson, mine neat, hers on the rocks.

We sat sipping them and talking, getting to know each other better.

"Nice button," she said, as I got up to get our next drinks.

"Thanks." I didn't know why she'd compliment me on a button she gave me.

"Come here," she said.

I leaned into her, curious as to what she wanted to whisper in my ear. But she didn't whisper anything. She kissed me. It was a light kiss, but it made my heart skip a beat.

"What was that for?"

"Your button told me to." She laughed.

"I'm glad you follow directions." I winked at her.

We finished our next drinks and I couldn't remember a time I'd felt so alive, so content and excited at the same time.

"You ready to go cut a rug?" I said.

"I don't know. I think we should buy some of this whiskey and go back to my place. I'm not sure I want to share you with a bunch of crazed lesbians."

"If that's what you'd like, then that's what we shall do."

We found a liquor store and I bought a bottle of Jameson. When I got to the counter to pay, I saw Tanya had a liter of Coke.

"What's that for?"

"I can't drink that stuff straight anymore."

"How unIrish of you." I laughed and paid for both.

She took my hand as we made our way back to her apartment. The sounds and smells of the festival accompanied us.

"You sure you don't want to go listen to music?" I asked.

"I'm sorry. I'm just really not in the mood for crowds."

"Understood."

"Besides, I have to work tomorrow. I don't know what I was thinking, suggesting we go dancing. I hope you'll forgive me."

"Tanya, as long as I'm with you, I'm happy."

She stopped dead in her tracks, and I worried I'd said the wrong thing. What if we weren't both on the same page?

"You mean that, don't you?" she said.

"I do indeed."

"Thank you."

"For what?" I said.

"For coming into my life."

"My pleasure. Believe me."

She smiled and started walking again. We finally reached her apartment building. We took the elevator to her floor and she leaned against me for the ride up. My whole body short circuited at the most minor of contacts, so feeling her whole body against mine had me trembling with desire.

Inside her apartment, I set about mixing her drink and pouring mine while she played with her stereo and TV.

"What are you doing?" I handed her the drink.

"You'll see. Have a seat."

I sat on the couch and set my glass on the coffee table.

"Close your eyes," she said.

I did as she asked and soon the room was pulsating with drum and bass. She didn't have it loud, but the beat was unmistakable.

"Open your eyes," she said.

The most amazing laser show was on the big screen. The lights exploded to the music on the stereo.

"How did you make them match?"

"A friend of mine set this up for me."

Jealous rage filled me. Who was this friend? How close were they? What else were they doing in the apartment?

"He's really into electronics," she went on. "He's also really into fashion. I love gay boys."

Relief flooded me.

"Me, too." I laughed. I couldn't believe how upset I'd been. I wasn't the jealous type. What the hell was going on?

"I'm bummed," Tanya said.

"How on earth could you be bummed at a moment like this? It's Saint Patrick's Day. We're drinking Jameson. The music and laser show are amazing. What's to be bummed about?"

"Honest?"

"Honest."

"You're going back to Houston tomorrow."

My heart skipped a beat. She'd miss me. She was really into me. And God knows, I was into her.

"Houston isn't that far away."

"But it's not here."

"No. It isn't. Let's not think about tomorrow. Let's just enjoy the here and now."

She snuggled up against me on the couch and sipped her drink.

"This is yummy," she said.

"It's sacrilege." I laughed.

"It's still Irish whiskey."

"That it is."

The music continued to pound out a steady beat and soon the area between my legs was keeping time. I was a throbbing mess. I needed Tanya like I'd never needed a woman before.

"Tanya?" I said hoarsely.

"Hm?"

"May I kiss you?"

"Like you need to ask?"

She turned her face up to mine, her eyes so dark they betrayed her own desire. I lowered my mouth to hers, claiming her in a soul-searing kiss. Our lips would surely be bruised after such a kiss, but I didn't care. She opened her mouth and I slipped my tongue in, tasting Tanya and Jameson. It was a heady flavor and I needed more.

I eased her back until she was lying down, and I was on top of her, grinding into her, my hands in her hair, my mouth on hers. I was in heaven. But I had to have more. I had to have all of Tanya. I had to make her mine.

"Your room," I whispered.

"Take me here."

It was tempting. I had to have her and could easily have stripped her and had my way with her on the couch. But I wanted to do this right. Tanya wasn't a couch-type lover. She was a woman who deserved to be pleased on a bed. Where she could be the pillow princess I sensed she truly was.

With what little self-control I had left, I pushed myself off of her. I stood on shaky legs and took her hand to help her up.

"Your bed," I said. "Now."

She stripped as we walked down the hall and naked, she lay on the bed, on display for me and only me. I stood admiring every inch of her before she interrupted my reverie.

"Will you be joining me?"

"Yeah."

I made short order of my own clothes and climbed up on the bed with her. The feeling of flesh on flesh almost caused me to implode. She was so soft. And so silky. And she was mine. At least for that moment. That night. Tanya was mine.

We kissed some more, fueling the fires within that were close to burning out of control. I began kissing down her body. Slowly, deliberately. I nibbled, sucked, and kissed every inch of her.

She propped herself up on her pillows.

"What are you doing?" I said.

"I want to watch you."

I didn't care. Let her watch me. I was about to taste the heaven that belonged to her and her alone. I rested my cheek on her inner thigh, admiring her in all her glory.

And then the pulsing was back. Funny, I hadn't noticed the music. But the pulsing was strong, undeniable. I realized with a start it was coming from Tanya. It was right under my ear. It was her femoral artery.

I wasn't thinking. I couldn't think. Instinct took over and I felt my fangs unsheathe. I buried them in her thigh and sucked.

"What are you doing?" She sounded scared, angry.

I pulled away from her leg and looked up at her. Terror showed in her eyes. I came to my senses and licked the wounds, my teeth marks disappearing.

"Shit," I said. "I'm sorry, Tanya."

I jumped off the bed and dressed as quickly as I could.

"Wait," she said.

"What?"

"Come back here."

"Tanya, seriously. I'd better go."

"You can't leave me here alone after that. You need to stay. You need to explain what the fuck I just saw."

"Tanya. Please."

"No." She wrapped the sheet around her and walked to the kitchen. She poured us each a drink.

"Why are you doing this?" I was so confused. "Why aren't you screaming in terror? Why aren't you calling the cops? Why are you wanting me to stay after what I just did to you?"

"You didn't hurt me," she said.

"How can you say that?"

"Well, I can't say it felt good..."

"Exactly."

"Rina. You owe me an explanation. You know you do. I'm confused. Curious. Tantalized even. But I need you to talk to me."

We sat at the small kitchen table. I shot my whiskey in one gulp.

"I'm sorry," I said.

"Don't be. Rina, right after you bit me, you looked up at me. I saw your fangs, saw my blood on them." I nodded, too embarrassed at losing control to say anything. "And those weren't your usual eye teeth. They were indeed fangs. Long, sharp, piercing fangs."

"I'm sorry," I said again.

"Tell me the truth. Who are you? What are you?"

I shook my head, unable to admit the obvious.

"Rina. Are you a… a *vampire*?"

I raised my head and met her eyes.

"I am."

"How cool is that? I didn't know vampires really existed."

"Cool?" I couldn't hide my confusion.

"I love vampires. At least what I've read of them. They're so romantic, seductive. Just like you."

"Tanya." I shook my head. "It's not all glorious. Sometimes it's gory and gross."

"So you feed off people? Like for real? Did you feed off the man who tried to rape me?" Her eyes were wide, like a schoolgirl hearing a ghost story.

"Drained him dry."

"Thank you."

"My pleasure. Now, I really should go."

"Pour yourself some more whiskey," she said. "I have so many questions for you. I don't know where to start. But I do know one thing. You owe me answers."

She had a point. The least I could do was answer her questions, assuage her curiosity. And then I'd be on my way. My lone existence back again. I sat down with another whiskey which I sipped.

"What do you want to know?"

"Everything. Tell me everything, Rina."

"Like what?" I smiled then. Her interest alleviating my fear and discomfort. I didn't see any wooden stakes in her apartment, so I didn't fear for my life imminently. And I didn't get the feeling she was going to turn me in to the authorities, so I relaxed somewhat.

"Tell me what it's like to be a vampire? Are you really from Venice?"

"I am. My parents arranged a marriage for me when I was fourteen. Even at that young age, I knew I wasn't like other girls. I couldn't imagine laying with a man." I shuddered. "So I ran away, dressed like a boy, and lived on the streets. It wasn't an easy life, but it was the only one I could conceive of."

"It must have been scary."

"I could hold my own. Eventually, I apprenticed with a blacksmith. Soon I had my own shop. No one questioned me. They assumed I was a man making my way in the world."

"Good for you," she said.

"Thanks." My chest swelled with pride at her approval. "One night, late, I was leaving the shop and crossing the Piazza San Marco when five men approached me. No one had ever bothered me, and I knew I could hold my own. But five men? I knew I was in danger. What if they knew my secret? What if they were going to rape me?

"I asked what they wanted as they closed around me. I offered them the money in my pocket, but they didn't say anything. Finally, one man grabbed me and pulled me to him. My back was against him and I struggled to get free, but he just laughed."

"Oh, God, Rina. Do I want to hear this?"

"I don't know, Tanya. Do you?"

"I think so."

"The man bit my neck," I went on. "He took a deep pull then passed me to the next one. I went around the circle twice before they let me drop to the ground, barely hanging on to a thread of life. I called to them as they walked off and begged them to help me.

The leader, the first one to take a bite out of me stood over me. He asked if I wanted to live. Of course I said I did and he bit his wrist and I drank from him. I knew in the back of my mind what I was agreeing to, but I didn't care. I just wanted to live."

"Wow. So you've been a vampire for how long now?" Tanya said.

"About four hundred years."

"Oh, my God. I can't even imagine everything you've seen. All you've done."

"I've seen a lot. That's for sure."

"What's it like?" she said.

"Being a vampire?"

"Living forever."

"It has its moments. But, for the most part, it's a very lonely existence. I refuse to be part of a coven and I can't get close to mortals, so it's very lonely."

"You've never had a vampire partner? Someone to spend eternity with?"

"Negative."

"Would you like one?" asked Tanya.

"I don't know. It would be wonderful, I suppose. But where would I find such a being?"

"Right here."

"In Austin? You think there are vampires in Austin?"

"No, silly. Me."

"But you're not a vampire." I was so confused.

"But I could be."

"But you're not."

"Please, Rina," she said.

"Please what?"

"Make me a vampire."

I stood.

"No way. No way. No how. You don't know what you're asking of me."

"I think I do."

"Tanya, I'm an older vampire. The need to feed is still real, but usually I can fight it. I only feed once or twice a week now. A new vampire has to feed all the time. You'd have to kill people, Tanya. Actually take their lives."

"I guess I hadn't really thought this through, had I?" she said.

"No. You obviously haven't."

"How do you choose who dies, Rina? How do you make that decision?"

"I punish bad people. I never feed on the innocent. Present company excluded."

She laughed.

"Right. Well, I'll do that too. I'll only kill people who deserve to die."

"Tanya, it's really not that simple."

"I think it is." She came over and sat on my lap. "Do you like me, Rina?"

"I barely know you."

"Do you want me?"

"Of course."

"Then take me. Take me every way you can. And I mean every way."

"Tanya…"

She kissed me and my libido took over. She was a beautiful woman and I wanted her. I needed her, craved her. And I was going to have her.

Tanya stood and I stood. She pushed me back into my chair, dropped her sheet, and straddled me. Her body was smoking hot and I wasn't going to mess up this time. I was going to have her completely.

We kissed some more, and I ran my hands all over her body. I caressed her shoulders, her back, her thighs. And she arched into my touch as her tongue got ever more demanding. I slid my fingers inside her and she threw her head back. I nibbled, sucked, kissed it. And then. And then all thought was gone.

Her carotid artery was pulsing hard. Bouncing under my tongue, my lips. I didn't think. I only did what came naturally. I buried my fangs and drank her almost dry.

I eased her almost lifeless body to the floor. Her eyes were closed, her breathing shallow.

"Tanya?" I said. "Tanya?"

She didn't respond. I bit my wrist and placed it against her mouth. She latched on to me and sucked. Her hands were like claws on my arm, pulling me closer, holding on for dear life. Or quite the opposite.

When I knew she'd had enough, I pulled my wrist away. I stared looking down at her body, now breathing heavily. Her eyes were still closed.

"Tanya?" I was filled with remorse. Sure, she'd thought it sounded nice, but now that I'd done it, would she forsake me?

She opened her eyes and stared up at me, questioning me with her eyes.

"Did you do it?" she said.

I nodded.

"Thank you."

"Really?" I said. "I can't believe I just did that."

She pulled me onto the floor with her and undressed me. I'd never been with a vampire before and had no idea what to expect. But it was mind blowing. By far the best sex I'd ever had.

When it was over, we lay together, arms and legs entwined.

"What now?" said Tanya.

"What do you mean?"

"What do we do now? Can we go to bed? Can you hold me while I sleep?"

I laughed sardonically.

"We can't sleep in beds. The light from the sun burns our skin."

"So what then?"

"Come on."

We dressed and walked to the cemetery. I let her test her new strength by removing the slab. She giggled with pleasure.

Once inside the now cramped space, I slid the cover back into place and held her tight.

"How do we know when it's safe to get up again?"

"We wake up as soon as the sun goes down."

"That's convenient."

"It really is."

We woke the next night and made frantic love, before leaving the cemetery and Austin behind us in search of new worlds to discover. Together.

RETURN TO ME

DEL ROBERTSON

"Your dress or your life."

She sank beneath the surface, saltwater coming up all the way to the tops of her eyebrows before she resurfaced with a sputter. "M-my what?"

"Did I not speak clearly enough, woman? Choose which you are willing to forfeit." Jeanne drew the knife from her belt.

"You did, but I do not believe the sheer audacity of your demand." She pushed a hand through a mass of straggly red hair.

"Very well, if you will not decide, I will." Jeanne's grip tightened about the knife hilt.

"My life, then." She tilted her chin defiantly.

"Wrong choice, my lady."

Jeanne thrust up with the knife, feeling the blade catch on thick material and strike whalebone. She twisted the handle, tugging down. The dress became entangled about her forearm and she struggled against the sodden weight.

She went down, under the surface, waves lapping over her head. She kicked, fighting her way up. As she broke the surface, she took in great, heaping gulps of air. She felt hands on her shoulders. The lady clutched her closely, as if afraid she might yet drown.

Jeanne expected a kiss of gratitude. Instead, she was shoved back beneath the surging waves.

†

Abigail sat on a narrow cot with the scratchiest of blankets draped over both shoulders. Despite standing exposed on the deck, shivering and shaking in nothing but her corset as the most unsavory group of men ogled her, she'd refused to surrender her dignity. As soon as she was confident that her voice would not tremble, she demanded to be taken to the captain. Instead, she'd been taken to the captain's cabin.

A man named Roche entered the cabin. She thought him to be the captain. Alas, he was merely the quartermaster. He brought her a bowl of lukewarm stew and promised someone would bring her dry clothes shortly. He ignored her repeated demands to see the captain.

He left and she lifted the spoon from the bowl. It was a mishmash of possibly beef, perhaps ham, definitely cabbage, and boiled eggs. She saw a fish eye looking back at her and she grimaced, dropping the spoon. She jumped as something made a noise and leapt at her.

"Mrr?" A black cat appeared beside her on the cot, rubbing its head against her arm and sniffing at the concoction. It leaned forward, stretching its neck, and took a tentative lick.

"By all means, help yourself," she told the cat, placing the bowl on a table stacked with papers, a compass, and a telescope.

"We don't usually let Petit eat on the table. Tends to dribble on the charts. I once tried for three days to find an island on the map, only to discover it was a salmagundi stain."

Abigail froze at the sound of the voice. She'd only heard it briefly and she'd been up to her ears in salt water at the time, trying her level best not to drown. Still, it was unmistakable. She looked up, seeing the woman that had all but molested her whilst hauling her out of the ocean and up the nets that trailed over the side of the ship.

"Y-you...what are you doing here?" She clutched the blanket tightly against her body, attempting to ignore the scratching of rough cloth against sensitive flesh.

"You asked for the captain, did you not?"

†

"I do not believe you."

"My lady, I assure you, I speak the truth."

"Don't call me *my lady*, you...you..."

"Jeanne de Bouchard, at your service." She removed her tricorne hat, revealing cascading blonde locks, and bowed with a flourish. "And, what shall I call you?"

"Abigail Sullivan, if you must," she said with as much an air of disdain as she could muster.

"A pleasure, Lady Abigail Sullivan." Jeanne reached out, lifted her hand, and pressed her lips against it in the same manner a proper gentleman would.

"I've asked you not to call me 'lady'."

"I heard you clearly, but I also recognize a lady when I see one. Do not fret, I do not intend to ransom you."

"Of that, I have no doubt, for I do not believe you to be a pirate."

"Why not?"

"Pardon?"

"Why not? Is *The Banshee* not a pirate ship? Does she not have a pirate crew? Is this not a pirate captain's cabin?" She extended both arms as if to encompass everything in the room. She leaned in close and winked. "Although, for purposes of amnesty, I must declare myself a privateer."

Abigail blinked, thinking that Jeanne had the most amazing eyes she'd ever seen. They were like honey. She caught herself staring, blushed, and hastily looked about the cabin.

"It's very...nautical. But, everyone knows that sailors believe it's bad luck to have a woman on board."

"Not if you're the captain," Jeanne said.

"Ha. See there? They would not allow a woman to be captain."

Honey-hued eyes hardened. She'd once seen something similar in a market; an insect encased in hard amber, trapped for all time. She felt ensnared like that, caught in this woman's gaze. "No one has allowed me to be anything. I am exactly as I choose to be."

"Well..." Abigail looked down, picking at the material of the blue dress she was now wearing. "Well, I don't know why anyone would choose to be a pirate and I think you probably aren't a very good one."

"And why would you possibly draw that conclusion?"

"For one thing, you have no shoes." She pointed at the other woman's bare feet.

Toes wriggled in response. "It's too slippery to wear shoes on deck. Do not fret over my wardrobe. I have fancier clothes to wear whilst in port."

"This dress." Abigail lifted the hem to make her point. "It's worn and frayed. It's of fine fashion, but it's at least three years out of style."

"It's a pirate ship. We plunder what we can. I don't keep a hold full of fancy dresses for every woman I should chance to rescue from drowning."

†

By the next day, Jeanne noticed her crew casting longing looks.

Lady Sullivan stood at the bow. She mirrored the ship's figurehead beside her; one hand shielded over her eyes, leaning forward, breasts jutting out. The only difference was that the wooden version was naked from the waist up.

"They make a lovely pair, don't they, Leone?" Roche elbowed the sailing master.

Leone stared. "They certainly do. Both of them."

It reminded Jeanne of why having women on board was a bad idea. It wasn't because she believed the superstition that females brought ill luck. After all, she was a female, also. So was Petit, for that matter. Nope, having women on board led to nothing but trouble. Distractions, accidents, fights; not to mention if she went and got herself with child.

Jeanne promptly had the small bed in her cabin removed and replaced with one the size befitting a proper pirate captain. After that, if any of her crew cast knowing looks, snickered, or muttered comments about hidden treasure, she ignored them.

†

After the fourth day at sea, Abigail at last believed she was on board a pirate vessel.

The sailing master had spotted a merchant ship low in the water. It was a sure sign she was laden down with cargo. *The Banshee* followed, shadowing her for days, her crew watching, counting how many men were on board and the strength of her armament. They matched the British ship's flag so that anyone that spotted them would believe them to be allies.

When at last they struck, it was with lightning fast certainty. The British flag came down and the Crossbones was raised. Two cannonballs chained together smashed through the main mast, rendering the merchant unable to flee even if she tried. The crew quickly surrendered their ship and cargo. Those deemed worthy were given the option of joining the pirates or being put to death. Many signed on, for conditions on board a pirate ship were not nearly as brutal as the discipline enforced on a British vessel.

It was later, over dinner in the relative privacy of the captain's cabin, that Abigail at last asked the question poised on her lips. "Were you going to sink the ship I was on?"

"No." Jeanne sucked the juice from a piece of gristle. "No profit in sinking the cargo. We get in as close as possible to seize the vessel whole."

"If I hadn't fallen overboard, if you hadn't dove into the sea to save me, you would have caught her."

"No doubt." Jeanne stopped chewing, spat something into her cloth napkin, and eyed it suspiciously. She folded the napkin and sat it aside. When she looked across the table at Abigail, there was a smirk on her lips. "Truth, did you fall from the ship by accident or did they toss you overboard on purpose?"

The slap of indignation left a welt forming on Jeanne's cheek.

Hand to stinging flesh, she said, "Perhaps I should have saved the ship and left you to drown."

She spent the night on deck while Abigail slept alone in the cabin.

+

"Is this correct?" Jeanne eyed the port suspiciously.

"It's the place she showed me on the map." Leone shrugged.

Petit stalked the length of the map and sat on the section of coastline the sailing master was pointing to.

"Petit, move."

The cat looked at her, blinked twice, put her leg in the air over her head, and proceeded to lick.

Jeanne rolled her eyes. "Where is she?"

"Already put ashore." Leone shrugged. "I thought that's what you wanted."

"It was. Is." She shook her head. The woman had her befuddled. "Let's scout the area, survey any inlets and coves. This might be a safe haven."

"Early reports indicate it's better than Barataria."

"Good. Never liked sailing into the bayou, anyway." To Jeanne, the swamps were too easy to get lost—and captured—in. "What do they call this place?"

"Galveztown."

+

"We need to parlay."

No sooner had the door to the governor's house opened than Jeanne was pushing her way inside. A lad in ill-fitting clothes, two sizes too small, stood gawking at her.

"You're not the governor, are you?" she asked.

"He most certainly is not. That is Walden Wallace, my manservant."

Jeanne looked past the lad. An older man with a cane was on the stairs. He was dressed in fashion, wore a monocle, a handlebar mustache, and looked every bit the part of a governor.

She removed her tricorne hat and cloak with a flourish and shoved both items into the shocked Walden's arms. The lad scrambled to keep from dropping them and rushed off to hang both on a stand.

"Governor." She smiled brightly and extended her hand.

"Sullivan," he said.

"Sullivan?"

"Sullivan," a voice drifted down the stairs behind the governor.

Jeanne gaped. Abigail was descending the stairs. She was wearing the most exquisite dress Jeanne had ever seen. Her crimson hair was done up, bouncy curls framing her face and falling about her shoulders.

"Abigail." She bowed. "I told you I recognized a lady."

†

During the parlay, an accord was reached. In exchange for allowing them to use Galveztown as a safe haven, Jeanne and her pirates…privateers…would offer protection from anyone seeking to enforce their rule over the island. The occasion was celebrated with a ball. A grand ball that had everyone dressed in their best fashion. As Jeanne was introduced as a privateer captain, many of the gentlemen balked. Those same gentlemen appeared at once scandalized and curious. She'd had more offers to share a bed that night than the prettiest whore at The Black Swan tavern.

The men held no interest for the pirate captain. The women, although pretty in their fancy dresses, paled in comparison to the only beauty in the room that she had eyes for. Some dandy had been dancing with her for most of the evening. Throwing caution to the wind, she at last crossed the room.

"Lady Sullivan." Jeanne bowed.

Hands never leaving their proper dance position, Abigail nodded. "Jay. Permit me to introduce Mycroft Yardley of His Majesty's Royal Navy."

Jeanne frowned. She realized now why Abigail had called her by the wrong name and why the British flag flew above the courtyard. No doubt, there was a gaggle of troops in the town. The flag had been changed from French to British to serve as warning.

"Lady Jay." The commander turned, bowed, and planted a slobbering kiss on her hand.

She grimaced and jerked her hand back. He looked up, clearly startled.

"Forgive my cousin's appearance," Abigail said, "She's foreign, you know."

"Ah, yes. I see. You are quite…unusual, aren't you, my dear?" he said.

"Yes and you're a poof, aren't you?"

The commander looked taken aback.

"How about some refreshment?" Abigail grabbed him by the arm and steered him away. "*Poof* doesn't mean the same in her country as it does here."

"Oh? And, where did you say she comes from?"

†

It was not until much later, when most of the revelers had gone, that dandy British officer amongst them, that Jeanne finally found her chance to dance with Lady Abigail. She seemed hesitant at first, looking about the room as if to see who might be watching, before extending her hand and allowing herself to be escorted onto the floor.

Thankfully, the orchestra played a waltz. It was one of the few dances besides a jig that Jeanne knew. It also permitted her to hold the shorter woman close and breathe in the fragrance of her hair. As the dance ended, she led Abigail from the floor, out a set of doors, and into the moonlit courtyard.

They stopped beneath the flagpole. Jeanne did her absolute best to ignore the gaudy British flag above her head. Abigail shivered and she moved closer to shield her from the wind. They stood gazing out at the bay, the full moon reflecting brightly on the midnight waves.

"You nearly gave yourself away," Abigail said.

"I was not expecting the British Navy to be in residence."

"You should not have called him a poof."

"He dresses as one and I do not suffer fools lightly."

"You're a fine one to talk." Abigail turned and faced her. "I am no fool."

"I was referring to your attire. Why would you dress so?" She reached out, fingering the satin sash worn diagonally across her chest and wrapped about her waist.

Jeanne looked down. She had aired out her best three-quarter-length coat so that it no longer smelled of sea turtle. She wore a bright-blue velvet waistcoat and tan breeches. She'd even polished her best shoes, the leather thigh-high boots without the hole in the sole.

She looked again to where Abigail's fingers were toying with her sash.

"I dressed in my finery to visit you," she said.

"You dressed like that to show off. You wanted to flaunt your independence before all the rich men you knew would be here. You wanted to shock them and scandalize their women."

"Do I scandalize you, Lady Sullivan?"

"Not at much as you wish."

Jeanne reached out, catching Abigail's chin with her thumb, raising her gaze to meet hers. Bright green eyes stared boldly back at her.

"I saw you watching me, even while you were dancing with him. I think you like the way I'm dressed tonight. I think there are a lot of things you like about me." Jeanne ducked her head, lightly touching her lips to Abigail's. Soft lips parted beneath hers and their kiss deepened.

†

Commander Yardley screamed and threw his dagger. It hit the doorframe, the steel tip embedding itself scant inches from his second's nose.

"I want her. I want her head," he said.

"Yes, Commander."

"*Yes, Commander? Yes, Commander?* As if it were so simple that I merely say I want it and you can hand it to me on a silver platter, Kentwood?"

"No, Commander."

"*No, Commander.* That's right, because you can't. Bloody hell, I can't either. Fifteen ships over the course of two years; fifteen loyal British naval, merchant, even fishing ships have been captured, plundered, or sunk."

Kentwood was sweating. He always sweated profusely when nervous. As of late, the commander's behavior made him very nervous.

"Mark my words, I will have her head. She's only a woman, after all."

†

241

Jeanne blinked one eye open. She had expected to be met with the harsh morning sun in her face, for she liked sleeping with the double doors wide open so that the fresh sea breeze might blow in. She hardly expected to wake to Abigail's face, mere inches from hers. Her brows were furrowed.

"You'll cause a crease here." Her fingertip traced the worry line.

Abigail turned her head, placing kisses against the inside of Jeanne's wrist and palm. "Shush before you ruin my concentration."

"What are you about, woman?"

"I'm braiding a lover's knot into your hair."

"You're what?" Jeanne pulled back as far as she could, which admittedly, wasn't very far with her back pressed against the bed and Abigail's body stretched out atop her.

"Plaiting a lover's knot. Oh, who will have frown lines now? You don't even know what one is, do you?"

"No, but it doesn't sound like something fearsome pirates should be sporting in their hair."

"In Ireland, it's a symbol of love. It's said to represent the unbreakable bond between two lovers. Ancient lore says that if the knot holds for a year, it means that our love will last."

"We've lasted three years so far, my love."

"And I would have it be three thousand more." Abigail leaned down, sealing their lips together in a kiss.

The bedroom door burst open. Walden rushed in. He froze three steps in, eyes widening. Abigail ducked her head, pressing her face into Jeanne's neck. Jeanne reached for the sheet, tugging it up and over their nakedness.

"Have you never heard of knocking?" she asked.

"S-sorry. Very sorry." With trembling hand, he extended his arm as far as he could.

Jeanne's fingertips barely grasped the parchment before he was taking several steps back. She unfolded the letter, noting the flourish of the royal signature at the bottom. She also noticed that the missive had not come in its customary accompanying envelope with the royal seal.

She was about to make mention of it when she saw Walden staring. One handed, she reached down and with a flourish of her wrist, flicked the sheet so that it was covering Abigail's exposed backside. She glared fearsomely at him until he retreated out into the hall.

"It's alright, my love. He has gone." Jeanne hastily read the missive. "I must go, my love. There is a ship, *The Conquistador*, bound for Spain. King Louis commissions me to capture her."

"Oh, Jeanne, no."

"I must. For king and country, I must. Do not fret," she smoothed out the line between Abigail's brows. "I shall not be away longer than need be."

"See that you aren't, my heart, and mind that you don't ruin that knot I've plaited in your hair."

"First, I plunder the treasure ship. Then, I return to plunder you." Jeanne gave a bold wink and rolled them over so that she was now on top. "Correction, first I shall plunder you."

"Repeatedly, you roguish pirate."

Womanly laughter filled the room and spilled out into the hallway. Petit sat on a dresser, a paw washing behind her ears. Walden leaned against the opposite wall, watching them make love in the reflection of the dresser's mirror.

†

Walden stood nervously at the bar inside The Black Swan. He had been there for hours, sipping liquid courage. A group of British troops was seated nearby, heartily raising toast after toast.

Galveztown had always been a free port, but it seemed as if the British had all but invaded the island. They made too many patrols and asked too many questions of the locals, particularly the fishermen and the tavern wenches. Word was they offered good coin to anyone with information about pirates in general and Jeanne de Bouchard specifically.

"If Yardley can't stop the pirate she-wolf, he won't be commander long." Though the redcoat leaned in close to his tablemates, his voice still carried.

"Nonsense."

"Then why's he offering gold from his own purse to anyone that comes forward? I overheard it when I went to give the officers their meal."

At last, Walden screwed up his courage and approached them.

†

The wind blew brusquely, lashing her curls about her face, creating a veil of crimson. She tossed her head from side to side. Had her hands been free, she would have simply brushed the hair out of her eyes. Instead, they were bound behind her back, securing her to the flagpole. She stood exposed in the open courtyard, her cloak crumpled on the ground at her feet, her bodice ripped, and her sleeve hanging off one shoulder. Her entire body shivered from rage, fear, and cold.

Commander Yardley stood tall, with one hand behind his rigid back. His starched, white military pants and polished black boots were pressed so tightly together that a shilling couldn't pass between them. The tails of his red coat remained stiff, despite the strong breeze. Eyes fixed on the horizon, he passed his spyglass to his second-in-command.

"Tell me the instant you see the whites of her sails."

"Yes, Commander." His second snapped to, taking the spyglass, fixing it to his eye, and training his gaze out to sea.

Yardley approached her. His shiny sword hung in its polished scabbard. Twin flintlock pistols were tucked into his belt, their grips within easy reach. He trampled her cloak beneath his boots as he stopped before her. His smile was twisted and cruel. He lowered his voice, as if his words were intended for her alone.

"Tonight, your pirate bitch is mine."

Abigail cursed herself for trembling before him. She had vowed to be strong. Squaring her shoulders, lifting her chin despite the dull ache she felt from the earlier slap across her face, she defiantly met his stare.

I will come to thee. The remembered promise made by her captain gave her the daring to speak through pain and fear.

"You will never have her, for Jeanne de Bouchard shall always return to me."

"That, my dear, is precisely what I am counting on. After she pillages *The Conquistador...*" He paused, as if searching her face for reaction. "She'll sail into Galveztown Bay, thinking nothing is amiss. When she is deep into the cove, three of King George's most heavily armed ships will flank her. Tell me, do you think we should hold a lengthy trial followed by a lingering death on the gallows or show mercy by simply blasting her from the sea?"

"You are indeed a witless, pompous dandy if you think she shall fall so easily into such a simple trap," said Abigail.

The strike landed hard and fast. It was loud, reverberating through her skull as her head was sent reeling to the side. She would have been knocked from her feet had she not been securely bound to the flagpole. She righted herself and met his steely gaze. She tasted blood in her mouth, could feel it spew from between her lips and down her chin.

His face was crimson and twisted with rage. His hand darted out. She flinched and his scowl turned into a grin. He grabbed her face between his thumb and fingers so hard that she could feel each digit press into her flesh.

"Stop, please."

Abigail tried to turn to see who had spoken, but her range of motion was restricted by the commander's grip. Out of the corner of her eye, she could just make out Walden holding a wooden chest, its lid open, revealing a mass of folded flags inside.

The commander tilted his head back, his eyes traveling the height of the flagpole. He grinned. Abigail's heart sank.

"Very clever." His gaze darted from the empty halyard to her. "Which flag signals that it's safe to enter the bay?"

She remained silent.

"Which flag, boy?"

"I...I..." Walden sat the chest down. He rifled through the flags, haphazardly strewing them about.

"Walden, no," she said.

From his kneeling position, Walden looked up at her. His hands stilled.

"I…I don't know…" Walden's answer was so pitiful that Abigail wasn't entirely certain whether he actually knew or not.

"Which flag do I hoist?" The commander's grip increased.

Tears welled in her eyes, stinging and blurring her vision. Her lips parted. He drew nearer. She spat at him, grinning as drops of crimson spittle stained the lacy collar beneath his chin. He drew back his arm and cocked his fist, as though he intended far more damage than an open hand could inflict.

"No! You said you would not harm her," said Walden.

His fist fell from sight. A flintlock pistol appeared beneath her nose, leveled in Walden's direction. The entire time, the commander's eyes never left hers.

"Woman, as Commander of His Majesty's Royal Navy, you shall respect my authority." His foul breath was hot as he punctuated each word with a squeeze of his fingers.

She knew Walden was in imminent danger. Still, she could not risk Jeanne's life for his. She struggled to speak from between clenched teeth. "Your King George does not rule here."

Too late, she realized her mistake.

"Who is dimwitted now, Lady Sullivan? How does it feel to be hoisted by your own petard?" He abruptly let loose his grip on her face. "Raise the French flag."

†

The hours passed slowly. Her head hung down, her chin nearly touching her chest. Despite her resigned position, her eyes remained alert and active, observing all that transpired in the courtyard.

Three redcoats worked at loading the massive cannon pointed at the bay. It took two of them to lift the forty-two pound iron ball into the opening. The third poked a wad of cloth into the muzzle, using a rammer to shove it down into place. The elevation was set, the barrel raised into position so that it would fire out over the sea. Jeanne had told her at its highest point, a properly packed cannonball from this gun could travel the distance of a mile. If Yardley told the truth of three enemy ships in the bay, then the forty-two pounder was superfluous.

He probably only intends to fire one shot so that he may say he had a hand in sinking The Banshee, she thought.

As the redcoats readied the cannon, two more made sport of hauling possessions from the house. They carried chairs from the sitting room, throwing them on the ground. The pieces that didn't break outright, they set to destroying with axes. An intricately hand-carved wooden bench was the next piece to be reduced to kindling.

She tracked their progress as they worked their way through the house. She noted that chairs and small tables were easily lifted over shoulders and heads and smashed about the courtyard. The considerably larger table from the main dining room had yet to make an appearance. She wondered if the heavier pieces were left unscathed or simply broken where they stood.

She realized they'd found the cellar when the barrels of rum came out. They each took an axe to a barrel, as if making a game of who would be the first to smash it apart at the seams. The largest of them broke through in three strikes, sending a river of liquid pouring forth across the courtyard. His cohort, a mousy looking little man with a thin moustache, lifted his axe double-handed over his head and sent it crashing down onto the lid of his cask. The wood splintered, bits and chunks flying into the air as he hacked at the lid. When at last he broke through, what was left of the lid caught on the neck of the blade and came loose as he wrenched the axe free. He embedded the head into the outside of the cask so that it was protruding from the barrel like a great handle.

Enlisting the help of his larger friend, they lifted and carried the barrel, rum sloshing over the sides with each step. They staggered an unsteady line to where Walden sat cross-legged, staring at the ground. When one of the soldiers nudged him with the toe of his boot, he looked up. The redcoats turned the barrel upright, sending a deluge of rum pouring out over Walden's head.

Walden sat morosely, his hair plastered down, the dark liquid staining his shirt as he continued to look down. She chewed her bottom lip, trying to figure him out. He was not bound the way she was. It did not seem as if they treated him as prisoner, yet Yardley had pointed his flintlock at him. She recalled that the trigger had been cocked. He could have easily shot Walden, had he so desired.

Walden had pleaded for Commander Yardley to not touch her.

His exact words were that Yardley said he would not harm me, she thought.

The soldiers laughed uproariously, drawing her attention. They had abandoned the rum barrel and were now rifling through a familiar clothes chest. They found great entertainment in removing each item and displaying her undergarments for all to see. Some pieces, they held in front of their disgustingly masculine bodies and posed. Others, they held up to her and made sniggering insults that impugned her honor.

Each item in turn was tossed upon the mound of broken furniture. The shorter man, the one she related to a mouse, added powder to the pile. He drew his flintlock, took aim, and fired, igniting the pyre like so much kindling.

Commander Yardley and his second were pacing the length of the courtyard, hands clasped behind their backs as they preened like a pair of peacocks. As the bonfire grew higher, the second-in-command stopped walking. He stared at the fire for several long moments before looking in her direction. She caught and held his gaze until he tore his guilt-ridden eyes from her.

"Commander Yardley, I must protest," he said.

"Very well. You men, use restraint. Destroy what you wish but do not build the bonfire so high that it draws the pirates' attention."

"Yes, sir." Mouse and his cohort smartly saluted before redoubling their efforts at terrorizing her wardrobe.

"Sir, a storm is brewing and the bay is treacherous enough on a clear day. Given the danger of crashing against the reefs, do you believe that de Bouchard's eyes would be fixed here?" asked Kentwood.

Yardley's gaze went to the French flag flying taut in the breeze before looking pointedly at her. "I'm certain she has a spyglass. Would your eyes not also be drawn to such a prize?"

Kentwood's face turned crimson and he huffed. "Yes, well…"

Yardley reached out, grabbing a handful of hair at the top of her head. He tugged until she was forced to look him in the eye. She noted that although he stood before her, he made certain he was out of range should she consider launching another barrage of spittle at him.

"Yes, well, no matter." His gaze flicked to the bonfire. "Once de Bouchard has been dealt with, this witch shall meet her fate. Come."

Yardley turned his back on her, as though she were insignificant, and walked toward the cannon. Kentwood followed like an obedient puppy. He gave pause and glanced back at her. His expression was one filled with regret.

As the fire burned brightly and the wood crackled and popped, Abigail's thoughts went to the tales she heard of witches dying at the stake. She twisted her hands behind her back, desperately working at the knots tied in the rope.

†

Thick storm clouds rolled in, blanketing the horizon, prematurely darkening the afternoon sky. Thunder rumbled. Forks of lightning stretched across the sky, resembling the long, fleshless fingers of a skeleton's bony hand reaching toward the sea. Grey sheets streaked the sky, touching the ocean as white-capped waves swelled, surged and fell.

"She's a fearsome storm, Captain," said Leone.

Jeanne shouted to be heard above the sound of the sails being lashed by the wind. "You've guided us through far worse, sailing master."

She knew the sea and her temperament. She could be calm and serene as a choir nun one moment and a cruel, merciless mistress the next. *The Banshee* had weathered storms in the tropics in the summer that threatened to batter her poor hull to pieces. She'd braved the frigid gales that blanketed the Eastern coast in the winter. She recalled one particularly brutal storm that had the bow of her ship creaking through sheets of solid ice, inch by inch, as her crew huddled on the deck, burning anything not essential to keeping her afloat lest they all freeze to death.

I should have heeded Abigail's wishes and not gone this time, she thought. She'd been commissioned, though. The prize had been too great. One last act of piracy and I'll return to you forever, she had sworn.

"Where's that damned cat, anyway?" Leone wiped the sea spray from his face with one hand while he kept the other securely on the ship's wheel.

"Thought you disliked Petit."

"Yeah, well, I do. But she's a good mouser and I awoke to one in my bed. Besides, if she's gone overboard, it's a sure sign we're in for a terrible storm."

Jeanne looked toward the ominous sky. "I hate to tell you this, my friend, but we are most definitely in for a terrible storm."

"If it's gone overboard and we survive the tempest, we're still in for nine more years of bad luck."

"You're as superstitious as an old wife and you worry twice as much. Belay your fears, for Petit is safe and dry in Galveztown."

"So, the maid's bewitched even that scurvy cat? First time we've sailed out of port without her."

She, too, had been taken aback when for the first time since she was a kitten, Petit did not follow her on board ship. She shrugged. "No matter, we are so near home, I can taste it."

"It...or her?"

"Keep your mind on your duty lest we all go down," she said.

He snickered.

She couldn't keep the smile from her lips as she recalled the adventures of the last night she'd spent in Abigail's embrace. *And into the wee hours of the next morn,* Jeanne thought. She'd never before had a woman like Abigail. She was intelligent, charming, and demure. She was stubborn, proud, and had a fearsome temper. She was a fiery temptress, lusty and wanton, and buxom. In bed, she was as gentle as a kitten and as savage as a wildcat.

Jeanne pulled the collapsible monocular from her belt and expanding it, lifted it to her eye. She adjusted the scope until the outline of land came into view. She looked beyond the shore and inland, focusing high. She soon spotted the familiar colors of the French flag.

"Hang on, lads. The coast is clear. We'll be home before you know it."

†

Abigail's eyes sought *The Banshee*'s sails. She did not know if she were more afraid to see them, or not. She feared for her captain. She worried that *The Conquistador* had managed to elude *The Banshee*. She feared more that it had not and Jeanne would unwittingly sail straight into the navy's trap.

Her fingers were slick, wet with blood as the rope mercilessly cut into her wrists. Still, she would not give up. The rope gradually began to loosen. She kept her gaze straight ahead, so that none would suspect she was planning her escape.

Not that the redcoats were vigilant. Hours of idleness and boredom must have crept in, for the soldiers had partaken of the rum. This was not the rum that was watered down in the taverns or even the grog that Jeanne spiked with lime and brown sugar. This was pure, undiluted rum, and all the redcoats were well into their cups. Even Commander Yardley had indulged. Although he had only partaken of one mug, it was enough to inebriate him.

Perhaps that was why he had boasted of his plans and how he had worked them out. He spoke loudly, as if he were already bragging in the tavern. An informant had confided to him that *The Conquistador* was bound for Spain, laden down with treasure, and that de Bouchard had plans to capture the prize. If she failed, the Spanish would then have both the treasure and the pirate crew. It was the least favorable outcome, as far as Yardley was concerned, for he personally wanted de Bouchard. If she succeeded, the British Navy would confiscate the treasure and capture her as she sailed into Galveztown Bay.

"If she refuses to surrender, then the treasure and de Bouchard can spend all eternity at the bottom of the sea," he said.

His vile threats made her stomach churn. Abigail struggled to keep from retching and attracting undue attention as she worked the last knot free and the rope slipped from her wrists. She remained perfectly still, as though she were still bound, and looked about. If she could just manage to slip away unnoticed...

Abigail's gaze went to Walden. He was sitting on the ground nearby, hands clasped about his ankles, rocking back and forth. He was not bound and no one was watching him, yet he made no move to escape.

From out of the shadows, Petit walked along the path, stopping in front of Walden, sniffing at him. She leaned forward, pink tongue tasting, before she set to whole-heartedly licking the rum from his face.

"Oy, look there."

The redcoats at the cannon were pointing at Walden and Petit. At first, Abigail thought their interest was merely one of novelty. Then, she saw one of them shoving his ramrod down the barrel of his musket.

"Petit. No."

The cat paused, looking at her through yellow-slitted eyes. In typical cat fashion, Petit turned up her nose as if in indignation. She sauntered to the split cask, rubbing her back beneath the axe handle as she went, and began drinking the rum in earnest from the pool on the ground.

Abigail heard the click that indicated the trigger was set to full-cock position. He raised his musket and fired.

"Petit! Get away!"

Abigail didn't know if it was her urgent scream or the actual musket firing, but Petit bolted. Ears pinned back, body low to the ground, she ran for the cover of the woods.

To Abigail, it felt as if time slowed to a crawl, though there were so many events transpiring at once. Three of the redcoats, two of those that were manning the cannon and the large brute that had wrecked her belongings, gave chase after the cat, yelling and shouting as they crashed into the wood.

"I see a ship," said Kentwood.

Yardley took the telescope, shoving Kentwood out of the way.

Abigail thought she saw whitecaps on top of the waves. Her blood ran cold as she at last recognized them as sails. With certain dread, she knew it was *The Banshee*.

She pushed away from the flagpole, grabbing Mouse's flintlock from his belt, knocking him to the ground as she charged past him. She pulled back the trigger so that it was fully cocked, took aim, and fired. The soldier at the cannon looked at her in shock before his grin widened, as though he thought she had missed him. Too late, he realized she had hit her mark. The fuse ignited. The cannon fired. The ball and shot were launched into the air.

She didn't wait to see if it hit anything. That had not been her intention.

Yardley and Kentwood were shouting, racing across the grounds toward her.

She turned and ran. Flintlock spent, she turned the grip around, and used it as a club against Mouse's head. She lunged for the barrel, using both hands to wrest the axe free. She sidestepped useless Walden. Her blow against the flagpole struck true, splitting the rope, sending the flag crumpling to the ground.

"Lady Sullivan."

She turned slowly, her back against the flagpole as she faced the commander. His face was beyond crimson. His eyes were wide and wild. He held both his flintlock pistols up, extended at arms' length. She raised her hands in surrender.

Twin puffs of smoke wafted on the air as flintlock exploded. She thought she could actually hear and see the musket balls take flight. One shot veered off, passing safely between her and Walden.

†

The waves swelled. Rain and sea spray collided, drenching everything. Crewmembers fought to stay at their positions and on their feet as the deck pitched erratically. Jeanne felt her legs going from beneath her and reached out, grabbing at part of the rigging.

A great booming sound nearly scared the life out of her. As it was, she jumped, a reaction most unseemly for a notorious pirate captain. She looked to Leone, hoping he had not noticed. His attention was focused straight ahead, white-knuckling the ship's wheel, fighting to keep the rudder under control.

Was that thunder or cannon fire?

The quartermaster rushed forward. "Captain, two British Navy ships ahead of us. What are your orders?"

Heart pounding, Jeanne lifted her monocular to her eye. Through the driving rain, she focused on the exact spot she knew the governor's house to be. The halyards were bare. The flag was down. Ice seized her heart, causing her to clutch her chest.

"Captain, what is it?' asked Leone.

"Abigail." Her lover's name was like a whisper swallowed by the wind.

"Turn to starboard," said the quartermaster.

"Belay that order. We're going in."

Jeanne attempted to wrest the wheel from Leone's hands. He was overpowering her until his eyes met her and he relented.

"Tis madness," he said, turning loose the wheel.

†

Abigail's legs betrayed her. She fell to her knees. There was searing pain beneath her breast. She looked down, seeing red blossoming across the fabric of her blouse. Her body weakened, crumpling backward. Head tilted back, eyes open, she felt the splatter of raindrops mixing with her tears.

"Lady Abigail, no."

Walden's face loomed above hers. Tears streamed down his face and she wished he would move so she could see the sky. She felt him holding her hand. It offered little comfort.

Walden moved away. Perhaps he was shoved. The next face she saw looking down at her was that of Commander Yardley. His expression was one of indifference.

"Commander, *The Relentless* has been disabled. She's sinking, sir." Kentwood's face joined Yardley's.

"There's still two more of our ships out there." He leaned down close to her ear. "Your pirate dies this night."

In a louder voice, he said, "Come along, Kentwood. No sense wasting any more time here."

Abigail wished she could yet again find the strength to spit upon him. Her eyes slid closed.

†

The Banshee's sails were on fire, the deck awash in flames, despite the rain and waves. They had sunk one ship. The other ran aground on the shallows, leaving her helpless. The pirate crew cheered, believing victory was theirs.

They hadn't known of the third ship. They hadn't seen her slip into the cove behind them. She was nearly broadside before she fired on *The Banshee*. There had been a barrage of cannon fire. The mainmast had been struck and split, smashing down on the deck. Jeanne hoped the crewman trapped beneath hadn't seen it coming, hadn't felt it pulverize his bones.

The ship tried to ram them. They took a glancing blow, but it was enough to cause damage. To both vessels, for the British ship sank quickly. *The Banshee* was out of control. Waves crashed over the bow as she sank lower and lower into the water. She was aiming for the jagged shoreline.

Jeanne fought against the spinning wheel, trying, but unable to right her. A massive wave crashed over the bow, washing part of the crew overboard. A mighty jolt knocked her from her feet. She was sent sliding forward, face first along the deck. Grabbing onto anything she could for support, she struggled to her knees. Eyes widened as the ship's figurehead was ripped away. Wood broke against jagged reefs and *The Banshee* wailed her death-knell.

†

Walden stepped out onto the widow's walk. She was exactly where he expected her to be. Bonnet blocking out the afternoon sun, red ringlets falling softly about her shoulders, she sat with her back to him. She dabbed at the canvas with a fine brush.

"Are you ready to come inside, Lady Sullivan?"

"Nearly. I need to finish this bit before she's gone from sight." Abigail added a touch of white to the full sail she painted on the ship's mast.

Walden looked past her to the horizon. It was a bright day, with puffy clouds hanging in the sky. The sea was calm, with nary a gull in sight. It was small wonder, with none of the familiar fishing boats on the water. With the navy having seized control of the shipping lanes, no sailing vessels, not even the smallest of fishing boats, ventured into the gulf cove.

No matter, the British shall not keep possession long, he thought.

He had already heard talk in the tavern that the French, the Spanish, even the Americans were looking toward Galveztown as an important port. Walden did not care who took control, so long as it was not the British. He had no desire to ever set eyes on a redcoat again so long as he lived, unless it was to see that treacherous Yardley hung by the neck.

"You must have your rest."

"Yes, Walden." She wiped her brush and placed it on the artist's table beside her chair.

Abigail gripped the chair arm and tried to rise. She winced and would have collapsed had Walden not been there to support her. An arm about her waist, he guided her inside and assisted her into her bed. He removed her slippers and draped the comforter over her outstretched form.

Her eyes drifted closed.

Walden returned to the widow's walk, packing up her paints and canvas, bringing them into her room. That damned black cat darted in front of him, nearly causing him to trip.

"You're lucky I don't paint a white stripe down your back," he said to the cat, even knowing full well he wouldn't. That cat had become Abigail's constant companion, keeping nearly as close an eye on her as he did, if not better. He closed the double doors and pulled the curtains to.

"Walden?" Without opening her eyes, she said, "Perhaps I can paint more later, weather permitting."

"Of course."

Her weak smile touched his heart. He knew there would be no more painting this day. Ever since…the image of her broken body on the ground, crimson spreading across her dress. Seeing her like that had spurred him to action, even if it was only after the redcoats had gone. He'd rushed her into the house, rode her horse into town, and fetched the doctor as quickly as he could.

After months of uncertainty, Abigail had recovered, even if she had not healed. The wound made by the musket ball had never properly closed, no matter how much the physician sutured it. She still wore a bandage because it continued to stubbornly bleed from time to time. It was as if, after the death of her beloved captain, her heart simply would not mend.

They'd searched. Nearly everyone on the island searched, in spite of the British troops attempts at warning them off. Wreckage washed up on the shore, the largest piece was the upside-down hull of a ship. It was lodged deep in the sand and could not be pried loose, no matter how many men put their backs to it. So, they simply agreed to leave it as sort of a monument to the lost sailors.

More debris would surface, usually after a storm. A barrel floated to shore, drifting on the tide. Pieces of timber drifted in, even a ship's figurehead bobbed upon the tide. Some drunken lads on the way home from the tavern had great fun with that wooden lady. That is, until the very next day when a bloated body, bits of its flesh missing from where the fishes had been nibbling, reminded them all that this was a place of the dead.

To date, they had taken thirteen bodies from their watery grave and laid them to rest in the cemetery. Jeanne de Bouchard was not one of them.

Walden had been spiteful and petulant in his jealousy of their love. He knew now that Abigail Sullivan's heart would forevermore belong to Jeanne de Bouchard. He had resigned himself to that, just as he had resigned himself to being Abigail's constant and loyal caretaker. Nothing more.

†

Abigail tossed and turned, restless in her slumber. Dreams, troubling dreams came to her, as they always did these nights. She heard tapping on glass and opened her eyes to see a shadow at the double doors. She stumbled from the bed. Tired, so tired, her feet shuffled across the floor. She turned the latch, opening the door.

Jeanne stood before her, soaking wet from the sea.

"I will come to thee."

Abigail reached for her.

†

When Walden came to bring her breakfast, he found Abigail passed out on the floor in front of the open doors. She was wet and there was water all about the floor. He dismissed it as having rained in last night. He picked her up and carried her back to bed, tucking her in. As he closed and latched the double doors, he noticed that the planks of the widow's walk were bone dry.

†

Autumn. Leaves fell from the trees, blowing across the grounds. Outside, Petit played like a kitten, chasing a swirling leaf across the boards.

She'll need her cloak.

Walden fetched it from where it was draped across the end of the bed. He stepped outside, approaching her, draping the cloak about her shoulders. He expected her customary, "Thank you, Walden," spoken in her soft voice.

She said nothing.

His gaze drifted. Her hand hung limply at her side. A brush was on the floor, paint staining the planks yellow.

Tears filled his eyes, losing focus, even as he took in the painted canvas. There was a full moon and cloudy skies. The black galleon's bow cut a swath through the waves, her white sails at full mast. There were two women standing at the ship's wheel, one redhead and one blonde. The picture was, at last, complete.

Walden carried her to bed, one last time. He tucked her in, as always, placing the comforter about her lest she should catch cold. He returned to the widow's walk, taking up the canvas and art supplies. The damn cat was nowhere to be seen.

Let it stay outside if it has a mind to, he thought.

Walden shut the doors firmly behind him and drew the curtains to. He placed the canvas on the easel in her room and covered it with a sheet.

†

A black cat raced along the overturned wreckage of what was once a ship's hull. It was broken and battered, the wood nearly rotted and overgrown with barnacles and covered in seaweed. The holes between the timbers made great hiding places for crabs to scuttle in and out of. Petit fearlessly chased after one and then another, her keen eyes easily finding her prey in the dark.

At last, she settled down on the wreck. Claws kneaded at soft wood, making well-worn grooves. Something caught her attention and her ears swiveled. Her tail swished. She sat down, yellow eyes reflecting moonlight as she stared out to sea.

Abigail stood on deck, at the ship's wheel. Jeanne was standing behind her, arms wrapped about her waist. Long, blonde strands of hair intermingled with shorter, red curls. Abigail leaned back and tilted her chin up, looking into soft, amber-hued eyes.

"I will always return to you." Jeanne lowered her lips to Abigail's.

Clouds moved in, chasing the moon from sight. When it returned, the ghostly galleon had disappeared.

GHOSTLY GALLEONS

YVETTE MURRAY

The soft sea breeze ruffled Kerry's short reddish curls as she topped off the gas tank of her Ford Escape. Thirty miles from her destination and she could already smell the salt in the air from the Gulf of Mexico.

Since taking the loop around the Bayou City, Kerry had been humming Glen Campbell's song, "Galveston." Although she had visited the Texas coast less than half a dozen times, something familiar always pricked at the edge of her consciousness whenever she was near the dark, cloudy waters of the Gulf.

The SUV was packed to the ceiling, plus a roof pouch on top, with necessities to last Kerry through her six-month lease. Her furry roommate, Molly O' Donnell, was sleeping somewhere among the piles of clothes, linens, and kitchen items.

The move to Galveston was both exciting and a little daunting. Kerry had spent most of her adult life in Austin. The sales of her last two novels were down, and Kerry felt that her writing had grown stale. She decided that a change, albeit temporary, would be a good career move. She was hoping that a change of scenery would jumpstart her creativity. Still, at age 42, she was a bit apprehensive about leaving her home and circle of friends.

After freshening Molly's litter box, Kerry climbed back into the Escape and checked her Google map. They were close to the Galveston Bay Bridge that connected the mainland with the island. Excitement and nerves made Kerry slightly nauseous. She had seen photos of the house which she would be sharing with the owner. The rooms were lovely, but Dr. Danika Lester was the unknown variable.

Kerry had to complete a very detailed questionnaire before Dr. Lester granted her an interview. The doctor was pleasant, yet succinct, during their one telephone conversation.

Since her new landlady would also be her next-door neighbor, Kerry was definitely curious. She was disappointed when an internet search yielded only professional information. Dr. Lester was Chair of the Psychology Department at the University of Texas Medical School. Numerous publications were listed covering a wide range of topics in clinical psychology. The faculty directory included a brief bio, so Kerry knew that she would be meeting a woman in her mid forties.

"Here we go, Molly," Kerry told the large fluffy cat when they entered the long Galveston Bay Bridge. "We're out over the water now." Molly promptly climbed on top of the duffle bag on the passenger seat to get a better look at the sea gulls who were swarming near the sides of the bridge.

With spatial separation from the mainland, Kerry felt that she was entering another country when she arrived on Galveston Island. It was very different from her familiar Hill Country. All types of boats were docked at weather beaten piers. Bait shops, liquor stores, and army surplus outlets advertised their wares. Various seafood restaurants boasted the best crabs, shrimp, and oysters.

"Food isn't going to be problem here, Molly," Kerry remarked. "How would you like some fresh flounder?" Chuckling, Kerry grinned at her furry companion. The cat's silence indicated her usual feline skepticism.

Kerry turned left on Broadway Avenue, and soon, they entered the East End Historical District. Magnificent examples of Victorian and Greek Revival architecture were interspersed in this residential area with more modest, remodeled dwellings.

"Wow, Molly, these mansions are magnificent! Somehow, they survived the 1900 hurricane which destroyed most of the city."

Kerry glanced over at her companion who restlessly kneaded the canvas duffle bag. "Hey, cool it. We're almost there." Kerry slowed down to read street numbers until she spotted their destination. She stopped across the street to survey the property.

The mint-green stucco house with white trim appeared to be two and half stories. Four large bay windows looked out in front, topped by two smaller dormers, which protruded from the sloping roof. On the left side, a two-car garage was connected to the house by a covered walkway. A brick driveway led to a large, wrought-iron gate on the other side of the property.

Gingerbread fretwork framed the covered porch that spanned the front of the house. The entrance consisted of a beveled glass door flanked by urns of overflowing asparagus ferns. Broad stone steps led up to the front porch. Dual flowerbeds flanked the stairs, each one sporting large philodendrons fronted by an assortment of pink and purple petunias. *Nice landscaping. I wonder who does the gardening.*

Kerry observed two women emerge, laughing, from the side of the house with a skinny teenager trailing behind. The taller woman was dressed in a short-sleeve, linen pantsuit and matching espadrilles. Her dark-blonde hair was swept up in a French roll. *That must be the doctor,* Kerry surmised. The other woman wore cropped pants and tank top. She was considerably shorter and a bit on the chunky side.

While Kerry watched, the taller woman hugged her companion and kissed her cheek as they parted. Moments later, the doctor backed out of the garage and zoomed off in a BMW convertible.

Oh, so Dr. Lester has a partner and a kid. Maybe that's why there was so little personal information available. Gee, I'm not sure where to park so I'll circle the block and stop along the curb in front.

"Time to meet the family, Molly," Kerry announced. She snapped the leash to Molly's harness and gently placed the large gray cat on the lawn. "Come on," she urged as Molly insisted on sniffing the petunias. Exasperated, Kerry picked her up and mounted the stairs. When they reached the front entrance, she put the cat down and rang the doorbell.

Moments later, the woman, whom Kerry had seen earlier, appeared with a shy young man lurking behind her.

"Hi! I'm Kerry O'Donnell, the new renter."

"Glad you made it. I'm Jessica and this is my son, Cade. Let me get your keys."

While Kerry waited in the vestibule, Cade noticed Molly. "What's a cat doing on a leash?" he asked.

Kerry grinned. "Oh, Molly is part dog. She was fostered with a golden retriever before I adopted her."

"She's really huge," Cade replied, "bigger than a lot of small dogs."

"Yes, I'm glad that Molly likes to walk on a leash because she's heavy to carry. Maine Coon cats tend to be rather large. Molly is about 18 pounds," Kerry remarked.

Jessica returned with a set of keys. "Danika had an emergency faculty meeting," she explained, opening Kerry's side of the duplex. "Cade and I will help you move any large items."

"Thanks, that's great! First, I need to get Molly settled."

"You could put her in the breakfast room behind the kitchen," Jessica suggested. "That way she won't be in the way when we bring in your things."

"Good idea. I'd better fetch her water bowl and litter box before she begins to complain."

"Cade, please unlock the iron gate so Kerry can pull in by the side entrance," Jessica instructed.

After numerous trips, the trio had the SUV unpacked, and Kerry's belongings were sorted by floor and room.

"Kerry, if you need anything else, I'm sure that Danika will check in when she gets home. We hope that you and Molly enjoy your time here."

"Thank you so much for the help, Jessica. It would have taken me a couple of days to unload the Escape. I don't know why I packed so much stuff."

After Jessica and Cade left, Kerry sank into a recliner. *I'm going to be so sore tomorrow. Thank goodness I had help with moving things. It was definitely worth the twenty-dollar bill I slipped to Cade.*

"What do you think about your new digs, Molly?" she asked the cat who was busy grooming her long-haired coat. "What, no comment? Yeah, so you're reserving judgment until you get to taste some fresh seafood. Well, you have to admit we have nice neighbors."

Molly looked at Kerry. She flicked her bushy tail, then resumed her toiletries.

The adrenaline which had fueled Kerry's energy dissipated and weariness settled over her. She sank into the plush cushions of the recliner and promptly fell asleep. Later, Kerry was startled from her nap by knocking. Groggy from sleep, she managed to collect her wits and answer the door. She looked up to see a tall, blonde woman standing in the foyer. A linen jacket was casually tossed over the woman's arm exposing a melon-colored sleeveless blouse. A necklace of polished shells rested on high round breasts. The woman smiled, her hand outstretched.

"Hello, I'm Danika Lester. You must be Kerry."

Surprised by the attractive woman holding her hand in a firm grip, Kerry mumbled, "Yes".

"Sorry I wasn't here when you arrived. I hope that Jessica and Cade were helpful."

Looking away from Danika's breasts, which were at her eye level, Kerry managed to mutter, "Uh, yeah, they were great."

Wow! My new landlady is an Amazon. She has at least eight inches over me. Such beautiful amber eyes. Come on, Kerry, engage your brain and say something reasonably coherent.

"Jessica mentioned that you had an emergency at the university. I hope everything is all right."

Danika snickered. "Emergencies in academia consist of faculty members hysterically complaining about not having a TA, or being assigned to morning classes. In other words, much ado about nothing."

Don't just stand there like a dummy, stop gawking and invite the woman inside.

"Dr. Lester, please come inside and meet my roommate." Kerry motioned to the big fur ball who was wrapped around her ankles. "Molly would probably like to shed a little fur on your pantsuit. Unfortunately, I'm not stocked up on beverages, yet, so I can't offer much in the way of hospitality."

"The doctor business is for the classroom. Call me Danika or Danny since we're neighbors now. I'd like to change into something more comfortable. What if I stop by in about twenty minutes with a soda or beer?"

"A cold beer would be much appreciated," Kerry replied.

After Danika left, Kerry raced upstairs to take a quick shower. She rummaged through her duffle bag for clean clothes and managed to locate a pair of cutoffs and a rumpled T-shirt.

Well, at least I don't stink now. Hopefully, I can manage an intelligent conversation. The doctor must wonder about my IQ after my pathetic first impression.

Kerry finger-combed her hair, knowing that any attempt to style the short curls was fruitless. As she spritzed on a dash of lavender water, a soft knock came from downstairs.

"Hello again," Danny said as Kerry welcomed her inside. She handed Kerry a chilled six pack of Michelob.

"Sorry, I guess we'll have to be bohemians and drink out of the bottle. I don't have any idea which box has the glasses. Gee, I don't have a bottle opener, either," Kerry apologized.

Danny chuckled. "I always come prepared." She pulled a Swiss Army knife from the pocket of her shorts and deftly opened two beers.

Molly was curled up on the sofa, eavesdropping. Kerry noticed that Danny carefully sat at the opposite end and ignored the kitty. *I guess Danny doesn't care for cats. At least she didn't ask for a pet deposit.*

"Kerry, did my sister mention that we have additional furniture in storage? After you're settled, please let me know if you need anything extra. We may have something you can use."

277

Sister! Jessica is her sister, not her roommate!

While Kerry's brain fixated on that surprising bit of news, Molly stood up and stretched, then she padded across the sofa and gave Danny a head butt.

Danny smiled and gently scratched the cat's back ending at the base of her tail.

"Works every time," she remarked. "You ignore a cat and the kitty comes to you."

Kerry was amazed that her usually reticent companion continued to rub against Danny. "I'm surprised that Molly is so friendly. It usually takes her quite some time and treats before she warms up to someone. She acts like the two of you are old friends."

Danny allowed Molly to curl up in her lap while she briefed Kerry on the best restaurants, the fish market, and the nearest H.E.B store. They were into their second beer, when Kerry unsuccessfully tried to stifle a yawn.

Danny stood up and remarked, "You've had a long day. I'd better leave now."

"Thanks! The beer was most welcome," Kerry replied as she accompanied Danny to the front entrance.

"Any time. Just knock if you need anything." Danny lightly brushed Kerry's shoulder as she passed through the threshold.

The brief touch was electric. Kerry closed the door and gasped as a warm current spread from her shoulder down her arm to her fingertips. She shrugged off the pleasant sensations. *It's probably the beer because I'm so tired. Molly does seem to be smitten with Dr. Lester, though.*

†

Over the next couple of days, Kerry kept busy sorting her things and stocking the refrigerator and pantry. Despite her attempts to stay task focused, thoughts about her landlady keep intruding. *That woman is truly an Amazon, so tall and strong. She has the physique of a power forward in basketball. Danny is pleasantly attractive, too. Those light amber eyes and honey-blond hair that just brushes the top of her shoulders. Gee, Kerry, listen to yourself. You sound like you're describing a character for one of your romantic novels. Stop mooning like a teenager! You need to clear your head. Perhaps some exercise would help. Try jogging. It will also be a good way to explore the neighborhood.*

"Molly, I'm obsessing too much over our landlady, so I'm going for a run. Yeah, I know, you're not interested. Your food bowl is full. Try not to knock anything off my desk while I'm gone."

Molly yawned and stretched. She wasn't making any promises.

Kerry began her excursion with a brisk walk, then progressed to a slow jog. It was late afternoon and the sea breeze cooled the temperature to a tolerable level. Kerry soon relaxed and settled into a rhythm, easily covering the distance to the sea wall. She stopped and sat on the steps leading down to a narrow strip of beach.

The gray Gulf was relatively calm. The sound of the waves lapping on the shore was calming. Kerry felt a sense of connectedness with the ancient waters and its creatures. Unbidden, images of Danny seeped into her consciousness. *There's something familiar about that woman that I can't quite resolve. It tickles my brain, like I know her from somewhere, but that can't be true. Ah well, it's a pleasant frustration. Time to head back.*

Thoughts of Danny continued to linger as Kerry jogged toward home. She fantasized about what it would be like to slip her hands under Danny's shirt and caress those lovely firm breasts until the nipples grew taut. Kerry imagined kissing her way up the bare skin revealed by an open collar, then nibbling her way along Danny's muscular shoulders.

"What the hell!" Kerry sputtered as she stepped on a loose fragment of the pavement. When her ankle rolled, she lost her balance. Kerry braced her fall with her left hand and landed hard on her backside.

"Great, just great," Kerry growled as she struggled to stand. Her ankle throbbed, blood dripped from cuts on her hand, and her butt felt bruised. She glanced around and was relieved to see that there were no witnesses to her embarrassing tumble.

At least this crap happened only two blocks from the house. I'd better get moving before I stiffen up. Kerry grimaced, hobbling gingerly on her sprained ankle. When she turned the corner, she spotted Danny in the front yard watering the flowerbeds.

Damn, my luck is really lousy today! I hate for the professor to see me in this sorry state. Can this evening get any worse?

When Kerry neared the house, Danny noticed her limping up the sidewalk. She quickly dropped the hose and hurried to meet her.

"Kerry, what happened to you?"

"Oh, I just twisted my ankle."

Danny saw the bloody hand and noted the discomfort on Kerry's face that she was unable to disguise. "Let me help you over to the steps where you can sit." Not waiting for an answer, Danny slipped her arm around Kerry's waist.

"Lean on me, Kerry. Let me absorb some of the weight off your ankle."

Close physical contact with Danny sent waves of tingling warmth spreading over Kerry's skin as if no fabric existed between them. She felt dizzy from the intensity. With Danny securely holding her, Kerry relented and leaned against her for support.

"There is an urgent-care center only a few blocks from here. I can drive you there for x-rays," Danny offered.

"No need for that, this ankle has caused problems before. It's an old tennis injury. My foot will be swollen and tender for a few days, then everything will be fine."

"Okay! I guess I'll have to play doctor." Danny grinned and winked. "Let's get you inside and ice the swelling."

Kerry sighed in relief when she reached the sofa in the den. Danny untied her shoes and carefully positioned a throw pillow under her injured foot.

"I'll be back with some first aid supplies and an ice pack. It'll only take me a minute to gather things. Don't move or try to do anything." Danny stared at Kerry until she nodded in agreement.

When Danny left the room, Kerry squirmed, trying to find a comfortable position on the sofa that didn't put pressure on her sore buttocks. *Whew, talk about a no-nonsense woman! When she gives an order, she obviously expects compliance. Usually, I don't care to be bossed around, but somehow, I like Danny's take-charge attitude.*

Molly chose that moment to come downstairs. She looked at Kerry and swished her bushy tail, hinting for treats.

"Sorry, not now, Molly."

The big kitty responded by jumping up on the back of the sofa. She peered down at Kerry, projecting a pathetic, neglected look.

Minutes later, Danny came bustling in carrying a small basin loaded with medical supplies.

"I see you have company," Danny remarked, pulling a foot stool next to the sofa. "First, let's soak your hand, then I'll tend to your ankle. Those cuts could become infected. They're encrusted with dirt and shards of shell."

"Yes, Doctor," Kerry replied, "I'm at your mercy."

Danny filled the basin with warm, soapy water. She placed it on the foot stool so Kerry could soak her damaged hand. Satisfied with that arrangement, Danny knelt on the floor to examine the ankle injury.

Kerry tried not to grimace when Danny slowly peeled off her tennis shoe and sock. *Dammit! It hurts but I'm not going to act like a wimp. It's bad enough having my new landlady take care of me. So much for my butch card.*

"Your ankle is definitely swelling. If it's okay with you, I'll use some arnica gel to limit the bruising, then I'll apply an elastic bandage."

"Sounds good to me, Doc."

Danny carefully spread the herbal gel over Kerry's ankle and the top of her foot. After the gel had penetrated the skin, she wrapped the injury. Next, she laid a cotton kitchen towel over the area and applied a slushy ice pack.

"Gee, Doc, you look like you know what you're doing," Kerry teased.

"Yeah, I spent some time in the trainers' room when I played basketball. I've had my share of mishaps, too. Let's take a look at your hand." Danny turned on the floor lamp and closely examined the cuts.

This is not the way, I'd like for her to be holding my hand. Ordinarily, I'd feel awkward in this type of situation, but somehow, I'm comfortable with Danny taking care of me. She's very gentle.

"You have pieces of shell embedded in these cuts. They really need to come out, Kerry."

"Yes, you're right. Go ahead."

"It's going to be a little unpleasant," Danny warned.

"I can handle whatever you do," Kerry replied, smirking.

Danny laughed at the double-entendre. She held Kerry's hand under the light from a floor lamp and picked at the shell fragments with tweezers. When Danny was sure that the cuts were clean, she applied anti bacterial cream and wrapped the injured hand with gauze.

"Is the torture over, Doc?"

"Yes, unless you have other injured body parts to show me."

Kerry blushed. *No way she is going to see my bruised butt.* "Thanks for the rescue, Danny. The only thing missing was your white horse."

"Despite being a redhead, you take orders well." Danny winked, patting Kerry's thigh. She stood up and gathered her first aid supplies. Pausing at the front door, she added, "Call me if you need anything."

"I will, thanks." When the door closed behind Danny, Kerry smiled. *Oh, sweet woman, I might take you up on that offer!*

†

After being cooped up inside for two days, Kerry decided to sit outside and read a new lesfic novel. When she approached the covered patio, Kerry was surprised to see Danny digging in a corner of the backyard.

"Is this where the bodies are buried?" she asked.

Danny laughed. She stopped working and gave Kerry her full attention. "You seem to have recovered fairly well from your mishap. I guess it's time to send the bill."

Kerry felt her face reddening. Danny was wearing short shorts and a sleeveless blouse tied under her breasts. *On my, what a gorgeous body! Danny has a six-pack midriff and nicely sculpted arms and shoulders, definitely the body of an athlete. I'd like to be the cause of that fine sheen of perspiration on those lovely muscles.*

"What about accepting liquid payment, Doctor? Maybe some freshly squeezed lemonade?"

"That sounds wonderful!"

"Do you prefer sweet or tart?"

"Oh, I definitely prefer the sweet version," Danny replied, her light-amber eyes twinkling.

I think Dr. Lester is flirting a wee bit. "I'll be back in a couple of minutes," Kerry replied.

When she returned, Danny was relaxing at a patio table in the shade. Handing her a tall frosted mug, Kerry remarked, "You look a little hot. Sweet lemonade should cool you off," she added, grinning. "What's your project?"

"This is supposed to be a fish pond. With all the hungry seabirds, I'll probably end with up with big turtles, though."

"That's really hard work to do by yourself."

"Gardening is a good way to stay fit. It's more fun than exercise machines."

Yes, you're definitely fit, Dr. Lester. Whew, I need to rein in my libido and change the subject.

"Danny, you mentioned having some furniture in storage. Would you possibly have a small table that I could use for my printer? The library table in the study is great for a desk, but Molly likes to lounge on it. She's such a big Maine Coon, there isn't much extra space when she sprawls out beside the computer."

"I probably have something that would work. Let's check out the storage area later in the day when it's cooler, say about six-thirty?"

"Great, thanks!"

Later in the afternoon, Kerry heard a soft knock.

"Ready to explore the attic?" Danny asked.

"In the world of fiction, that could be interpreted as a sinister invitation."

"My intentions are harmless, well, most of the time," Danny replied with a quick wink.

Oh, she's definitely flirting, now!

"I guess I'll have to take my chances," Kerry quipped as she followed Danny up the stairs leading to the attic.

After a few minutes of searching, they located an oak end table that would be perfect for the printer. Rejecting offers of help, Danny carried the table down the stairs to Kerry's apartment.

"It's beginning to cool off outside. Would you like to have drink on the deck?"

"I didn't know you had a deck!"

"Yep, it's a modern version of the widows' walks that are perched on the rooftops of some of the old mansions here in the historical district. As the story goes, mariners' wives would wait up there hoping to see the sailors' ships returning from their voyages at sea."

"Sounds like a good opening for a romantic novel."

"I'm sure that you could come up with a good story," Danny replied, wiggling her eyebrows. "What about my offer? I make a terrific mojito with my own organically grown mint."

Kerry smiled. "Okay, I'm game."

"Follow me. Access to the deck is through the storage area on the third floor."

When Kerry emerged from the attic, she was surprised to see a spacious terrace. Half of the space was covered. It contained a complete bar set-up with a sink, refrigerator, and cabinets. The open portion of the deck sported two, comfortable, chaise lounges flanking a small table. When Kerry stood at the wrought iron banister, she could see the Gulf less than a mile in the distance.

Danny busied herself at the bar, muddling mint which she eventually scraped into a cocktail shaker. She added freshly squeezed lime juice, super-fine sugar, rum, and ice. After shaking to cool the ingredients, Danny strained the mixture and poured the contents into two, tall, bar glasses. She topped off each glass with club soda and a sprig of mint.

Kerry curiously watched the preparations. When Danny handed her the mojito, she eagerly took a sip.

"This is absolutely heavenly! I've never had a more delicious rum cocktail."

"Shall we take advantage of the view?" Danny asked, settling into one of the chaise lounges facing the water.

Kerry relaxed in the adjacent chair and inhaled the unique, salty smell of the sea. The breeze from the water was pleasantly cool after a hot summer day. Squawking sea gulls swirled overhead looking for scraps.

"Danny, this is a lovely home. How long have you lived here?"

"About 12 years."

"The divided floor plan creates privacy, but also affords the possibility of companionship. Did you do the design?"

"Yes."

Hmm, Danny's not very forthcoming. I think there's a story here. Let's see if I can ferret out more details.

"I love the way my rooms are furnished. You're taking chances with the antiques, though. Renters don't always take care of things."

"You're actually the first renter," Danny admitted. "Are you and Molly planning any wild parties?"

"I'm not, but I'll have to check with Molly. You never know what cats are up to."

What? It's a little odd that she's been living in the house for 12 years without a renter?

Danny noticed the puzzled look on Kerry's face. She downed the last of her drink and moved to the edge of the deck. She stood there, quietly staring at the rolling water in the distance. After a few minutes, frowning, she turned to face Kerry.

"When I designed this house, the plan was for a faculty colleague to share the space with me. She wasn't 'out' and insisted on a separate living area. Last year, she accepted a research position at an out-of-state university."

It sounds like Danny is telling me that she was in a committed relationship that ended. Perhaps it would be best to move this conversation to a less sensitive topic.

"I really admire your taste in furnishings, Danny. The painting of the old galleon in my study intrigues me. Whenever, I visit the Gulf Coast, I invariably think about Alfred Noyes' poem, 'The Highwayman.' My imagination turns to the line about a 'ghostly galleon tossed upon cloudy seas. For me, that artwork is a visual image of the ship in the poem."

Feeling a pleasant buzz from the rum in the mojito, Kerry moved next to Danny and leaned on the top railing of the banister. "When I look at the painting," she confided, "I can feel the rocking of the ship. I hear the creaking of the rigging and the snapping sound of the canvas sails billowing in the wind."

Danny rested her hand on Kerry's forearm. Her eyes took on a faraway look. "Yes, there is the pervasive smell of fish and oil, the thrill as the ship knifes through dark waters, and the excitement of adventures to unknown places."

"Spoken like a romance writer," Kerry teased.

"No, I'll happily leave writing to you. When I spotted the original painting in an antique store on the Strand, I confess that it spoke to me. The dealer didn't know anything about its provenance. She sold it at a very reasonable price because considerable restoration work was needed. Interestingly, when the artwork was professionally cleaned, two figures were revealed standing on the deck of the ship. Although we couldn't identify an artist's signature; special lighting revealed that *Banshee* was the name of the vessel. Since Jessica liked the painting, too, I had several prints made and hung one of them in your apartment. The original art work is in my bedroom."

A wave of dizziness swept over Kerry. She held on to the wrought iron railing to steady herself. *What's happening here? Sparks seem to arc between Danny and me, connecting us. There's this soul-deep ache in the pit of my stomach that demands more closeness. Am I smashed after only one drink? Time for a reality check.*

"Either the mojito was very potent, or something unusual is happening. I'm usually very reticent to trust people, or to reveal my feelings, but you seem to be the exception. For some inexplicable reason, Danny, you feel safe and familiar to me. There's a sense of connectedness that I don't understand."

When silence ensued, Kerry felt foolish. "Occupational hazard, I guess I'm conflating romance stories and real life."

"No, this is real. I feel it, too," Danny confessed. "I'm as amazed as you are."

"How can this be happening? We met only a few days ago."

Danny paused for a minute, then replied, "Some of my colleagues in the psychology department would probably theorize that we're experiencing an artifact leftover from a previous life."

"Is that what you think?"

"I don't know, but this is an adventure that I'd like to pursue."

Danny lightly gripped Kerry's shoulders. When she made eye contact, Danny cupped her cheek and pressed a delicate, feathery kiss on her lips.

Tingly sensations immediately suffused Kerry's body, traveling down her limbs, their power immobilizing her.

"I hope that wasn't too presumptuous of me."

Kerry encircled Danny's waist and rested her head on the taller woman's shoulder. She yearned for more, but she was reluctant to go further.

"I'm a little overwhelmed right now. Danny, I've known you for such a brief time, yet my feelings are so intense. It's a little frightening. I can't seem to process everything right now."

Kerry was trembling, but she gradually relaxed when gentle hands caressed her back, stroking in small circles.

"There's no rush," Danny whispered. "Sometimes the journey can be as pleasant as the destination."

Yes, time is what I need to get my brain and my feelings in sync. Kerry released Danny. Putting a little space between them, she replied, "Thank you for understanding."

Danny gave her a quick reassuring hug. "It's getting late, and I have to pack for a trip tomorrow. I'll be presenting a paper at an APA convention in Dallas."

Kerry immediately experienced a letdown until Danny added, "I would like for you to reserve Friday evening."

"What do you have in mind, Doctor?"

"It's a surprise!"

"What, no hints?

Danny chuckled. "Think of a full moon and ghostly galleons!"

†

Kerry tried to stay busy in Danny's absence. She cleaned the apartment, stocked the pantry, and did laundry. Thoughts of Danny kept intruding, however, and the research for her next novel was going nowhere. She looked at the big ball of gray fluff sprawled out next to the keyboard.

"Molly, I think I'm really falling for Dr. Lester."

The cat stared at her, briefly, then began licking her paws.

"Hey, don't act like you're disinterested. You make a fuss over Danny every time she visits."

Molly ignored Kerry. She busily focused on working out tangles in her undercoat.

"You'd make a great poker player," Kerry grumbled, "you never show your cards."

When she turned her attention back to the computer screen, Kerry noticed that she had email. Her mood lightened when she saw that the message was from Danny:

Looking forward to Friday evening. Is 6:00 okay? Wear beach attire. D.

Gee, what a brief note. Well, at least Danny is thinking about me. I wonder what she's planning. I'll wait a few hours to send an acknowledgment. I don't want to appear too eager. Now, what to wear?

†

Promptly at six, a knock sounded. Kerry playfully called out, "What's the password?"

"Uh, how about ghostly galleons?"

"Permission granted to come aboard," Kerry quipped, opening the door. She was about to hug Danny when Molly intervened. The cat wedged herself between the two women.

Danny laughed. "It looks like somebody missed me! I have a treat for you, Molly. How about some fresh shrimp?"

As soon as Danny emptied the morsels from a plastic bag into Molly's bowl, the kitty was fully engaged in wolfing down the goodies.

"You're spoiling my cat!" Kerry protested.

"Suppose I spoil you a bit, too?" Danny hugged her. "Come on, my car is already packed for our adventure!"

"Aye, aye, Captain," Kerry replied. She followed Danny outside, noting that the top was down on the convertible. A picnic basket lay on the back seat.

Since Danny wasn't forthcoming with any details, Kerry decided to be nonchalant.

"How was the conference?"

"I drank a lot of coffee trying to stay awake. Too many pretentious male egos presenting esoteric research that doesn't have any practical applicability."

"By any chance, were these self important fellows sporting Freudian style facial hair?"

Danny laughed. "Kerry, I think you completely understand."

"Literary conferences are much different. At GCLS events, I like to make bets on which authors will be doing horizontal research."

"Oh, that sounds much more interesting! Tell me more."

"Well, Kerry explained, "there's a well-known author who always seduces some young novice writer. What's so hypocritical about the situation is that this particular author always dedicates each of her books to her wife. In the dedication, this author professes total love and devotion."

"Are you disclosing professional trade secrets?" Danny asked. "Do these literary conferences provide source material for your romance novels?"

"No, of course not," Kerry retorted. "I actually have an imagination."

When Danny burst out giggling, Kerry realized that she was being teased.

"Dr. Lester, I'll have you know that I'm no easy lay!"

"Well, damn, there goes plan A, and I don't have a plan B for this evening," Danny confessed.

"What was plan A?"

"A picnic on a deserted beach, moonlight, wine." Danny stopped the car and parked along the sea wall.

"Well, since you obviously put a great deal of thought into it, I suppose we could try plan A." Kerry grabbed Danny's shirt and pulled her close. She planted a quick, assertive kiss on Danny's lips, then released her.

"Let's find a more private spot to watch the moon rise," Danny suggested. "Tonight will be a super moon."

"What's a super moon?"

"At certain times, the moon's orbit is closer to the Earth, so it looks larger," Danny explained, grabbing the picnic basket and an insulated bag from the rear seat of convertible. She added,

"Please take the blanket. It's likely to be cooler after the sun sinks below the horizon."

Kerry complied, following her to a flat spot near the end of the long jetty. Waves were breaking on the rocks below, but the ensuing spray couldn't reach them.

For the next hour, the two women feasted on shrimp po' boys, cheese, and fruit. Danny had also packed some exquisite Belgian chocolates for dessert.

Satiated, the two women sipped wine while the day ebbed into twilight. The stars began appearing to perform their nightly voyage across the sky. Eventually, a huge golden orb rose majestically, dispelling the darkness. The insistent waves lapping up against the jetty turned to silver, reflecting the moonlight.

Peacefulness drifted over Kerry. She felt a sense of belonging. The empty places in her soul no longer ached. She turned to Danny and pressed her down on the blanket. Kerry's fingertips explored the planes of her face. She moved on to delicately trace the contours of Danny's ears with the tip of her tongue. Drifting downward, Kerry nibbled tender skin. Her lips felt the passion throbbing in the veins of Danny's neck. Emboldened, she loosened a couple of buttons and kissed the valley between her breasts.

Before Kerry could explore further, Danny rolled over and pinned her. Kerry's hands felt the bulge of strong biceps holding her in securely in place.

"It's my turn, now!" Danny whispered.

She kissed Kerry deeply, their tongues dancing a sensual duet. Kerry wanted more, to merge completely with her. It had been a very long time. She had finally found her other half.

Danny responded by biting Kerry's neck, marking her, claiming her. Moments passed before she managed to find some measure of control. She released Kerry and sighed.

The women lay still, breathing heavily. Eventually, Danny broke the silence. "Kerry, we need to take this somewhere more private. It's all I can do to keep from tearing off your clothes."

"Who would think that two middle-aged women would be caught up in such passionate activities on a public beach?"

"Well, I suppose we could always tell the beach patrol that we're doing research for a romance novel," Danny joked.

Kerry turned serious. "This is a case of reality being stranger than fiction. I can't explain this feeling of closeness and familiarity. Danny, you fill the empty spaces in my soul."

"I don't question unexpected blessings, Kerry, but if you must have an explanation, perhaps our souls have unfinished business."

"Spoken like a psychologist."

"And what would a storyteller say?"

"We'd probably say that the adventure continues."

The two women held hands and looked out over the restless Gulf waters. The ambient light of the full moon revealed the dark silhouette of a large, wooden, sailing ship resting peacefully at anchor.

The End

ABOUT THE AUTHORS

Dena Blake:

Dena Blake is an eternal optimist, would-be chef, tech nerd, and occasional auto mechanic. Her books are steamy, sometimes funny, and always full of angst. Dena's first novel, *Where the Light Glows*, is a Rainbow Award winner for Best Lesbian Debut. Her third novel, *A Country Girl's Heart* was a 2019 Goldie finalist. Contact her at DenaBlakeBooks@gmail.com

Kris Bryant:

Kris Bryant is a multi-award winning author who pens lesfic novels for Bold Strokes Books. She lives in Kansas

City, MO. Kris enjoys binge-watching movies, Netflix, and television shows for her podcast, "Queerly Recommended" with her co-host, Tara Scott. In her spare time, Kris likes to bike trails, hang out with friends and family, and spend summers in her hammock. She can be reached at krisbryantbooks@gmail.com.

Julie Cannon:

Julie Cannon divides her time by being a corporate suit, wife, mom, sister, friend and writer. Julie and her wife have lived in at least half a dozen states, traveled around the world, and have an unending supply of dedicated friends. And of course, the most important people in their lives are their three kids, #1, Dude, and the Diving Miss Em.With the release of *The Last First Kiss*, Julie will have twenty books published by Bold Strokes Books. Her first novel, *Come and Get Me*, was a finalist for the Golden Crown Literary Society Best Lesbian Romance and Début Author Awards. Several of her books have additionally been finalists for the GCLS Best Lesbian Romance, and *I Remember* won the GCLS Best Lesbian Romance in 2014. *Rescue Me* and *Wishing on a Dream* were finalists for Best Lesbian Romance from the prestigious Lambda Literary Society. "The Last Roundup" was Julie's short story in the first *Lone Star Collection*. Contact Julie at: www.JulieCannon.com.

Renee MacKenzie:

As a Navy brat, Renee MacKenzie lived on three continents before her family settled in Virginia. She currently resides in Naples, Florida, with her partner and their poodle. Renee enjoys wildlife photography, pickle ball, reading, and hiking. Even though Renee has been paid to do all sorts of jobs, ranging from dental assistant to bartender, field sampler to pet-sitter, and maintenance worker to property officer, she insists she's only had one job—writer—and all the rest has just been research. Renee is the author of nine novels: *Confined Spaces, Flight, Nesting, 23 Miles, Anywhere, Everywhere,* and *Pausing,* and three books in the Karst Series, *Kai's Heart, Naomi's Soul,* and *Misha's Promise.* Renee's short story, "Finding My Muse," can be found in *The Lone Star Collection* (2018). Contact her at ReneeWrites@gmail.com.

Annette Mori:

Annette is an award-winning author who lives in the beautiful Pacific Northwest with her wife and their five furry kids. She has twenty-one published novels and thirteen short stories, including *Coochie Couch* from the first Lone Star anthology. In addition to a Goldie Award for her fourth novel, *Locked Inside,* Annette has several Lesfic Bard Awards for her other romance novels. If someone picks up one of her books and it touches them, Annette believes that she has achieved her goal as an author. To see her other publications visit the Affinity Rainbow Publications website at www.affinityrainbowpublications.com. Annette loves to hear from readers. Contact her at annettemori0859@gmail.com or visit her blog at: https://annettemori0859.wordpress.com.

Yvette Murray:

Yvette Murray, PhD. is a retired university professor with 25 years of clinical experience in psychiatric social work. A native of Central Texas, she currently resides in Austin. Yvette's hobbies include rock collecting, gardening, and jewelry design. Her favorite pastime is reading lesfic novels with Elly, her feline family member. Yvette discovered lesbian fiction in the 1980s. Since that time, she has been involved in various literary and promotional activities, serving as an awards administrator for the Golden Crown Literary Society and organizing the Lone Star LesFic Festivals. In 2005, she formed the Sapphic Reading Group and presently serves as the facilitator. The short story, "Under the West Texas Stars" in *The Lone Star Collection I*, is her first lesfic publication. Contact Yvette at: drmurray729@yahoo.com.

Del Robertson:

Del Robertson has always been an avid reader, particularly of fantasy, history, the unusual, the offbeat, and the simply odd. She enjoys mixing all these elements into the stories she writes. Thanks to the women in charge at Affinity Rainbow Publications, she's found a place to tell her tales: From the swash-buckling pirate adventure in *Taming the Wolff* to the sword-wielding *My* Fair Maiden, to the *real* story of St. Nic in *Thundersnow and Lightning*. Del is a ongoing supporter of the Lone Star Literary Society. She is proud to have her short story, "Remember Me", included in their first anthology, *The Lone Star Collection I*. Contact her at delrobertson@ymail.com

Lacey L. Schmidt
Lacey holds a doctorate in industrial-organizational psychology and has published numerous acclaimed texts in that field. She resides in Houston with her wife and fur children. Her hobbies include sailing, photography, and scuba diving. Previous creative publications include a poetry book, *The Nightshade Lexicon*, a creative non-fiction story called *Pride and Prejudiced* in *Unbroken Circle*, plus three romantic short stories, "Love's Luck" in *It's In Her Kiss*, "Peaches for Honey" in *Christmas Medley*, and "A Lone Star" in the first Lone Star anthology. Lacey has three lesbian romance novels published by Affinity Rainbow Publications: *A Walk Away, Catch to Release*, and *Playing With Matches*. Lacey's website: http://laceyschmidt.blogspot.com/ contains free new poetry, fiction, art, and essays each month.

MJ Williamz:

MJ Williamz grew up on California's central coast, which she left at age seventeen to pursue an education. She graduated from Chico State where she rediscovered her love for writing. It wasn't until MJ moved to Portland, however, that her writing really took off with the publication of her first short story in 2003. In the initial Lone Star anthology, she penned "Meeting Miranda". MJ is the author of fourteen books, including three Goldie Award winners. She has also had over 30 short stories published, mostly erotica, with a few romances and horrors thrown in for good measure. She lives in Houston with her wife, fellow author Laydin Michaels, and their fur babies. Contact MJ at mjwilliamz@aol.com, or look for her on Facebook at MJ Williamz, or on Twitter at @mj_williamz.

Barbara Ann Wright

Barbara writes fantasy and science fiction novels and short stories in between naps. Her Pyradisté Adventure novels (starting with *The Pyramid Waltz*) have made recommended reading lists on Tor.com, Book Riot, and Syfy.com. She's won five Rainbow Awards and has been a finalist in the Foreword Review Book of the Year Award, the Goldie Awards, and the Lambda Awards. Barbara is excited to be in the second *Lone Star Collection* after her story, "The

Heartbreak State," appeared in the first anthology. She would love to hear from you at: barbara@barbaraannwright.com.

OTHER BOOKS FROM AFFINITY

<u>Footprints</u> by Ali Spooner

Sandy, the youngest sibling of Gator Girlz, Inc., has worshipped her older sister Cam all her life and wanted nothing more than to be just like her hero. *Footprints* provides readers with Sandy's story of growing up in the Bayous of Louisiana. When the devastating floods of 2016 impact the Baton Rouge area, Cam and Sandy join the Cajun Navy to help rescue families trapped in the rampant floodwaters. The story also revisits Sandy's victory over Bubba Gump and how Sandy's injuries started her down the path to find the love of her life. Food, adventures, and great family relationships fill the pages of *Footprints.*

Love at Leighton Lake by Samantha Hicks
Tallulah 'Tally' Roberts decides that a few weeks staying in a cabin at Leighton Lake will help mend her shattered pelvis and broken heart.

Caitlyn Matthews works at the lake resort her mother owns, loving nothing better than spending her morning swimming in the lake. That is until she meets Tally. Their attraction is instant, but both are wary of these new feelings with their history of previous relationships.

As they get to know each other, secrets from Caitlyn's past come to light. Caitlyn fears her mother has been lying to her and together they search for the truth.

Love at Leighton Lake is packed full of love, drama, and a cow called Houdini who likes to roam the cabins, much to Caitlyn's delight.

The Others by Annette Mori
As a seer and brilliant scientist, Em convinces her wife, Lise, to prepare for the inevitable conclusion, after the chaos caused by foreign countries attacking the United States. Leaving behind a wake of destruction and a new world order, forcing them to navigate a frightening reality. After ten months in their cozy bomb shelter, they emerge to a world where the vegetation is surprisingly unaffected. Should they band together with other survivors, or try to make it on their own? There are others in this unknown world. On the first day outside of their shelter, they meet members of an alternate society. Are they friend or foe? Change is

inevitable. But will they change in ways Em and Lise can live with, or will this altered world change them into something unrecognizable?

Three Mile Cache by Jen Silver

The story is set in Australia circa 1988. When archaeologist Carolyn Wells returns home to Sydney after several months away at a dig in Tunisia, she expects to be reunited with her lover, Detective Inspector Alex Graham. But she soon learns that Alex has been wounded in a hostage incident and is recuperating at a Royal Flying Doctor Service hospital at a place in the outback of New South Wales called Three Mile Cache. Carolyn decides to fly out there and surprise Alex with her arrival. Surprises abound when she gets there. One of the doctors treating Alex has a rather intimate interpretation of a bedside manner. There are mysterious goings-on at a local homestead and Alex's injuries haven't stopped her from probing into the lives of the locals, much to their annoyance. When Carolyn and Alex meet again, things don't quite work out as either of them would like. Can their relationship recover from the series of events in Three Mile Cache that threaten to keep them apart?

Sculpting Her Heart by Annette Mori

On the surface, it appears as if Zari Woods has achieved everything, she set out to accomplish fame, money, a supportive best friend, and loving parents. But to a person on the neurodiverse spectrum, a loving woman is elusive. When the right woman comes along she's already taken.

Soul on Fire by Ali Spooner

A perfect summer ends with danger on the Appalachian Trail for Whit, Mitch and Brad. Once safely home, the relationship between Eli and Whit continues to strengthen as the boys return home and they grow as a couple. Eli falls deeper in love with Whit and North Carolina as the trees come alive with autumn color. The first Christmas at Cast Iron Farm is celebrated with Eli's family as a new chapter in all of their lives begins. Join the family for the third book in the Cast Iron Farm Series.

The Boss's Daughter by Samantha Hicks

Vivian Westfall, CFO of *Bridger Holdings*, meets her boss's estranged daughter, Lauren, when a disturbance at the company spring party piques her interest. Lauren is clearly drunk and making a fool of herself. To prevent embarrassment, Vivian forces Lauren away from the party. They have angry words, and things take an unexpected turn when Lauren kisses her. Months later Lauren pitches a proposal to her father to loan her the funds to start her own health club. Her father reluctantly agrees with a caveat; Vivian must go with her to Scotland to keep an eye on the money. It doesn't take long for the sparks to fly in all emotional directions. When Gregory Bridger finds out about their relationship, he does everything in his power to break them apart. Trust is at the heart of this love story, a fragile emotion that without it, things can and do fall apart.

The Ghost of East Texas by Ali Spooner

Agent Blair Cooper and her partner, psychic Tally Rainwater (Terminal Event), are back in a gripping new murder mystery investigation. When the serial killer Casper Caruso, known as The Ghost of East Texas, was sent to death row, Agent Blair Cooper was adamant that there were more victims of his killing spree. As his execution day approaches, Casper reaches out to Blair. If she agrees to a face-to-face meeting, he will give the whereabouts of 10 additional bodies left in his wake. Blair and Tally must piece together the clues to bring closure for some of the victim's families. However, when you bargain with the devil, there is always a price to be paid.

Terminal Event by Ali Spooner

Tally Rainwater was born with the gift of second sight, something she never understood. A near-fatal accident, at age twelve, makes her visions clearer, but not the reason for them. As she matures, Lisa, a spirit, enters her visions to guide her in using her gift, but still not the reason why. Can Tally and Blair's budding romance survive the possibility? Read this intense murder mystery romance and find out.

The Star Child by Ali Spooner

Eli and Whit are enjoying their life together on the mountain when Whit is called into action for a secret mission at the Pentagon. While she is gone, the Cast Iron Farm comes to life, literally, when Eli discovers a mysterious cave that has a connection to Whit's past. Younger brother Brad joins the gang. When Whit returns, she plans an Appalachian Trail adventure with Brad and Mitch. Join Eli and family as their adventure at Cast Iron Farm continues.

<u>My Dear Vet by JM Dragon</u>

Ava Lawrence, a research veterinarian, is thrown in the deep end when her uncle asks her to cover his country practice while he has a vacation of a lifetime. How could she refuse? His team shouldn't be any different than the crew at her parents' practice, oh, was she so wrong. What she now has to work with is a sassy nurse, an obnoxious receptionist, and an animal whisperer, or so it seems. Ava finds herself embroiled in taking care of animals in the area and local issues outside her experience, making her question her sanity. Throw in chickens, cats, dogs, and a donkey named Theo, along with various other animals. This turns out to be Ava's unexpected adventure with far reaching romantic benefits.

Affinity
Rainbow Publications

eBooks, Print, Free eBooks

Visit our website for more publications available online.

www.affinityrainbowpublications.com

Published by Affinity Rainbow Publications
A Division of Affinity eBook Press NZ LTD
Canterbury, New Zealand

Registered Company 2517228